I'M FINE
AND
NEITHER
ARE YOU

OTHER TITLES BY CAMILLE PAGÁN

Woman Last Seen in Her Thirties

Forever is the Worst Long Time

Life and Other Near-Death Experiences

The Art of Forgetting

PRAISE FOR *I'M FINE AND NEITHER ARE YOU*

"Camille Pagán's novels are compulsively readable, and her latest may just be her ultimate page-turner. Smart, witty, and exacting, *I'm Fine and Neither Are You* examines the high price of perfection and the rewards of getting real—even when doing so jeopardizes your most important relationships. I loved it."

—Sarah Jio, *New York Times* bestselling author

"With amazing insight into what it's like to balance marriage, home, and career, Camille Pagán has shined a spotlight on the stark truth, which is that it's much harder than we make it look. 'Mother's little helper' takes on a very modern—and unsettling—meaning. This is one relatable tale."

—Tracey Garvis Graves, *New York Times* bestselling author of
The Girl He Used to Know

"A senseless tragedy causes a woman to reevaluate her entire life in *I'm Fine and Neither Are You*—a beautiful novel that is equal parts hilarious and heartbreaking. Camille Pagán's latest is a must-read for any woman who has tried (and most likely failed) to have it all."

—Liz Fenton and Lisa Steinke, bestselling authors of *Girls' Night Out*

I'M FINE
AND
NEITHER
ARE YOU

Camille Pagán

LAKE UNION
PUBLISHING

Published by Lake Union Publishing, Seattle

www.apub.com

Amazon, the Amazon logo, and Lake Union Publishing are trademarks of Amazon.com,
Inc., or its affiliates.

ISBN-13: 9781542042550 (hardcover)
ISBN-10: 1542042550 (hardcover)
ISBN-13: 9781542042239 (paperback)
ISBN-10: 1542042232 (paperback)

Cover design by David Drummond

Printed in the United States of America

First edition

For the women in my life—especially Pam K. Sullivan

ONE

Mistakes were made. The first wasn't even something I did; it was only a germ of an idea, fleeting but infectious. I had just sat on the toilet and was mulling over the day's to-dos and why-didn't-Is when a single thought shot past all the rest:

I want out.

Maybe it was the photo I had seen on my phone moments earlier. One of my college friends was on vacation yet again, and had posted a shot of the vast Caribbean horizon beyond her sandy, pedicured toes. A novel was on her lap, closed to highlight the cover (and, presumably, her sculpted thighs). The caption noted that a cabana boy had fetched the cocktail she was holding in her free hand.

I glanced down at my own legs, which were not so much toned as two-toned. I had recently read that making it through mothering alive required putting on your own oxygen mask before assisting others. Alas—I had failed to make the connection between survival and sunscreen.

But my sudden desire to be somewhere else was probably less envy and more the result of my second child screaming through the half-inch gap where the bathroom door failed to meet the frame. "Mommy! Mom! Maaahhhmaaay!"

"Miles, can I not have one whole minute of peace?" The answer to this wasted breath of a question would remain no for another twelve years and two months—not that I was counting. "Go attempt to wake your father up."

The knob twisted. Then the door flung open and there stood my son, tight fists resting on his narrow hips. His face was contorted with a mix of lingering rage and the fresh pleasure of ratting out his older sister. "Stevie called me Rumpleforeskin!" he announced.

Still perched on the toilet, I turned and tucked my chin to my shoulder to stifle a laugh. When I had composed myself, I looked over at him. "Well, that's a silly thing to say. What do I always tell you about how to respond to someone who's mean to you?"

He smiled angelically. "Punch them in the tenders?"

"Sweetheart, if you do that and tell people I told you to, you're going to end up living with Cookie."

His face immediately crumpled and he began to cry. It was true that my mother-in-law, Riya, who preferred to be identified as a baked good rather than a grandmother, smothered my children to the point of terror when she bothered to see them. Still—Miles' tears were a reminder of the microscopic line between being six and having borderline personality disorder.

"Oh, sweetie, come on. Just ignore Stevie," I said, as though the four hundredth time I uttered this advice would be the one that finally stuck. "Go pour yourself a bowl of cereal."

"I want waffles," he said, sniffling. His cheeks, which bore the high color of indignation, were streaked with glossy tear trails. I would have pulled him to me and hugged him, but I hadn't wiped yet.

Instead, Miles stalked off, leaving the door wide open. It was just far enough away that I couldn't close it myself, so I quickly reached beside me. My fingers landed on a cardboard roll where paper should have been. The basket beside the toilet was empty.

I needed someone to trek to the dungeon, as my children referred to our basement, and retrieve toilet paper.

"Miles!" I called. "Come back!"

Radio silence.

I decided to try my daughter instead. "Stevie! . . . Stevie?"

Still no response. I was ready to revert to yodeling empty threats into the hallway when Sanjay appeared. He wrinkled his nose. "What died?"

Romance, I thought. But instead of saying this, I reached behind me and flushed, which sent toilet water spraying everywhere. Who needed a bidet when you had decades-old plumbing? "Good morning to you, too. Can you please get me some toilet paper?"

Sanjay shook his head, which had yet to produce a single gray hair. At thirty-nine, his stomach was still as flat as the day we met sixteen years earlier. His bronze skin was nearly as unlined as it had been then, too. Only the dark half-moons beneath his eyes hinted at a string of midlife disappointments. "We ran out yesterday."

I stared at him. "And you just decided to tell me that now?"

"I told you we were low last week, Penelope," he said, and since he was using my full name, I knew he was officially annoyed. "Remember?"

I did not.

"I didn't have a chance to remind you again last night, because you were passed out by nine," he added.

Yes, yes, I was, because I had been up at two the night before to change Miles' pee-soaked sheets. And the night before that, I had stared at the ceiling for nearly an hour, wondering if whatever material had been used to make it look as though we were sleeping a few feet beneath the moon would give us mesothelioma. A popcorn ceiling, our Realtor had called it when we bought the house. Sanjay had purchased a mask and spraying solution and a special scraping tool, and stood on a ladder with his neck bent backward for eight minutes before giving up. I had found the number of a guy—a wall guy, as opposed to the roof guy or the lawn guy or, for the sake of parity, the painter gal. Four years later, Sanjay still swore he was going to call him; on principle, I refused to do so myself. Every once in a while, I awoke to find a chunk of plaster at the end of the bed.

Sanjay disappeared. I was about to unleash a string of expletives (under my breath, lest the children hear) when he reappeared and tossed a package of baby wipes at me. "Use these," he said as the wipes whizzed past me and hit the shower curtain.

I reached over to grab them, flashing Sanjay in the process. I recognized that my doing so was at odds with our having marital relations anytime soon. But he had seen me in the middle of giving birth, and we had still managed to conceive a second child. So.

"Not flushable," I pointed out.

"But more sanitary than toilet paper," he said. "That's research proven."

Sanjay Laghari Kar, patron saint of useless trivia. "Thanks," I said.

He shrugged. Then he dropped his clothes in a pile and stepped into the shower.

I glowered at the shower curtain before looking down at my phone, which was at my feet. I had seventeen minutes to make lunches for the kids to take to camp, get dressed and ready, and run out the door . . . *Forever,* I thought for a brief, shameful second before banishing the idea from my mind.

I had planned to rinse off quickly, but now I would either have to accept that Sanjay would be in there until I left, or deal with the attitude he copped when I suggested he leave a bit of water in Lake Michigan.

I ran back to the bedroom and yanked a dress over my head. I had just pulled a muscle in my shoulder trying to zip it up when Sanjay, humming and wrapped in a towel, walked into the bedroom.

"How do I look?" I asked. I had a meeting with my supervisor, Yolanda, at nine, and it was either this dress or my bank-teller pantsuit.

He sat on the bed and glanced up at me. "You look great," he said, but I was pretty sure his eyes hadn't risen higher than my knees.

I sighed. My closest friend, Jenny, called Sanjay Thing 3. If it had been anyone other than her, I would have been offended. Of course, anyone else wouldn't have known that I sometimes felt my husband was, in fact, my third and arguably least affectionate child. Now I called him Thing 3, too—though only to Jenny.

Anyway, her husband, Matt, wasn't perfect. Since I had mostly grown up without a mother and had been raised by a father who spent more time at work than at home, I would never have been able to handle Matt's being on the road all the time. But Jenny said she loved him so much she was willing to put up with it, even if she did occasionally feel neglected. That was one of the best things about having a friend you shared everything with: It gave you a bird's-eye view of another person's life. Which in turn reminded you that the bad you had was your choice, and better than the alternative.

In truth, I sometimes wondered about the better part. There was plenty about Jenny's marriage that was covetable, including but not limited to the fact that she did not have to rush to work every morning, because Matt made oodles of cash. Jenny did, too—her "little website" had become a juggernaut—but she didn't have to. And though she had never said as much, I was pretty sure she didn't feel like the walls of her large and tastefully decorated home were closing in on her, or that Cecily, her one ridiculously well-behaved child, was trying to strangle all whimsy from her life. Jenny did not look across the table at Matt (who never masticated chicken nuggets with an open mouth as he scrolled his phone) and wonder what had happened to the clever, cultured man she had married.

Because she did not serve chicken nuggets for dinner.

(They had sex all the time.)

I didn't really want out, I reassured myself as I dashed to the kitchen to finish the lunches. My childhood had been such that I knew how fortunate I was to be a part of a nuclear family and own a home in a good school district in one of the least generic parts of the Midwest— even if I did sometimes long for the bucolic, childless existence Sanjay and I had once enjoyed in Brooklyn. I recognized the windfall of two healthy, mostly manageable offspring. Our neighbor Lorrie, who let herself into our house more often than I cared to acknowledge ("Just saying hi!" she would announce as I wet myself from the shock of discovering I was not alone and in fact someone who I had once mistaken for a friend was lounging on my sofa), was a single parent. I understood how hard this was—my father had become one himself after my mother decided she wasn't cut out for family life.

But my father knew I could be trusted to hold down the fort when he was working and my little brother, Nick, needed to be fed, bandaged, or otherwise tended to. Whereas Lorrie only had young Olive, who seemed perfectly average until you realized her supertight hug was the first step of an orchestrated plan to disembowel you with her teeth. As such, I made a conscious effort not to complain to Lorrie about Miles and Stevie cage-fighting in the netted trampoline in our back-yard, nor to mutter to her about Sanjay's fervent belief that plucking wrinkled clothes from the dryer to wear was the same thing as "doing the laundry."

Still. I was well aware that the semicharmed life I led was one part luck to three parts effort. I had left Brooklyn and traded a beloved but barely paying editing job for a more lucrative position in development at a major Midwestern university—the same institution where Sanjay had spent nearly a year in medical school before admitting that he really didn't want to be a doctor (never mind that I had pointed this out back when he began an expensive premed preparatory program years earlier).

When it became evident that we could not move back to New York with two children without selling an organ on the black market, I had researched the best neighborhoods and schools in our college town. I had located the only house we could afford in our desired district, and now spent 29 percent of my post-tax paycheck covering the mortgage. (Sanjay had finally started getting paid for a few of the music reviews and articles he wrote, though I had pushed him to bolster our anemic savings account with that cash instead of putting it toward the house.)

Those decisions had paid off. Stevie was getting the reading intervention she needed. She and Miles had a yard that was not made of concrete. Our life was not so expensive that Sanjay's being mostly unemployed had left us destitute. And I had met Jenny, which had made my suburban, child-centered existence infinitely more tolerable.

I loved my husband. I loved my kids. I mostly liked my life.

But I was so damn tired.

And maybe that was why on that June morning—as Sanjay lounged in his towel and checked his phone while I ran around like I was on uppers, curling my eyelashes while shoving vegetable straws into lunch boxes and zipping backpacks for two sloths in human clothing—I allowed myself a tiny, terrible indulgence.

Which was to admit that in that moment, I actually did want out.

TWO

Sanjay and I met sixteen years earlier at *Hudson*, a now-defunct glossy magazine that envisioned itself as the love child of *Harper's* and *Vanity Fair*. I had been working as a junior editor for nearly a year when he was hired as an assistant to the music editor. The attraction had been instant—I could still recall the electricity that shot through me when our eyes locked as we were being introduced, and the flutter that stayed in my stomach long after he sauntered away, all long limbs and quiet confidence.

Within months we were a couple. We had seemed so perfect for each other that I remember wondering why we hadn't come together even sooner. We both aspired to be writers—me, children's books; him, music journalism—and wished to one day have families happier than the ones we had grown up with. We talked for hours before lapsing into the most comfortable silence, and traveled well together. Any arguments we had were swiftly resolved in bed.

But after two years of dating, I abruptly decided I wasn't ready to settle down—which really meant "I'm only twenty-five and I'm scared of how serious this is." I knew the minute I broke up with him that I shouldn't have, but the wheel was in motion and I did not allow myself to consider that I might have made a mistake. We were too young to choose life partners—and besides, he probably would have broken up with me eventually. Wasn't it smarter to preempt him and deal with the loss on my own terms?

That was the story I told myself for several years. At first, I proved just how not ready I was to settle down by dating a succession of jerks. Then I entered a semiserious relationship with a stoner who loved me even more than weed and wanted to know why I refused to say those three words to him. I finally told him it was because I didn't, and spent the following year solo. It was then that I realized that living without Sanjay was far worse than living with the fear he might leave me. I'd made a terrible mistake—possibly the biggest of my life. But it was too late.

He had left *Hudson* several months before we broke up, and through our friends I learned he was still working as a research assistant for a historian at Columbia and dabbling in writing on the side. He had moved from Harlem to Greenpoint, a neighborhood in Brooklyn, and had a serious girlfriend—a woman of Indian descent I bet he loved, even if our friends were too nice to tell me as much.

Then one rainy September evening we bumped into each other outside his favorite bookstore in the East Village. I would call it a coincidence, but it was really the consequence of me indulging myself by walking past his old haunts, as I occasionally did on my way home from work or when I should have been doing something productive. I didn't really think I would see Sanjay—not on a random Friday night. Yet just as I was approaching the shop, he emerged from it.

I remember thinking my eyes were playing tricks on me. How could the tall man in dark jeans and a corduroy blazer possibly be Sanjay? Surely this was another handsome if awfully thin Indian guy. Had I conjured him up? Maybe I would duck behind my umbrella and scurry past so I wouldn't look like the stalker I sort of was.

Then he called out to me: "Penny."

Our eyes met and I gave him a self-conscious smile.

"Hey," we said at the same time. Then we both laughed.

He was holding a book wrapped in a paper bag in one hand, and he gestured with it. I folded my umbrella and joined him under the bookstore awning, which was sending water cascading down in front of us. We watched it for a while before speaking.

"How have you been?" he said.

"I've missed you," I confessed.

"I've missed you, too." Though he was sheepish, I thought I saw something else in his eyes. After three years, he probably didn't love me anymore. Yet as I stared deeper into the black pools of his pupils, I allowed myself to consider that maybe he did.

"Do you want to get out of here? Go get a cup of tea, or whatever you'd like?" I said, and I meant it. This was nothing if not love at second sight. When I saw him striding out of the bookstore, I understood my life would never be the same—if only he would take me wherever he was going.

He did not respond for several seconds, and my heart gave a little lurch as I prepared to hear him say no.

"Yes," he said.

We were engaged two months later and married within the year. I had never been one for weddings, and the three hundred people Sanjay's parents invited to our reception put me off of them for good. But we emerged from the experience as blissful newlyweds. Finding and furnishing an apartment; hosting dinner parties and our first Thanksgiving dinner; traveling to new places, whether it was a Puerto Rican restaurant in the Bronx that purported to have the best *empanadillas* in New York, or to Mumbai to be feted by his father's family—it was all an adventure with Sanjay at my side. And though that giddy pace slowed when his premed classes began to eat up his nights and weekends, it remained a heady time, brimming with possibility and promise.

I had never wanted out back then.

~

I was thinking about this on my way to work as the driver behind me began honking like a maniac. As my eyes refocused, I realized I had drifted a teensy bit out of my lane. But it wasn't as though I had swerved to the other side of the road while texting and driving. And at least I had not been fantasizing about making not-so-sweet love to a stranger, as I sometimes did during my commute or while I pretended to watch Stevie clod-hop her way through ballet practice.

The driver who had been tailing me skidded into the next lane and flashed me the finger. Always eager to demonstrate my black belt in passive aggression, I gave him my best pageant wave and zipped past him.

The drive from my house to the development office at the far end of the medical campus was just three miles, but it took twelve to twenty excruciating minutes to get there depending on what time I left and how many roads were closed. Sanjay was constantly telling me to bike— it would be faster and good for me, he argued. He was probably right, but I was afraid of navigating traffic on two wheels and did not want to give my husband an opportunity to sleep with other women after I was flattened by a truck.

I'm grateful to have a job, I reminded myself as I began a claustrophobic spiral through the employee parking garage. Even at 8:32 in the morning, the only spots left were for electric cars. I pulled my gas-guzzler into one of them and scribbled a note on a piece of paper explaining that I had circled the whole garage to no avail and had to get to a nine o'clock meeting.

I am grateful to have transportation, I thought as part of the windshield wiper came flying off when I lifted it to tuck the note beneath it. I sighed, picked the rubber strip up off the pavement, and tossed it on the hood so I could deal with it . . . *Tomorrow!* I thought, recalling the Frog and Toad book I'd read to Miles and Stevie the night before. *I will do it tomorrow!*

As a child, I had loved the way books transported me into another world. As an adult, that magic had not worn off, and Frog and Toad remained my favorite children's book characters. Jenny adored them, too, and no surprise—she was so clearly Frog to my Toad. Reminding myself I was thankful for the very things that were irritating me was a move stolen straight from her website, Sweet Things.

Just the week before, she had posted about how she was anxious for Matt to get home from his latest business trip. She had paired the post with funny pictures of her staring at herself in the mirror, cursing the fact that she spent her teens coated in baby oil instead of sunscreen. She was prone to these kinds of corrosive thoughts when she was alone too long, she said.

It was only after she reminded herself she was grateful for Matt's position at a small venture capital firm—which kept him on the road for at least half the month—that she had immediately realized that all of her best ideas were the result of, as she had written, "the mental space that comes from being by yourself for stretches of time."

I wouldn't know. Since Sanjay worked from home (and lately he *was* working more, I had to admit), the only alone time I had was in the car. Yet the point stood: gratitude was at least mildly effective. And on a day like this one, I needed to remind myself that there was a good reason a sane person would pull herself out of bed at the crack of dawn, spend all of her waking hours tending to the needs of other people, and then do it again and again and again.

It was a labor of love. Or something like that.

"Morning, Penny."

I hadn't yet turned my computer on when Russ came barging into my office. It was a luxury having an entire windowless, shoebox-sized office to myself. Especially since it was rumored that soon we would all be working side by side at long tables so we could collaborate—or however the university would fictionalize the latest cost-reduction initiative.

As long as I had a door, however, I expected Russ to knock before throwing it open.

"I didn't mean to spook you," he said, sitting on the edge of my desk.

I glanced pointedly at the chair across from my own. "Who said I'm spooked?"

"Baby keep you up last night?" he said, looking down at me. I would never understand how a man who spent hours on his pecs each week could so blatantly fail to address his nose hair situation. Russ was the co-director of medical development—a title that had been created just for him after he protested when I was promoted to the same position first. However, he was sharp as a scythe and had taught me a lot about the art of closing a difficult "give," as we referred to charitable donations made to the university's hospital and medical school. As such, I tolerated more of his antics than I probably should have.

"He's *six*, Russell. So no, he did not," I said, as though my champion sleeper of an infant had not evolved into an elementary-aged insomniac with a chronic bedwetting problem. Sanjay felt this was the result of my coddling Miles; he said I had created a reward system in which our child was given attention and affection in exchange for destroying any semblance of REM sleep I might have otherwise enjoyed. I didn't know what else to do—I couldn't lock him in his room and insist he roll around on wet sheets until morning. And Sanjay was such a heavy sleeper that by the time he was conscious enough to be of any use, I was already wide awake and finished with putting Miles back to bed.

Russ regarded me skeptically. "You just look tired."

I leaned back in my chair to escape the cloud of his coffee breath. "You know when you say that you're basically telling someone they look awful, right?"

"You don't look awful. Just like you could use a night or two in a hotel room away from your kids."

I was not about to point out how inappropriate this comment could come across. "I'm swamped, and you and I already have a meeting on the books today. What's up?"

Russ clapped his hands, and I had to force myself not to wince—long-term sleep deprivation had made me skittish. "George Blatner just called. He's in town and wants to swing by tomorrow morning, which means we're going to need a proposal polished and ready before then. Medical initiatives, potential impact, supersad patient story—the whole nine. I'd write it, but I'm closing with the Rosenbaums this afternoon. And you know Adrian can't handle it," he said, referring to our staff writer, who took days to draft a single page.

"I'm on it," I said, because that's what I always said when there was work to be done.

Russ grinned. "Pediatric cancer's a goldmine—I'm willing to bet Blatner will drop close to a mil. You're welcome."

"Russell?"

He looked at me expectantly. "Yeah?"

"Please shut the door on the way out."

This meant I had even less time to get through the day's work than I had budgeted for, and just a few minutes to prepare for my nine o'clock meeting with my boss, Yolanda. Yet I still pulled my phone out of my bag and texted Jenny.

Please end it for me

Jenny usually wrote back right away, even if I texted late at night. But nearly an hour passed before I heard from her.

No can do, my love

Pretty please? There's a free latte or three in your future if you do

They don't serve coffee in heaven

Your point

Then I added, Russ dropped another unexpected project on my desk.

Another hour passed before she wrote back.

You could quit

It was such an un-Jenny-like thing to say that I actually checked to make sure I was looking at the right chain of messages. Yes—the text was from her.

Everyone had an off day, I reminded myself. Then I wrote:

I wish

To which she responded, Don't wish. If you're not happy, make a change.

Now *that* sounded more like Jenny, who spouted inspirational quotes the way some people recited Bible verses. Still, I couldn't say I agreed. Change was a privilege reserved for people whose families didn't rely on them for food, shelter, and health insurance. I thought she'd know that by now.

I stared at my phone screen, which was lit with a photo of Stevie and Miles frolicking on the beach during our last family vacation two years earlier, wondering how to respond. Jenny meant well, I reminded myself, so I texted her a heart symbol and set the phone beside my keyboard so I could continue chiseling through my workload.

But rather than working, I imagined myself in front of the ocean. Only this time I didn't fantasize about being alone. Instead I was with Stevie, Miles, and Sanjay. And in this fantasy, my children were building a sandcastle together instead of competing to see who could tear the other's limbs off first; and my husband, who was happy and fulfilled—or perhaps just gainfully employed—was gazing at me from his beach towel the way I often caught Matt looking at Jenny.

Which is to say with a look of love I had not seen in quite some time.

THREE

Sanjay called just before five, minutes after I had finally started writing the proposal I would be presenting the next morning. There would be no time to edit it, but just as well; I would be spared one of my supervisor's infamous revisions in which nouns were forced into verbitude. In Yolanda's world, you were expected to logic a problem, then inbox her the answer.

"Hey," I answered. "What's up?"

"Just reminding you that you're picking the kids up from camp today."

"Crap."

"You forgot."

I could barely remember my middle name half the time, let alone events he failed to put on our family calendar. "I did," I confessed. "Is there any way you can do it?"

"I have a jam." As a teen, Sanjay had dreamed of being the Indian Stevie Ray Vaughan—hence our daughter's name—and had recently joined a local garage band in what I assumed was a last-ditch attempt to recapture his youth before turning forty. "Remember?"

I was tempted to make a crack about how I was too busy keeping our family afloat to stay on top of his leisure activities. But then I glanced at the three lines I had just typed in an otherwise blank word processing document. If I left work at five and actually paused for dinner and to tuck in the kids, I would be up until at least eleven trying to wrap up the proposal. I could ask Russ for help, but he was probably already out golfing. If memory served, he was playing the back nine with Yolanda. How was it that everyone else managed to find free time?

I was nearly ready to curse with frustration when I remembered that Cecily was in camp with Miles and Stevie this week. Jenny would be happy to pick up the kids for me. "I'll handle it. Have fun with your band," I said to Sanjay, and though I had not meant this to come out as bitter as it sounded, I hung up without saying so.

I called Jenny from my office line. When she didn't pick up, I sent her a follow-up text and returned to the proposal. By 5:15 I still had not heard from her, which meant I should have left at least seven minutes earlier in order to make it to the kids' summer camp before they began charging me a dollar per child for each minute I was late.

I emailed the document I had been working on to myself, grabbed my purse, and speed-walked out of the office, praying no one would see me. The official end to our workday was five o'clock, and the department liked to flaunt this so-called perk when recruiting new hires. But ever since I was promoted, my coworkers gave me the side-eye if I was spotted leaving before the night janitor arrived. This frequently made me wonder just how much I really needed a fancy title and an extra eight thousand dollars a year. (On the latter count, the unfortunate answer was *a lot*.)

Russ did not seem to be subject to the same scrutiny. Maybe it was because he was a man. Or maybe because he waltzed through life expecting that things would go his way—and they mostly did. I sometimes wished I had it in me to emulate him and loudly announce I was going to a VERY IMPORTANT MEETING every time I left the building.

I made it to the parking lot without a single questioning glance and had just begun contemplating which route would get me to the kids' camp fastest when I realized my car was no longer where I had left it that morning.

Was there another area designated for electric cars? Maybe stress had short-circuited my mental compass. But as I looked beyond the concrete wall, the glowing sign for the buffalo wings bar where my colleagues insisted celebrating every birthday and business deal was blinking back at me—exactly as it had been that morning.

"This cannot be happening," I said aloud. I knew talking to myself made me look crazy, yet I usually did it anyway, which suggested that I should be more concerned about my mental health than how my muttering looked to other people.

"What can't be happening?" Russ came sauntering out of the elevator, swinging his keys on his finger. He stopped abruptly and cocked his head. "Uh-oh. What's wrong, Penny?"

I will not cry, I told myself. *I will not cry. I will not . . .* I felt a single tear escape the corner of my eye, which I quickly wiped away. "Aren't you supposed to be golfing?"

"I got held up in a meeting," he said. "So, what happened to you?"

"My car is missing," I said.

"Well, can you Uber?" Russ grinned at me. "You *do* know what Uber is, don't you?"

"It's not a good time for jokes, Russell. I'm late to get my kids, my car has been . . ." Now that my aging hatchback was no longer occupying the parking space, I could see the sign on the wall that clearly stated nonelectric vehicles would be towed at the owner's expense. "Impounded, and—" I had to stop because I was about to blurt out all sorts of vulnerable things to a man who probably ate baby bunnies for breakfast.

Then I had an idea. Granted, it was a terrible idea, but I was low on options and out of time. "Russell, can you drive me somewhere?"

From his expression, you'd think I just asked him to whisk me off to Wyoming. "I'm already late."

19

"I know, but this is really important. I have to pick my kids up from camp, and I don't have time to wait for an Uber. If I don't pick them up before six, I'll have to deal with a whole mess of paperwork and fees, and I'll be even further behind on the Blatner proposal. There's even a chance I won't finish it before he arrives tomorrow."

Now Russ was regarding me like I was leaning over the wall, threatening to splatter myself on the sidewalk in front of a bunch of people dining on dollar hot wings. I suppose I did sound a little frantic. "Okay," he said, making no effort to hide his reluctance. "Tell me where you need to be."

Asking Russ for a favor struck me as the epitome of stupidity. It was also the best decision I'd made all day. "It's about twenty minutes away," I said. I pulled my phone from my bag and sent up a last-ditch prayer that Jenny had called me back.

She had not.

"We'll be there in ten," said Russ, pointing a key fob at his recently waxed black sedan. The car beeped. "What's the address?"

I gave it to him and, with equal parts reluctance and relief, sank into the buttery leather passenger seat. A glance behind me confirmed that his backseat was so small, it had not been intended to accommodate any living thing, let alone two small children. It didn't matter. When I got to camp I would call Sanjay again, or maybe Jenny would be there. In that moment, all I needed to do was get to my kids.

"No GPS?" I said as Russ zipped down one side street only to turn abruptly onto another. I wanted to tell him to be careful—of my myriad worries, a child darting out in front of the car was one of the most pervasive and potent—but I bit my tongue and pushed my foot into an imaginary brake on the floor mat.

"I'm a townie, remember?" said Russ. He had been raised in town and had purposefully never left. "You practically are, too, at this point. You should know your shortcuts."

Was I practically a townie? Stevie would be eight in the fall, which meant we had lived here for . . . seven years. Through the car window, one Craftsman bungalow blurred into the next, and the next. Had it really been so long? In theory, I saw no problem with our having resided in the Midwest for nearly the same amount of time we had lived in New York. But in reality, it was not just that every year here felt like an erosion of the person I had been prior to having children—though there was certainly that. It was that I was not sure what all of those years represented. Was this it? Was this the goal, the reason, the sum total of two decades of adult decisions?

"Here we are," said Russ as he pulled up in front of the brick community center where the kids were attending the summer camp Sanjay's mother had subsidized so he could spend less time on what she deemed the womanly art of tending to one's children. "Nine and a half minutes. You're welcome."

"Thanks. I owe you," I said, hoisting myself out of the deep seat.

"You'll make it up to me," called Russ, but I was already running through a double door. The clock hanging in the lobby revealed that I had arrived with one minute to spare, which almost excused Russ from saddling me with the Blatner proposal.

The victory was short-lived. "You're *late!*" said Miles as he barreled toward me. I gasped as his forehead slammed into my stomach.

"Where were you?" said Stevie in a whiny baby voice from beneath the table where she was . . . hiding? Foraging for leftover lunch crumbs? It was anyone's guess.

"I'm not late," I said to my ungrateful spawn once I had regained the wind Miles had just knocked out of me. "I'm on time. And I was at work." *The same as every other day, except today I left early to get you because your father is busy living his best life.*

I was about to direct them to the hurricane of clothes and food storage containers they had scattered under their cubbies when I realized that there was a little girl sniffling on a beanbag in the corner—and this girl happened to be Cecily.

"Cess?" I called. "Where's your mom, sweetie?"

Her big blue eyes were brimming with tears. She sniffed. "I don't know."

"Aww, honey, it's okay," I said, kneeling beside her. I put my hand on her back.

"No touching, please," called the camp counselor, whose name started with a *B*—Brittany, maybe, or Becca—from across the room.

"She's my best friend's daughter," I said.

"I'm sorry, but it's against Knowledge Arena's policy. Only parents and counselors are allowed to have direct contact with the campers."

I was pretty sure I was first on Cecily's emergency forms, which made me the next closest thing to her parents, but arguing with the counselor wasn't going to help. Besides, Jenny would swoop in any second and save Cecily as well as me and my children, who still needed a ride home.

"No touching," I said, holding my hands palms up like a crime suspect. I winked at Cecily, who managed a small smile. "How about Stevie, Miles, and I hang out here with you until your mama shows up?" I asked, and she nodded.

We sat on the rug and read one book, and then another, and even after a third there still was no sign of Jenny. I called her again, but she didn't answer. Then I texted Sanjay to say that we needed a ride and to call me immediately.

Twenty dollars in late fees later, neither the camp nor I had been able to reach Jenny or Matt. He was home this week, so he was probably in the middle of a meeting or a conference call.

But where was *she*? Had she forgotten? That had happened once a few months earlier, but unlike me, she generally did not need to be reminded about things like picking up her children. Had she been felled by E. coli, or gotten in a car accident, or stopped to rescue a random person from something terrible? Only the last scenario was actually feasible—I could already imagine a self-deprecating post about how she had been walking through her neighborhood and happened upon an elderly woman who had fallen and couldn't get up.

I had just stood to look outside when the door opened. "See?!" I said triumphantly to the kids, who were rooting through my bag for snacks; even Cecily was peering into it with the wild eyes of a woman in the middle of a weeklong juice fast.

But it was just Russ. His tie was missing and the top of his shirt was unbuttoned, and for a second I wondered if he had returned from the golf course. "Everything okay?" he asked. "I've been waiting for you."

I stared at him, as incredulous as I was grateful. "You've been waiting? For me?"

"And your kids," he said. He did a double take. "There are *three* of them?"

"No, Russell. That's my best friend's daughter." I glanced back at the counselor, who was sighing heavily and repeatedly looking at the clock. "I should be listed on Cecily's emergency forms. Can I sign her out?"

"Let me confirm," she said.

She returned with her approval, and I refrained from making a remark about whether I was allowed to make contact with Cecily while taking her home. Then I texted Jenny to update her and hustled the children out of the building.

"Now what?" said Russ, looking in bewilderment as Stevie, Miles, and Cecily ran around the parking lot.

"Now I call my husband for the seventeenth time," I said.

Sanjay, who was probably blowing out his eardrums beside an amplifier in his friend Christina's garage, did not pick up. Nor did Jenny respond to my text. I was starting to feel shaky, and while I wanted to believe this was the result of my having three cups of coffee for lunch and the fact that the past hour had been a complete catastrophe, the truth was that a different sort of dread had come over me.

Motherhood had primed me to anticipate unlikely worst-case scenarios, and I tried to reassure myself that my internal disaster sensor was on overdrive, as per usual. But this feeling wasn't like when you realized your house had been quiet for thirty seconds too long only to find your beloved son practicing his penmanship in permanent marker on your beige sofa cushions.

It was something else entirely—something dark and unnamable.

Russ stared at me, and I was too rattled to look away. "Okay, Penny," he said, his pale-green eyes still locked with my own. "I know you're going to say no because we don't have five-point safety bubbles, or whatever it is you're supposed to trap the rug rats in, but how about we pile them into my backseat and I take you to wherever you need to be?"

I did not allow myself to think twice. "Yes. Thank you."

We got the kids into Russ' car and explained that, yes, they really did need car seats, but every so often rules had to be broken for a good cause. Miles began to cry, as he was known to do after missing an hourly feeding. "I don't want to die," he wailed. "I don't want to—"

"No one's going to die," interjected Russ. "I'm the best driver in this whole damn town."

"Really?" said Miles, instantly calmed.

"Mommy, that man said *damn*," said Stevie, who had once detonated an f-bomb in the middle of her school's pan-denominational holiday play. (The boy beside her had stomped on her foot, and her mommy and daddy used that word when *they* were in pain, she explained when Sanjay and I were called in for a family meeting with her principal.) Now she pretended to be the morality police whenever adults were present.

"That man's name is Russ," I said over my shoulder, "and he's nice enough to drive us to Auntie Jenny's, so zip it."

"Russell," corrected Russ, who had begun going by his full name around the same time he had decided we should share a title.

"Sorry," I said, checking my phone again. "Russell."

When we arrived at the Sweets', Jenny's white SUV was in the driveway. She must have just gotten home, I told myself, because I had been swimming in desperation long enough that any shape in the distance was now a lifeboat.

"You sure you don't want me to wait?" Russ asked as I helped the kids out of his car.

"No, you've done enough," I said, even though I was ever so slightly tempted to finally introduce Jenny to the coworker I had been complaining about. "Thank you."

"Awfully swank place," he said as he took in Jenny's midcentury ranch. With its floor-to-ceiling windows and sloping, manicured lawn, it looked like the kind of house you'd expect to see in *Architectural Digest*. Jenny and Matt had bought it for a song at the bottom of the market, and from what I had gathered spent hundreds of thousands transforming it into their "forever home" (as opposed to the FEMA trailer they must have thought our bungalow was, I sometimes thought when they said this).

"Yes, it is."

"Even Yolanda's house isn't this nice." He kept staring straight ahead. "Don't you wonder sometimes?"

"About working in development?"

He shrugged, and I understood that he meant that, but also everything.

"Yes," I admitted. "All the time."

No one had answered the door, and the kids, who had run up the stairs, were banging on the windows on either side of the door. "That's my cue," I told him. "Thanks again for saving the day."

"Don't mention it."

"Stop pounding on the glass, you guys," I told the kids as I joined them at the front door. I pressed the doorbell once, and then a second time. I was still jittery, but my mind was already leaping ahead. If Sanjay didn't call me back sometime soon, hopefully Matt or Jenny could drive us home; otherwise I would end up dragging the kids on the mile-long walk. Of course, I still had to find out where my car had been towed and pay what was sure to be an exorbitant fine in order to retake possession of it. But that would have to wait until the following afternoon, because I needed to spend the entire rest of the evening working on the Blatner proposal, then wake at dawn, at which point I would spackle over my exhaustion with concealer and caffeinate myself into—well, if not a charismatic state, then a competent one—

The whir of a car engine cut through my thoughts. I turned to see Matt pulling up in the driveway.

"Penny?" he said as he came striding toward me. Jenny's husband was movie-star handsome, with a thick head of salt-and-pepper hair, hazel eyes, and a zero-to-sixty smile that seemed more like a flash of generosity than a facial expression.

"Am I ever glad to see you," I said. "Have you talked to Jenny? I've been trying to reach her for hours now."

"No . . ." He looked at me curiously, then over at his daughter, who was attempting to work Miles' curls into a tiny ponytail. "So, you *weren't* supposed to pick Cess up?"

Cecily lifted her head at the sound of her name. "Hi, Daddy."

"Hey, Pumpkin," he said.

I shook my head. "Jenny didn't show. The school called you, and so did I. I thought maybe you had surprised her with a trip to Paris."

Rather than the reassuring laugh I had been aiming for, his eyes glinted with concern. Then he opened the front door and waved us in.

The kids trailed behind me like ducklings, then decamped to the kitchen. As I watched Cecily retrieve snacks from the cupboard, I had a momentary flashback to childhood—scraping the remains of a tub of margarine onto stale, crumbled crackers and placing them in my brother Nick's hands because there were no clean plates or napkins to use. Cecily had probably never tasted margarine. She certainly knew nothing of the insatiable hunger of being motherless. And yet she was so careful—opening each pack of gummies and handing it to my children before doing the same for herself—that I had the uncanny sense of having rewound and watched some secret footage of my past.

I sat on one of the stools at the marble island separating the kitchen from the rest of the first floor as the kids wandered into the living room.

Miles and Cecily were on the rug, where he was pretending to be some sort of animal to her sadistic zookeeper. Stevie retrieved a book from a bookshelf and sprawled on one of the Sweets' sofas, which almost made up for everything else that had happened that day. I had been reading to her since she was a baby, waiting anxiously for a sign that she understood the magic that happened when you could interpret the scribbles on a page. But it wasn't until she started seeing a reading specialist the year before that she began picking up books without me pushing her to do so.

"Jen?" Matt called out in the distance just as Sanjay's name lit up my phone.

"Aww, you thought of little old me?" I said to my husband when I picked up.

"Want to tell me why I have thirty-two missed calls from you?"

Cecily had mounted Miles' back, and with a vaguely Russian accent was commanding him to buck like a bronco. "Want to tell me why you didn't check your voicemail?" I asked Sanjay.

"No one checks voicemail, Pen." *Duh,* I heard him add mentally. "So?"

"So, my car got towed."

He cursed. "That's going to cost a fortune, you know."

It took everything in me not to point out that I would be the one paying for it, and that in fact I had already spent the past hour paying for it. "Can you please come get us? We're at the Sweets'."

He sighed just loud enough for me to hear. "Okay."

Behind me, Miles was whinnying. "We're excited to see you, too," I said.

"Please don't give me a hard time. I'm doing what you want without complaining."

Technically this was true, and it was the exact thing I was always asking him to do. What I had not said—and felt he should have understood—was that I did not just want compliance; I also wanted a hint of enthusiasm. Though by that point, even his not sighing would have been something to celebrate. This was on the tip of my tongue when Matt appeared in my peripheral vision.

"I need to go," I told Sanjay.

"Traffic is probably nuts right now. It'll take me at least ten minutes to get there."

"No problem. Thanks."

The Sweets' stairs were large, gleaming slats of hardwood hung on a stainless-steel frame. The gap between each step was wide enough that a small child could easily slip through them; they were "lovely and lethal," Jenny had said apologetically one of the first times I had come over. She and Matt planned to fix it before they had a second child, she told me, but years had passed since then.

Matt was at the foot of the stairs. The expression on his face instantly reminded me of the blank stare Miles wore when he was sleepwalking and was seconds from mistaking a corner in my bedroom for a urinal.

"Are you okay?" I asked. Stupidly—it was clear he was not.

"No." He was holding his phone out toward me. I could hear that someone on the other end was speaking, though I could not decipher what they were saying.

The fine hairs on the nape of my neck were still standing at attention. "What is it?"

"It's . . . Jenny."

Stop there, I thought. *Don't let your beautiful mouth utter another word. Let's have one more minute where life is what I believe it to be and everything is fine.* And yet I said, "What about her?"

Matt's eyes were on me, but he was still looking right through me. "I think she's dead."

FOUR

But I didn't have *time* for Jenny to die.

It was a terrible thought—the selfish, overly rational sort that surfaces before you've allowed yourself to admit everything has changed and trivial matters like space and time no longer matter. It was still what first popped into my head as I ran toward Matt.

He stood there, frozen, then handed me the phone and sat down on the last step. I glanced at him before stepping around him.

Upstairs, the hallway looked the same as it ever did: crisp gray walls decorated with a variety of framed candids and professionally shot photos; the wide, gleaming mahogany floor and its Persian runner, which probably cost twice as much as our monthly mortgage payment. No blood anywhere, let alone signs of chaos, I noted, though my heart was still galloping in my chest: *dead-dead, dead-dead, dead-dead.*

I lifted the phone to my head and heard a voice say, "Sir? Sir, are you there?"

To my left, the spare bedroom was empty. Just beyond it, Cecily's room was empty, too. "This is Penelope Ruiz-Kar," I said quietly into the receiver. "I'm . . ."

I'm looking for my friend, who may or may not be alive.

"Can you confirm your location?" asked the woman who had answered what I assumed must have been Matt's 911 call.

I rattled off the Sweets' address.

"Ma'am, are you in a safe place?" asked the woman.

Was I? "I think so."

"Does there appear to be an intruder in the house?"

This possibility had not occurred to me. If there were, Matt would have been behaving differently . . . wouldn't he? "I don't know. I'm pretty sure there isn't."

"Ma'am, I'm going to have to advise that you take yourself and anyone else in the home outside while you wait for the police and emergency personnel to arrive."

"Okay," I said as I walked into Jenny's bedroom.

The room was supposed to feel like a sanctuary, at least in its current iteration—Jenny had redecorated it twice since she and Matt had moved in, each time for a feature for her website. In this latest round, she had the walls painted a delicate gray, and the heavy velvet drapes had been replaced with pale cotton curtains and Roman blinds. Her king-size bed was a sea of white linens, and there were plants everywhere—tall fiddle-leaf figs in ceramic pots on the floor, air plants in delicate glass bubbles hanging in front of the windows, orchids in matte-glazed planters on the dressers. Jenny said Matt told her he felt like he fell asleep in the rainforest every night. I had never been clear whether this was a good thing.

At any rate, Jenny was not on the bed, or anywhere else in the room. I braced myself as I opened the door to their master bath, but she was not in their claw-foot tub, or in the spacious shower stall.

The woman on the phone was still speaking, but I was no longer listening. *Her office,* I thought at once.

I found Jenny sitting—sprawled, really—in the cream-colored armchair in the corner of the room. With her arms gracefully outstretched, legs straight and bare feet resting just so, she looked like a dancer. The chair was beside a window, and the last of the day's sun cast a strange light over her face, which was—

The phone slipped from my hand and hit the rug with a thud.

Her face was all wrong. Though they were closed, her eyes appeared to be looking in opposite directions. But her mouth, which was not the usual bright pink but so pale it nearly blended into the rest of her skin, was gaping open—too wide, I thought, much too wide. There was a dribble of something—food, or maybe vomit—on her bottom lip. For all her fretting about sun damage, she had already tanned to a golden brown in mid-June, but now her limbs looked like pale putty.

Worse, her chest wasn't moving. And when I put my hand over her mouth, I couldn't detect even the thinnest stream of air.

But she didn't *look* dead, I thought ridiculously—I'd never actually seen a dead person outside of a funeral home. If she was dead, her eyes would be wide open . . . wouldn't they? She had to be napping. Passed out, maybe.

"Jenny," I said softly, like I was trying to gently wake her. "Jenny!" I said, this time loudly. By the time I took her by the shoulders to shake her leaden body, I had realized that Matt was right. She was not alive.

Which meant she was right in front of me . . . but not there. Not there at all.

A terrible, strangled sound escaped me, and I touched Jenny again—poked her, really—in the stomach. I don't know why I did it, and thank God no one was there to see me prodding her. Maybe I just needed to be sure that I had not been mistaken. My fingers were met with the thinnest layer of soft flesh over a plane of muscle. Had she really grown so slim? *I need to take her out for a burger,* I thought. Then I reached for her hand, which was no longer a hand at all but rather a cold and lifeless thing, and realized there would be no burgers in her future.

But how stupid was I? What if Jenny had only been dead a few seconds? Or had suffered a heart attack or stroke and was still just the tiniest bit alive? (Was there such a thing as a little alive? Obviously seven years of working for the medical school had given me no real insight into matters of life and death.) I needed to try to resuscitate her. Immediately.

I had gone through CPR training right before I had Stevie, but like so many other things stored in my mind, motherhood had overwritten that file. Did I pinch her nose and put my mouth to hers? Press her chest . . . yes, but at the same time I was breathing into her mouth?

"Ma'am?"

I jumped straight up in the air. A police officer was behind me, and a man and two women were wheeling in a stretcher through the door. It took me a second to realize that they were emergency medical technicians or paramedics.

"We're going to need you to leave the room," the officer said.

"Going," I mumbled, slinking to the door, like I was somehow responsible for Jenny's condition.

In the hallway, Matt was walking toward me. His face was etched with a distant sort of pain; it looked almost as though he were watching this unfold from somewhere far away. I immediately recognized the feeling, even as I told myself to stay present—if not for Matt, then for Cecily.

"Don't go in," I told him.

His eyes welled with tears. "Then I'm right."

"I don't know, but don't go in there."

"She's dead," he whispered.

I stared at him. Yes, I was pretty sure she was dead. But . . . maybe the emergency responders had an antidote to bring her back to life. Maybe we would all wake up any minute now and realize this was a terrible dream. Or—well, I didn't know what, but something other than this.

Then I saw another set of policemen marching up the stairs, each with a hand on his holster, and reality came rushing back at me.

Matt must have felt that way, too, because he suddenly said, "I might throw up. Can you find Cecily and keep her away from this?" He didn't wait for my response as he ran toward the bathroom.

I could keep an eye on Cecily.

But who would be there for me?

~

As I descended the stairs, I found myself thinking back to how Jenny and I became friends—a story that began even before we met. The night before Sanjay and I left Brooklyn, our closest friends threw us a farewell dinner at our favorite restaurant. Stevie was six months old and at that point a wonderful child, the kind that tricked you into thinking that you had this parenting thing figured out. I bounced her on my knee as small plates were passed and wineglasses were refreshed again and again. At one point my friend Alex smiled at me with bright-red lips and said in her odd Wisconsin-by-way-of-West-New-Guinea accent, "Don't worry, darling. You'll be back."

"Of course we will," I said, though I knew nothing of the sort. "If all goes as planned, maybe even as soon as four years from now for Sanjay's residency."

We three Ruiz-Kars were headed West—not even halfway across the country, though at the time even New Jersey seemed like Timbuktu. But our course was already set. After years of preparation, Sanjay had been accepted into the ninth-highest-ranked medical school in the country, where he planned to become a neurologist or nephrologist or maybe even a psychiatrist like his father.

To say I had reservations about this plan, however glittering, was a vast understatement. Sanjay and I had known each other for almost a decade and had been together for seven of those years. All that time he had been a seed—ripe with potential but drifting unsown on the wind. How could a man who spent hours watching documentaries about Jimi

Hendrix and reading Charlie Parker and Chet Baker biographies believe that yet more schooling would magically transform him into a person who was passionate about physiology? Why couldn't he accept who he was and find something useful and well paying to do with his real interests, which were music and the arts and—well, not medicine? Didn't he see that there was a reason he had gone to work at a cultural magazine instead of attending med school after graduating from college?

And yet. Being a doctor was what his parents wanted for him. *Expected* of him. Moreover, his fulfilling this plan would provide a good, stable life for the family he and I had just started. While I harbored no fantasies about being a doctor's wife, I did not loathe the idea of being able to go to the grocery store and buy what I wanted without thinking about how much it would cost, nor the possibility of taking vacations with Sanjay and Stevie without running up credit card debt that would take years to pay off, if we ever did at all. Maybe later down the line, I thought, I could even take a whole year off just to write children's books.

Even so, my short-term worries far outweighed any hopes or fears about how the rest of our lives would unfold. As I looked around the table at Alex, Harue, Jon, and Malcolm—people we had known for almost a decade, four of the six of us having met at *Hudson*—I felt an aching, preemptive loss.

Alex and Malcolm had been with me in the *Hudson* break room on 9/11, glued to the television with horror as we learned our city was under attack. Despite her vocal distaste for children, Alex had held my hand as I caterwauled my way through Stevie's birth. And when Sanjay and I broke up, Harue had been the first to tell me I was a fool to leave him—a tragedy of sorts that she had retold as a comedy when toasting us at our wedding.

"You'll be back," said Harue. She drained her wine, then wiped her mouth with the back of her hand, having had so much to drink that manners were a distant memory. She added, "You'll be back, because you'll miss us too much, and you'll run out of things to do there."

Harue was right, I thought miserably as I drove past the forests and fields of Pennsylvania, through the flat expanse of Ohio, and north to the Michigan college town that was to be our home. We were making a terrible mistake.

That first year I quickly discovered she was wrong on one count: a dearth of things to do would never again be a problem. My husband disappeared into his coursework, I started a new job, and Stevie became mobile, revealing that the first year of parenting was not the hardest, after all. Then one December morning I threw up into my wastebasket at work and realized—with a horror that still fills me with shame—that I had gotten pregnant during the sole occasion Sanjay and I had slept together that fall.

I *was* lonely, though. Cripplingly so, and the email chain I kept up with Alex and Harue did little to ease the feeling that I had been marooned on a landlocked Midwestern island. I had taken a midlevel fundraising position in the university's medical development department, and to my surprise I liked the work well enough—if only because I was good at it. But most of my coworkers were younger than me and childless, and those who were the same age or older were bachelors or men who behaved as though their children were hobbies. Even before I was pregnant with Miles, no one seemed to understand why I really— *no, really*—couldn't grab a cocktail after work or join the development association's golf league. As I would quickly come to realize, having a child—and then another—was a professional liability for a person like me, which is to say a woman.

I tried going to moms' groups on the weekends, but I always felt awkward and out of place. When a brute of a toddler in the music-with-mommy class repeatedly played the role of Little Bunny Foo Foo to Stevie's field mouse while his mother cheered his innate leadership skills, I decided I would have to get comfortable with going it alone.

Then I met Jenny.

It was a Saturday, or maybe a Sunday. I had recently had Miles and was still oozing from too many places, but I had used up my maternity leave, which meant Sanjay had already dropped out of medical school and I was adjusting to life as a working mother of two. (This consisted of overparenting at night and on the weekends, and thinking self-defeating thoughts while huddled over a breast pump in a bathroom stall scrolling through photos of my children's life without me several times a day during the workweek.) I was pushing Miles, who was screaming his head off, in his stroller through a nearby park. I had just wheeled past a play structure when I came upon a woman with a baby in a sling, bouncing from one foot to the other with the kind of energy I had not had since before Stevie was born.

Of course, this woman was Jenny and her baby was Cecily. For whatever reason, I paused in front of them.

"Sounds like your little man's not too happy," said Jenny with a warm smile.

I shook my head. "Nope. He's been like this for weeks. I've tried everything short of an exorcism."

"What about probiotics?" said Jenny. She looked down at Cecily, who was the sort of pretty, peaceful infant that triggered ovulation in unwitting women. "That worked wonders for Cecily's colic."

"I haven't tried that yet."

"Get the drops—it's practically a miracle cure. Your first?" she asked, nodding in Miles' direction.

"Second." I pointed at my waist. "Hence my two spare tires."

"Don't say that. You look fantastic."

"For someone who's six months pregnant," I said.

She laughed. Her laugh was throaty and bright; it was easy to imagine her cast as the ingénue in a romantic comedy. "Cecily's my first."

She was awfully chic for a new mother, I thought, taking in her caftan-style dress, long sweater coat, and highlighted hair, which was artfully piled on top of her head. Even more than her clothes, though, she seemed like a parenting pro. But she probably had a mom who had shown her what to do. Nick was four when my mother left; I was six. I'd been winging the mothering thing ever since.

"How old is your daughter?"

"Three months," she said. "This little peanut won't let her mama sleep more than two hours at a time."

"Miles is four months," I said.

The corners of her mouth shot halfway across her cheeks as she grinned. "Practically twins!" She stuck out her hand, which I shook, not without noting that the paint on her nails was worn but most definitely the work of a salon professional. "By the way, I'm Jenny Sweet."

"Penelope Ruiz-Kar," I said. "But you can call me Penny."

"Jenny and Penny," she said, still smiling. "We should be friends."

And so we were. Almost as soon as Jenny came into my life, things took a turn for the better. There is something about seeing someone like you thrive that helps you to do the same. It was true that even then, Jenny and Matt were financially comfortable in a way that Sanjay and I were not. They were, well, polished—whereas Sanjay wore T-shirts and track pants most of the time, and though I tried to make an effort, I inevitably found a Cheerio stuck to the back of my pants hours after I had sat on it.

Yet Jenny, like me, was a mother in her early thirties. While I longed to return to New York, she pined for San Francisco; she and Matt had uprooted after he took a position with a financial firm run by a former business school classmate. Though she stayed home with Cecily, hiring a sitter only when absolutely necessary, she had recently started a website—though back then it was just a blog, sans sponsors and professional-looking photos—and worked constantly.

As for my loneliness, Jenny quickly put an end to that. She seemed to know everyone, even though she and Matt had moved to our town six short months before we had, and she was eager to connect me. Here was a hairdresser who knew how to turn the frizz on my head into a sleek chestnut bob; there was a yoga teacher who could fix my postpartum back problems. She also introduced me to Sonia and Jael, who were also relatively new mothers, and soon the four of us had a standing brunch date on Sundays.

"You have a crush on this woman," remarked Sanjay as I applied tinted balm in front of the mirror one Sunday morning in preparation for brunch, which had become the highlight of my week.

"Isn't that how all friendships begin?" I asked before pressing my lips together to even out the color. "With some degree of platonic infatuation?" What I did not say to him was that it was not so much infatuation as deep relief at having a friend in the thick of it with me—and who seemed to hold the answer to my heart's hidden question: how to be a good mother.

Sanjay looked at me quizzically for a moment. "I don't know," he finally said. "But you seem good lately. Happier."

Happier wasn't what he really meant. At peace, maybe, or at least accepting of my lot in life.

A few days after dropping out of medical school, Sanjay had surprised me by offering to become a stay-at-home dad. He would write during the kids' naps or whenever he could find an opportunity, he explained. If all went well, by the time Miles was ready for preschool, Sanjay would have figured out the next step of his life.

I readily agreed. I didn't really want to hire a stranger to watch my children or drop my months-old baby off at a daycare center for all of the hours he would be awake. More important, Sanjay was offering to be the father my own father had never been. Why *wouldn't* I give my family this incredible gift? My job paid enough that we could just make it work in the short term.

But after a few months, it began to sink in that for all the perks of our arrangement, it did not reduce my parenting load one bit. Sanjay was just as exhausted as I was at the end of the day—so how could I blame him for not having done the dishes or scheduled Miles' next pediatrician appointment? And if Stevie still wanted me to make her breakfast and help her get dressed and tell her stories until my voice was hoarse, could I fault her? I *was* gone most of the time she was awake.

One morning I was trying to pry Stevie off my leg so I could make it to work on time when it struck me: as wife, mother, breadwinner, and chief of operations chez Ruiz-Kar, I had become the fulcrum of my family's health and wealth.

And frankly, that was kind of terrifying.

But having a friend who understood that made it easier to keep marching forward—day after day after day.

~

The children. What was I supposed to do with the children?

Sanjay was in the foyer, clad in athletic shorts and a Cornell T-shirt he'd owned since attending there as an undergrad. "Where are they?" I whispered when I reached him.

He jerked his head back, indicating that the kids were elsewhere in the house. "Pen, what is happening?" He looked up the stairs. "The police . . . the ambulance . . ."

I couldn't bring myself to say it. I just stood there waiting for something to change.

"Cecily is upset," said Sanjay. I knew he wasn't directing this comment at me, and yet it made me feel guilty. "She saw them come in, obviously, and she's hiding in the bathroom. The kids are in there with her."

I put a hand on the wall to steady myself. The house was air-conditioned to the point of refrigeration, and the drywall was cold to the touch. "Does she know . . ."

"Know what?" Now Sanjay sounded irritated. "What the hell is going on?"

"Matt thinks . . . I just saw . . ."

His eyes bulged, commanding me to finish.

"Jenny." I had to push the words out. "She's dead."

He let out a low curse. "Did you see her?"

I thought of Jenny's tongue, prostrate across her bottom teeth. No wonder Matt had run off—I wasn't sure I wouldn't vomit right then and there. "Yes."

"Aneurism," Sanjay said, more to himself than to me. "Or a heart attack. But she's so healthy. Genes. You just never know."

"Stop, please," I said. Matt had asked me to take care of Cecily. I needed to focus—which meant that by extension, so did Sanjay. "Can you take the kids home?"

"And *leave* you here?"

"I can't go. What if she needs me?" I was sure Sanjay thought I was talking about Cecily, but in truth I meant Jenny.

But she didn't need me. She couldn't—not anymore.

Another paramedic had just entered the house with a police officer. Now they were in the foyer, asking me to move aside so they could get through.

"I don't understand," said Sanjay, though he was gently pulling me toward the living room.

"There's nothing to understand," I said. "Right now I just need you to go into the bathroom." I could hear myself talking—I sounded like a flight attendant cheerfully reading safety instructions that would keep absolutely no one safe in the event of an actual crash. "Go in there and entertain the kids until I knock on the door and tell you it's okay to come out."

He looked at me, almost like he was waiting to see if I was kidding. Then he jogged off.

Less than a minute later, Matt appeared at the top of the stairs. He stepped aside as one of the first medics who had entered the house walked past him.

"Where is my friend?" I said to the medic.

She didn't look at me.

"Excuse me!" I said loudly. "Why are you leaving?"

Now she turned my way. "I'm not leaving," she said evenly. "Our team will be on hand until the medical examiner arrives and the police are done conducting their investigation."

My stomach dropped at the phrase *medical examiner*. "Are they doing CPR on her?"

"Yes, ma'am. We do everything we can in cases like these."

Cases like what? I wanted to say, but I couldn't make my mouth form the words.

"If you'll excuse me, I have to get something from the ambulance," the medic said, and let herself out the front door.

Matt had descended the stairs and was staring past me blankly. I reminded myself that he was in shock. People acted in all kinds of strange ways in situations like this. At least, some people did. Others understood they had to keep it together for the sake of everyone else.

"I can stay here if you'd like. For Cecily . . . or whatever you need," I said. Jenny and Matt had no family nearby; hers was in Utah and California, and his was on the East Coast.

"Can you take Cecily home with you?" he said. "As soon as possible. Go out the back door and have Sanjay pull around the back alley. I don't think she should see any of this."

"Of course," I said.

He was still looking out the door. "She'll hate me one day."

He was definitely in shock.

"What? No," I said. "She could never hate you."

"She will. I could have prevented this."

Now he was just talking crazy. "Jenny—" Is? Was? I wasn't sure what to say. "She's healthy as a horse. This was some freak thing, maybe something genetic. A heart attack, or an aneurism," I said, repeating what Sanjay had said. "I'm so sorry this happened, but you absolutely cannot blame yourself right now."

Matt sighed and met my gaze. The whites of his eyes were now flooded red. He no longer resembled a movie star. No—now he looked like an ordinary man at the tail end of a several-day bender. "Oh, Penelope," he said. "Jenny had serious problems. And I let her keep pretending everything was fine."

FIVE

Problems? Everyone, no matter how perfect they seemed, had problems. Almost none were the kind that landed you in the morgue. I had no idea what Matt was talking about, but there wasn't time to ask. "I'm going to find the police," he told me. Then he disappeared.

I stood in the space between the foyer and the living room, staring at the stairs. Except rather than glass and steel, I saw Jenny splayed out in her armchair.

Any false hope I had been clinging to when I first found her was long gone.

Please end it for me.

Why had I texted her that? What if I had somehow planted the idea of death in her head? Forget Matt's inexplicable guilt—what if *I* had done this to her? I had spent much of the day wishing for an escape, but now I really wanted to beam myself into an idyllic reality. No need for a white-sand beach and well-behaved kids. Jenny being alive would have been more than enough.

"Ma'am?" said a police officer as he approached me. "Can I ask you a couple questions?"

I had watched a few procedural shows in my day, and I guess I was expecting him to tell me I should come to the station, wherever that was, and had already begun panicking about what I would do with Cecily and my kids. Instead, the officer pulled out his notebook and shot off a series of questions: What was my relationship to Jenny and the rest of the Sweet family? What time had I arrived at their house? Had I seen anyone suspicious in the area at that time? What about the house itself; how had that looked? When had I last spoken to Jenny? Had I noticed anything amiss about her then? Then he stopped scribbling on his notepad, looked up, and said, "Was your friend known to have a drug problem?"

"Jenny?" I said. "No way."

The officer was nearly a foot taller than me, with a neck the width of his head. "Sorry," he said, not sounding the slightest bit so. "I have to ask."

I hadn't been offended. Whatever Matt may have implied, I knew for a fact Jenny was a lightweight; I couldn't remember the last time I saw her have more than a second glass of wine. She wouldn't even be photographed with a glass in her hand—it was off brand for her site, she once explained before setting down her goblet to prepare for a picture. She did not want to run the risk of ostracizing her followers, many of whom were young religious women who did not drink coffee, let alone alcohol.

"It's fine. I've never seen Jenny—" I did not have the vocabulary to finish my sentence. Snort? Inject? I didn't know what drugs he was talking about. "I've never seen her do anything illegal," I finally said. "She barely drinks. I have to assume this was a freak health problem."

The officer nodded, which seemed to imply that I was correct. Then he took down my contact information, closed his notebook, and said it would be best if I left the house while the investigation was underway.

He was halfway up the stairs when I called after him. "My friend," I said lamely. "She's dead, right?"

"That's for the medical examiner to decide."

"So . . ." *What do I do now?*

He looked me in the eye. "Your friend? She had a little girl, right?"

Had.

I nodded.

"Go be with her," he said.

~

In the bathroom, Sanjay was playing a video on his phone with the volume turned on high. This had placated the kids, but only so much.

"Where's Mommy?" Cecily demanded when I let myself in.

I stared at her, willing myself not to cry. It was a question I remembered all too well.

Worse, I knew what came after the answer.

"Why are we stuck in the bathroom?" said Miles.

"What was all that noise out there?" demanded Stevie.

"It's a long story," I managed.

"Golden arches?" whispered Sanjay.

I nodded, and he announced we were going to get Happy Meals. The chorus of questions was replaced by my children cheering— McDonald's was a treat.

Cecily didn't seem half as thrilled, but she didn't keep pressing for answers, even after I made them wait in the bathroom while Sanjay brought the car around back and when we shuffled them out the back door. I tried not to look at her too much on the short drive to the restaurant. It wasn't just that she was the spitting image of Jenny. To see her was to be reminded of what she no longer had.

"Aunt Penny?" said Cecily as I placed her Happy Meal in front of her.

"Yes, love?" I said.

"Mommy doesn't let me go to McDonald's."

My eyes smarted, and I blinked furiously and made myself think of Russ' nose hair. "I know, sweetie," I said as Miles slipped beneath the table. "But I think this one time will be okay. All right?"

"Ow! Miles, *stop* right *now!*" yelled Stevie before Cecily could respond.

There was a thump under the table, and then my son reemerged, bawling. "You're mean!" he said to Stevie. "*Mean!* You're a—"

"Miles, please," interjected Sanjay. "Sit and eat your cheeseburger."

"She kicked me in the brain," he said, starting to cry again. He glowered at Stevie. "You're a fat turd log, and you smell like one, too."

"Penny," said Sanjay, staring at me. I stared back, imagining throwing a carton of fries at him, because what he was asking was for me to parent them. Of all the days—of all the times—could he not step up? His argument was always the same: our children didn't listen to him when I was around. They didn't listen to me, either, but Sanjay was counting on me to pull out my bag of mothering tricks and either guilt or cajole them into compliance.

"Do you guys want a story?" I asked the kids. My voice sounded wooden, but my kids didn't seem to notice. They stopped squabbling and began making requests—mutant alligators, a princess who only wore pants, kryptonite. This was our routine: they supplied the characters and key elements, and I devised a plot. Even Cecily began chiming in to say she wanted the princess to have a pet frog.

I had just had the princess' frog swallow the kryptonite in order to defeat the alligators when my phone began buzzing in my bag. I steadied myself, expecting to see Matt's name or maybe even a hospital number on the screen.

It was Russ. Checking in to make sure you actually got home, he had written.

"One second, guys," I said to the kids, trying to sound as though my heart had not just sunk yet again. Russ' text had just reminded me that there were nearly a million dollars riding on a proposal that I had not yet written and would not write at any point that evening. Worse, I had forgotten to tell Russ, who would have to be the one to inform George Blatner that we had nothing to show him. I began to type.

So sorry! I didn't, because—

I quickly erased this and tried again.

I'm really sorry. I'm not going to be able to do—

I erased that, too. Thumbs trembling, I wrote, My friend Jenny is dead. I haven't done the proposal and I won't be in tomorrow. I'll make it up to you.

Damn, Russ wrote back seconds later. I'll take care of it. I'm sorry, Penny.

His uncharacteristically gracious response made the situation feel . . . real, somehow. I took a long drink of my soda to wash down the sob in my throat.

Beside me, Sanjay was shoveling fries down his gullet. "Anything?" he said, half a fry still hanging from his mouth.

"No. It was work."

Across the table, Cecily had removed a miniature knock-off Barbie from its plastic packaging, but was still regarding the rest of her cardboard-box meal with suspicion. I expected her to ask me to finish my story, and honestly, I was hoping she would—even a world with mutant alligators was preferable to the red-and-gold blur of the restaurant, where children were screeching, the odor of burger patties and fries was permeating my clothes, and I was forced to grapple with the reality that I no longer had a best friend.

But when she looked up at me with saucer-wide eyes, Cecily said, "Aunt Penny? Where's Mommy?"

Storytime was over. "I'm not sure, Cess, but I think she's with your daddy."

Who was aware your mommy had a problem that I knew nothing about.

SIX

Our Happy Meal trick may have worked, but the kids were markedly less enthused about the sleepover Sanjay and I proposed on the way home. Stevie, who took sleep almost as seriously as Sanjay did, complained that she was too tired. Miles whispered that he didn't want Cecily to know if he had an accident.

And Cecily—well, Cecily was no fool. "Mommy said I can't spend the night at someone else's until I'm ten," she said crossly from the backseat. "I'm not ten for another three and a half years. I want to go home."

"Well, this is . . ." I couldn't exactly call it a special occasion. "This is an exception. Like McDonald's," I said, though Cecily had barely touched her meal. I cringed as I began my next lie. "Your parents are in the middle of something important. So, you're going to stay with us, just for a little bit."

"Mommy would have told me that," she insisted. "I want her to come get me. Right. Now."

My throat tightened. My mother used to go missing for hours at a time, until one night she disappeared for good. But while I had certainly watched Cecily for a day at a time in the past, Jenny had always informed her daughter of her plans beforehand.

I swallowed hard, searching for the same courage I'd had to summon when telling Nick not to worry, that our mother wasn't there but everything would still be okay. Like then, I didn't buy what I was trying to sell. But acting like I did with every fiber of my being was the only way to get through this night and let Matt be the one to break the news to Cecily.

"Sweetie," I said, turning toward the backseat, "I don't blame you for being angry. But your daddy asked if you could hang out with us for a little longer. Let's try to make the most of this, okay?"

Cecily's eyes were narrowed, but she nodded. "Okay," she said quietly.

Sanjay turned on a television show for them when we got home. As soon as it was over, he announced it was time to hit the hay.

After I tucked Cecily into Stevie's bed (which I had been permitted to do only after allowing Stevie to pass out in *our* bed), and then fought with Miles for two minutes before giving in and letting him pass out beside his sister, I poured myself a glass of wine. Then I sat at the kitchen table, waiting to finally shed the tears I had been holding back for most of the night.

But my eyes stayed dry.

What I had believed to be true—that my best friend was dead—just an hour earlier now felt like a terrible tale I had spun of cobwebs from the darkest corners of my imagination. After all, if Jenny had the kind of problem that killed a person, I would have known.

Wouldn't I?

"I can't believe it," I said to Sanjay after I finished telling him about my brief conversation with Matt. Gone were thoughts of Russ and George Blatner; camp and lunches and the rest of my scroll-length to-do list were already a distant memory.

"Me neither," he said. He was sitting across from me drinking a beer. For once, his phone was nowhere in sight.

"What do you think he meant by 'serious problems'?" I said, almost whispering.

Sanjay's eyes met mine. "I'm afraid to guess."

"But it wasn't a heart attack or an aneurism," I said. "And I know she had endometriosis, but that couldn't possibly have been life threatening."

He shook his head. "No."

"Maybe it was a mistake," I said lamely. "Maybe she slipped into a coma."

Sanjay looked down at his beer. That alone should have told me everything I needed to know. But I couldn't imagine the next day, let alone *my life*, without Jenny.

And somehow—even though I had seen her limp body with my own two eyes—being unable to envision a Jenny-less future made it feel almost as though her death couldn't possibly be real.

We couldn't have sat at the table for more than an hour, but it felt like days. Years, even. Finally, Matt knocked on our door.

I let him into the house. He had clearly been crying; he still was a little. Seeing him like that was a shot of reality I must have been waiting for, because my eyes immediately flooded.

Matt wiped his nose on the sleeve of his button-down. "Where is she?" he said.

"In Stevie's room."

"Sleeping?"

I nodded.

"Good." He glanced at Sanjay, who was hanging back in the living room.

"Hey," said Sanjay.

Matt nodded in his direction. "I'm going to take her home. Hopefully she'll go back to sleep easily. And then tomorrow . . ."

And then tomorrow he would tell her that her mother was dead. A sob bubbled up from deep within me. I pressed my hand to my mouth. "I'm sorry," I said after I had composed myself.

"I am, too." Matt's voice was hoarse. "She . . . they think she had already been gone for up to an hour when I got home. If I had gotten there sooner . . ."

If either of us had gotten there sooner, we might have saved her.

"I'm so sorry, Matt. How long will it take until they know—" I could not bring myself to say *cause of death*. "Until they figure out what happened?"

He stared at me.

I stared back, waiting for him to explain what he had meant earlier. I knew Jenny had suffered from anxiety when she was in her teens and early twenties, and that the issue had resurfaced after Cecily's birth. She had taken antianxiety medication for a while, but that was years ago now.

Jenny had been prone to overthinking things—just like me, and really most of the women I knew—but over the past year or two she seemed to have taken a turn for the better. Cruel comments on her blog posts, which once rattled her for days at a time, rolled right off her. I assumed her increased focus on gratitude, coupled with life experience, had given her the ability to put minor crises in perspective.

No, other than endometriosis, I couldn't think of any issues Jenny had faced.

Could it have been suicide? I wondered suddenly.

The idea was an arrow through my heart, but it was gone as fast as it had come. It seemed highly unlikely that a woman who talked about being there for her daughter's wedding and caring for her grandchildren would abruptly bring an end to her own life. Not without having shown at least some sign of depression.

The generic jingle of an overpriced cell phone broke through my thoughts. Matt pulled his phone from his pocket. "It's Jenny's mom," he said. "I'm going to step outside."

"Should I not have asked?" I whispered to Sanjay.

Sanjay looked like he'd been awake for days. I probably did, too. He ran his hand over his head. "I don't know. Maybe it was a little soon."

"She's my closest friend." *Was,* I told myself. *Was. Was. Was.*

"He probably doesn't know much more than you do, though," said Sanjay. "Try to stay calm. Breathe deep if you can." This was our old routine—him calming me when I was ready to climb up a tree. At least, it had been before I started calling Jenny whenever I needed to talk something out. "The how doesn't really matter, does it?"

I wanted to agree with my husband—what was done was done. Except I didn't think that at all. There was some self-protective part of me that needed to know exactly what had happened (*Now!* I wanted to yell. *Right this very minute!*), so I could process this terrible thing and start to grieve.

So I could prepare myself to help Cecily. Because I knew all too well that life without a mother would be the opposite of easy, even for a child who otherwise had the world at her fingertips.

So I could immediately begin taking steps to avoid the same fate—or at least assure myself I was in the clear on this particular issue. Because that was part of it, wasn't it? It was not unlike learning a friend was sick. Breast cancer? Time to schedule a mammogram. Lung cancer? Whew—thank God you never smoked.

I shook my head to clear the last thought. Shock or not, that was not what I wanted rattling around in my mind at a time like this.

Matt had let himself back inside. "I'd like to get Cecily now. Can you take me to her?"

"Of course." I led him to Stevie's room, where Cecily was in a ball at the foot of the bed. Matt scooped her up as if she were no heavier than a doll and kissed her forehead. In the dim glow of the lamp Cecily had asked me to leave on, I could see he was struggling not to sob.

"Daddy," said Cecily groggily, and then closed her eyes again and fell back asleep.

"I'll be around tomorrow," I said quietly as I opened the front door for Matt. "Or this week . . . or whenever. Please don't hesitate to let us know how we can help." In an instant, I had transitioned back to planning mode. Matt and Cecily would need support. A lot of it. A funeral or memorial service would need to be planned. (Would she be buried? We had never had that conversation.) I could help make arrangements for anyone who was flying in. Friends and close connections would need to be told this terrible news. Eventually there would be a stream of emails and social media posts to respond to.

He had just stepped on the stoop when I added, "Matt? What did you mean by 'serious problems'?"

He turned to me, Cecily still nestled in his arms. "You really don't know?"

I shook my head.

"It was an overdose."

"Pardon?" My mind was right back in the direction it had just come from. Had she killed herself? No—still impossible. Did she go back on anxiety medication?

Matt held up a finger. Then he walked Cecily to the car, buckled her into her seat, and quietly closed the door. Beneath the glow of the street lamp, I could see Cecily slumped sideways, still blissfully asleep.

Matt jammed his hands into his pockets and hunched his shoulders as he walked back to me. But then he raised his head, looked at me head-on, and said, "Jenny overdosed on painkillers."

I stumbled backward like he had just hit me. "She wasn't taking painkillers."

"She was," he said. "They were for her endometriosis. And she took way too many."

"I don't understand. I thought—I thought that hormone she was taking had been working. She said she was feeling better."

He shook his head slowly. "Not better enough. Or maybe she was just trying to block out another kind of pain."

The ground swayed beneath me. "What do you mean?"

Matt squeezed his eyes closed. When he opened them again, he was wincing. "Then she didn't tell you that, either."

"No," I whispered.

Matt looked up at the sky, which was dark and cloudy. "Our marriage was a disaster. It had been for years, but Jenny wouldn't admit it, let alone address it. And I—instead of telling her we needed to get real and deal with our problems, I just stayed away." He let out an awful choked sound. "Now she's dead."

SEVEN

After Matt left, I drank my second glass of wine in two gulps. Then I told Sanjay what Matt had said and fled to the bathroom, where I cried with the faucet running for fear I would wake the kids or somehow suggest to Sanjay that he should come in and comfort me. Comfort would have its place. For the time being I didn't want to be touched or talked to. I wanted to be what I was: alone.

When I had dehydrated and depleted myself, I trudged to the bedroom, left my dress in a pile on the floor, and crawled into bed in my bra and underwear. Sanjay, who had already moved the kids back to their rooms, was lying there stiffly with his arms at his sides.

"I really had no idea," he said.

"Yeah, me neither." I was just trying to be matter-of-fact, but the words shot out like spears, punctuating the air with my anger.

Wasn't it early to start cycling through the stages of grief? Not to mention completely inappropriate to feel angry, given how tragic this situation was?

But I *was* angry. I was so angry that I wanted to scream. How could Jenny have kept so much from me? I could have helped her.

Suddenly I understood why Matt said what he'd said earlier, because I was having the exact same thought: *I could have prevented this.*

"I'm really sorry, Penny," said Sanjay.

He slipped his left hand beneath the duvet and reached out for me. I let his fingers rest on my wrist for a few seconds before flipping onto my stomach. "Thanks," I said into the pillow. "Good night."

"Pen . . . ," he said softly.

I did not respond.

There had been a time when I would have clung to him like the mast of a boat in a squall, and he would have pulled me even closer and kept me safe.

But something between us had shifted over the course of our marriage, particularly the last two to three years. We had gone from being lovers to best friends to . . . roommates who routinely irritated each other. If I was honest with myself, that was what it felt like most of the time.

Stress was part of the reason we were slowly self-imploding; that I knew. Simply figuring out the logistics of any given week was enough to send my blood pressure soaring—and that was before I tore open the quarterly statement for our retirement account and was reminded we had saved roughly one-tenth of the recommended amount for a couple on the cusp of forty who didn't want to work until they were both a hundred and three. As such, I wasn't always a peach to live with. In response, he wielded his sarcasm like a weapon.

There was a bigger issue, though: most days I had the sense that, while I was frantically dog-paddling to keep our family afloat, Sanjay was sailing by. Our short-term agreement had morphed into an indefinite arrangement: after Miles began preschool, Sanjay had applied for a few jobs at local publications and an arts organization but hadn't received a single callback. He hadn't minded, though, because after years of dabbling, he had decided to pursue a freelance writing career in earnest.

That was nearly three years earlier, and while he had just a handful of bylined stories, things were looking up in terms of the number of assignments he received.

But as he'd gotten increasingly engrossed in his writing, my husband had become markedly less involved in our household. I had waited so long for him to find something to replace what would have been his medical career that I didn't want to dissuade him from sticking to his Official Career Plan—even if I wished I, too, could stay home to write all day. I didn't want a sink full of dishes to be the reason he didn't land a feature in, say, the *New York Times*.

I loved Sanjay. I felt fortunate to have a husband who was happy to be home with his wife and kids. And maybe that's why, while I was happy to complain and yes, occasionally nitpick, I never said the truth outright, even to Jenny: Sometimes I deeply resented him. Sometimes I wondered if I had it in me to maintain our status quo for even one more year, say nothing of a lifetime.

But even more than I wanted my husband to chip in, both financially and around the house, I wanted a peaceful home for my family. (And let's face it—for myself.) So instead of yelling, I rolled up my sleeves and finished the pots and pans and then ran to the market to buy eggs and milk. I kept my lips zipped about just how heavily life had been weighing on me lately.

I had told Jenny almost everything. But maybe if I had skipped the *almost* part of that statement and said, "My marriage is drowning me," she would have opened up fully and completely to me, too.

Then maybe I could have saved her.

A few minutes later, the rhythm of Sanjay's breathing slowed and his leg began to twitch.

I stared at our lumpy ceiling, half wishing to be crushed by falling plaster. Sometime later I was still alive and awake, so I got out of bed, went downstairs, and poured myself another glass of wine.

Then I sat on the counter in my bra and underwear, drinking in the dark and thinking about the last time I had seen Jenny.

~

It had been a Sunday afternoon, just four days earlier, and I was there to pick Miles up from his playdate with Cecily. I had knocked, and Jenny, as usual, had hollered for me to come in.

I found her in the kitchen, dropping raw chicken thighs into a large ceramic glazed pot. Like the rest of her kitchen, the pot was white.

"Sorry. I'm a disaster," she said, looking over her shoulder from the stove.

I laughed. "You look great."

"I don't. But can you do me the biggest favor?"

"Anything."

"My phone is next to the bread bin. Will you grab it and get a few shots of me? I'm attempting a chicken and shallots dish that I want to run as a feature. But as Tiana reminded me this morning, she doesn't do Sundays," she said, referring to her assistant, who had a minor in photography and usually played paparazzi while Jenny went about the parts of her life that she chronicled on her website.

"Easy," I said. Jenny was more cute than beautiful—she had glossy brown hair that she had recently cut just so at her shoulders, and a sprinkle of freckles across the bridge of her nose that made you look right at her bright-brown eyes—and if anything, this made her especially photogenic. (*Approachable* was the term people often used to describe her particular brand of pretty.) Though I was no photography wiz, she had taught me enough about composition that I knew one of the images I snapped would work.

"You're the best," she said. "Don't zoom in on my face. Do we need to move anything?"

The kitchen island was a mess: shallot skins discarded at random, a splatter of tomato paste not yet wiped from the marble, sprigs of an herb I couldn't identify strewn about. It was unlike Jenny to leave even a few grains of salt in her wake, but I didn't think anything of it then. No one could be perfect all the time, and anyway, the other counters were pristine.

"We're good," I said as I unlocked her phone by pressing the number seven until the screen changed. I opened the camera and directed it at the pot; Jenny had taught me that pictures looked more authentic when the person being photographed was slightly off to one side. On Jenny's site, only Cecily was allowed to serve as the visual center of photos because Jenny took those herself, and as she said, what mother would fail to home in on her own child?

"Smile with your eyes," I said, and then she laughed because that was what she always said when she took pictures of me. I pressed the photo button again and again, moving from one end of the kitchen island to the other in an attempt to capture a deliberate moment in a whimsical and unscripted way.

"There's a nice Sancerre in the fridge if you want some," she said when I was done. She had left the stove and was washing her hands in the sink. "The recipe called for some white. I would hate to waste the rest of a decent bottle."

"Like I can say no to that." Sanjay had taken Stevie out grocery shopping. I still needed to get the kids ready for their first week of camp, check our bank account balance, go through my inbox, and get a head start on a memo for a midday meeting the following day. But it had been a while since I'd had a glass of good wine, and I wasn't ready to deal with the fit Miles would probably throw when I tried to pull him away from Cecily and her Legos.

The scent of a meadow wafted up at me as I poured the straw-colored wine into a glass. "Mmm," I said as I took a sip. "This is nice. Thank you."

Jenny pulled a wooden spoon from a drawer and began pushing the chicken around in its sauce. "My pleasure."

"What's Matt up to?"

"Oh," she said, peering into the pot. She sniffed at the chicken and then said, "He's home this week."

"That's good."

She put a lid on the pot. "Did I tell you Sonia asked me to sit on the board of the Children's Literacy Society?"

"No. Huh." Sonia had recently come into money—so much money that even Jenny's eyes grew wide when we discussed it, and she had been raised to want for nothing. Sonia's grandfather had accumulated a great fortune, and she and her brother were his only surviving heirs. Sonia claimed the inheritance wouldn't change anything, but she had quietly stopped working and joined a tennis league as well as the boards of what seemed to be every other charity in town. I hadn't seen much of her lately. "Will you do it?" I asked Jenny.

"It's important work."

"Kids do need to read," I quipped, though Stevie's struggles had been anything but funny.

Jenny had begun cleaning off the island. "They have a really lovely signature event in the fall—Matt and I attended a few years ago. So that would be nice. But Sonia warned that it's a major time commitment. I need to find out how much time exactly."

"Are there ways to get involved that don't involve sitting on the board?" I asked, as much for myself as for Jenny. Dipping a toe into children's literature—in some capacity, even if I couldn't find the energy to actually write out my ideas—had been one of my New Year's resolutions. The year was closing in fast and I had not taken a single step toward my goal. But maybe volunteering would be a good way to make progress, and reconnect with Sonia in the process.

"I'm going to look into that." She stopped wiping the counter, cocked her head, and looked at me. "Why, you want to join me?"

"Maybe," I said.

She went back to sponging the marble. "You're so lucky, you know."

I was sitting on a barstool that I happened to know cost more than every single item I was wearing as well as the purse I had left on a hook in the foyer, and sipping fine wine out of an expensive glass that was part of a set that one of Jenny's sponsors had sent her as a thank-you for allowing them to advertise on her website. (That the company thanked *her* for letting them pay her still boggled my mind.) "And how's that?"

She tossed the crumbs in her hand into the garbage and put the sponge in the dishwasher. "Never mind."

"No, spill it," I pressed. "I could use a refresher on the perks of being Penelope."

"Well . . ." She scrunched up her nose for a split second. "It's just nice that if you want to volunteer, Sanjay will support you." She quickly added, "Not that I'm at all trying to minimize your issues."

One of these issues was that while Sanjay would support the *idea* of me volunteering, when I got home from having done so, the kids' lunches would not be made, and though I had asked him to pay the water bill, I would sort through the mail that had been left in the mailbox and find a notice informing us that our repeat delinquency would cost an additional twenty-five dollars—and that was provided we sent payment within the next two business days.

There was a reason that instead of daydreaming about my husband taking me passionately against a wall, I fantasized about replacing him with a wife.

I looked at Jenny, and over at the pot, which had the kitchen smelling like a French bistro, and then back at her. Matt was nothing if not supportive. Jenny said he was overly tied to the idea of coming home to a clean house and a hot meal—but I could barely fault him. After a long day at the office, I yearned for the same things, though I would have made do with someone (it didn't necessarily have to be Sanjay) greeting me at the door with a just-shaken martini.

What I would never dare admit to Jenny was that it seemed to me *she* was the one who was most concerned with her domestic duties. Instead of grumbling about the house, I heard him crow about Jenny's success—how she had managed to do what so many people could only dream of and turn her passion for lovely things into a well-paying career.

(If the online murmurs were to be believed, her website brought in several hundred thousand in advertising revenue each year.)

I never did have the opportunity to gently tell Jenny I thought Matt supported her, because Miles and Cecily came running into the kitchen to show us the kitten hospital they had just built. I drained my wine as they finished, and then it was time to go home and get on with the less pleasant parts of my day.

Jenny and I said goodbye in the kitchen and that was that; I don't even remember if I looked at her after I hugged her, let alone noted her expression before I dragged Miles out the door. He was begging to stay, and I said no—not even a little longer. Because it was Sunday and we had things to do, and I had no idea that my friend needed me and that our rushed goodbye would be the last time I would see her alive.

~

Back in my own kitchen, drinking seven-dollar-a-bottle chardonnay, I racked my mind trying to remember what I had missed. It was a fool's errand; you can't hit a rewind button in your head and suddenly spot all the things you had overlooked in the first place.

And yet I tried. Jenny hadn't responded when I said it was good that Matt was home for the week. At the time, I had barely thought anything of it. Like anyone else, Jenny occasionally redirected the conversation for no apparent reason.

If I had paid more attention, would I have noticed she was grimacing when I said this about Matt? Or if I had looked closely, would I have seen that she had seemed . . . high? That was what painkillers did to you, wasn't it? (The last time I had taken something stronger than Tylenol was in high school after I had gotten my wisdom teeth out. I could recall the Popsicles I lived on for a week, but not how the medication had made me feel.) Had there been a subtle, drugged glaze to her eyes? Was her speech ever so slightly slurred?

She had looked a bit thin lately, maybe a little distracted at times. But she had not seemed doped up, if that was even what you called it—not on Sunday, and not any other time.

I simply could not imagine perfectly crafted, always-in-control Jenny abusing painkillers. Taking them? Sure—I knew her endometriosis had been hell to live with, even though I had also been under the impression that ibuprofen and the hormones she had been prescribed had been enough. If she switched to a prescription painkiller, why wouldn't she just tell me that? Had she developed a problem right off the bat? Had she felt ashamed for needing something more than a drugstore remedy? I knew she hated to take pills.

At least, that's what she had told me.

I would have thought her not telling me about the painkillers was an unintentional omission—at least when she first started taking them, whenever that was—were it not for the additional whopper of her so-called blissful marriage.

Aside from her hinting that maybe Matt wasn't as supportive as she'd like on the last day I saw her, she had never given me the slightest impression there was trouble in their glossy paradise. She hated his frequent absences, or so she said, but she had acted like that was an unavoidable fact of life—not the consequence of a deep rift between them.

In just a few hours, all of the things I thought I knew about Jenny had been replaced with question marks and uncertainty.

I tipped my glass back. The last of my wine bypassed my tongue and hit the back of my throat. I sputtered and coughed, which made my nose burn and my eyes, still wet with tears, water even more.

When I had finally stopped hacking, I slid off the counter and put my wineglass in the dishwasher, because to leave it in the sink was to make twice as much work for myself. Then I walked upstairs and got back in bed beside Sanjay, who was still knocked out. The clouds must have cleared, because moonlight streamed through the blinds. I squeezed my lids shut, seeking darkness.

But a few minutes later my eyes sprang open in defeat; I would not be sleeping anytime soon. I twisted onto my side and then onto my stomach as I attempted to process the truth.

And that was that while I had told Jenny almost everything, she had told me next to nothing. The anger I'd felt earlier was still there, but now it was competing with heartbreak and the shame of having been so naïve—to think what I had been told was the whole story. Really, I felt as low as I ever had, and that was quite a feat for someone whose own mother didn't love her enough to stick around to see her through childhood.

The last time I'd seen Jenny, she had greeted me by saying she was a disaster. Maybe she hadn't meant anything by it.

But maybe she had. And my response had been the same as Sanjay's when he was pretending to pay attention: *You look great.*

EIGHT

When I awoke the next morning, I was in Sanjay's usual spot, and he was already out of bed. Panicked, I glanced over at the alarm clock. It was after nine, which meant I was late for . . . everything.

Then I remembered why I had slept so late and what I had woken up to, and my panic turned to dread.

I combat-rolled to the other side of the bed and retrieved my phone from the floor so I could email Yolanda and Russ. I couldn't bring myself to write out what had happened, so I left it at "major emergency," with the assumption that Russ would fill Yolanda in on what he knew. He was probably presenting to George Blatner at that very minute, which was problematic for a few reasons: not only would Russ call in a favor later, but I needed Blatner's donation to strengthen my case for something beyond a 3 percent raise when I came up for review in September. (Like the good Lord Himself, the cost of Stevie's ballet classes had risen again, and Miles was planning to do soccer in the fall, which was at least three hundred dollars for enrollment and gear he would outgrow before the season's end. If that wasn't enough to have me jingling a cup of pennies in front of Human Resources, our hot water heater was not long for this world.)

I retrieved a T-shirt and a pair of shorts from the dresser and put them on. Raises, extracurriculars, warm showers—what did any of it matter now? Jenny was dead.

Sanjay was at the kitchen table, typing furiously on his laptop.

I guess I must have been expecting him to be weeping over a box of tissues, because seeing him tapping at his keyboard sent a rush of anger through me. "You're *working*?" I asked as I walked into the room.

He looked up at me and flipped his computer screen down. "Not anymore."

"But you were," I said. "How can you possibly focus at a time like this?"

"I had a few minutes and thought I would use them."

On any other day, I would have given him a gold star for productivity. I rubbed my swollen eyes. "And where are the kids?"

"At camp. I just got back from dropping them off."

"Thank you. Did you . . ." My voice caught.

"See Cecily?" he said.

I nodded.

"No. I didn't tell the counselors what happened, either. I'm assuming they don't know."

"I'm assuming no one knows yet," I said. I would need to tell Jael and Sonia. And our hairdresser—*my* hairdresser, I realized with a jab of sorrow.

"I made coffee," he said.

He never made coffee—I always beat him to it. But instead of feeling like a victory, it was one more reminder of what was wrong with this day. "Thanks," I said.

He walked to the kitchen and pulled a mug from the cupboard, which he handed to me. "How are you doing?" he asked softly.

I didn't look at him as I poured coffee into my mug. I couldn't. "I don't know. Hanging in there, I guess."

"Are you? Because I feel completely shell-shocked."

Now I glanced up at him with surprise and handed him the coffee carafe. He did look shell-shocked, and in a backward way that was comforting.

"I know we're all operating on borrowed time, but I never expected—well, something like that to happen to someone like Jenny," he said as he filled his mug.

"I know," I agreed. Rationally, I understood that I was lucky it had been her and not one of my children; my worst fear was that I might outlive them. Hell, I was even glad it wasn't me. Stevie and Miles needed me, and truth be told, Sanjay would be up a creek if he became a widower.

But knowing it could have been worse did not ease my grief—not even a little. Because Jenny hadn't been felled by an incurable form of cancer. She hadn't been caught in the line of fire while fighting for our country. Her death had been entirely preventable.

"It just makes me think," Sanjay added.

I looked at him over the edge of my coffee mug. "About what?"

"Life," he said, meeting my gaze. "How ridiculously short it is, even if everything goes right."

How long had it been since we had last locked eyes? Since I had felt like he understood how I felt, and maybe even shared those feelings?

"Maybe it's too soon for any big decisions, but this . . . it just makes me feel like maybe I should be doing some things differently," he added.

"Yes," I said, because I agreed—even if I had no idea yet what those things might be or how they needed to change. I stood at the counter, drinking my coffee in silence as Sanjay did the same. I wondered if he was still thinking what I was thinking.

Which was that it was a crying shame it had taken something so terrible for us to enjoy one lousy connection.

After I had finished my coffee, I picked up my phone. Was I supposed to call Matt? Email or text him? What was the etiquette for reaching out to a newly bereaved person?

I settled on a text. It's Penelope. Just checking in. How is Cecily?

As soon as I hit "Send," a wave of nausea came over me—true nausea, like the kind that I got when I was pregnant. Cecily no longer had a mother. Because Jenny was dead. Yet again, it was almost as though I was realizing it for the first time.

Phone in hand, I dashed upstairs to the bathroom. Once I was propped over the toilet, however, I couldn't even retch; I just kept gulping air and feeling like my heart was seconds from giving out. Was this how Jenny had felt as she was dying? She had looked peaceful, but that didn't necessarily mean she was at the time. She might have been alert. She might have been in pain. Maybe she even knew those moments were her last.

"Pen?" I could see the shadow of Sanjay's feet coming through the crack of the bathroom door. "You just bolted back there. Are you all right?"

"Fine," I gasped. As I turned back to the toilet bowl, I spotted the bare toilet paper holder out of the corner of my eye. "Seriously?" I said, even as my stomach continued to roil.

"What is it?" he called.

I had been forced to use paper towel the night before, as we had run through the wipes, and had asked Sanjay to go to the store in the morning. Clearly that hadn't happened.

It wasn't worth the fight. "Nothing," I croaked.

My phone had begun to ring, so I took a deep breath and righted myself. The call was from an unidentified local number, and I immediately wondered if it was about Jenny. *Inhale,* I told myself. "This is Penelope." *Now exhale.*

"Mrs. Kar?"

It's Ms. Ruiz-Kar, I thought, but at least my nausea had started to let up. "Yes?"

"This is Brittany at Knowledge Arena."

"Is everything okay?"

"I'm not calling about anything urgent. Miles is fine, though he's having a bit of a tough time this morning. He seems very tired. Stevie is working on an art project right now."

Neither child had broken a bone, had suffered a head injury, or was freaking out about the previous night's events? I was immediately impatient. "So?"

"Oh," said Brittany, like she had forgotten why she was calling. "It's just that neither of your children brought a lunch. We are able to provide a nut-free meal for them, but there's a fee of fifteen dollars per child. This is a onetime courtesy call. In the future, we'll simply make them lunch if one isn't provided and send you the bill."

"Fifteen *dollars*? Are you serving nut-free foie gras?"

"Mrs. Kar? I didn't get what you just said."

"Never mind. I'll bring them food."

"Awesome! We eat at eleven thirty."

Of course they did. "I'll be there as soon as I can," I told Brittany. Then I hung up and stared into the vanity mirror. I looked like I hadn't slept in a week, which was about how I felt. Lunches to make and deliver. Toilet paper to buy. A car that needed to be retrieved from whatever far-flung lot it had been towed to. It didn't matter if none of it mattered. It had to be dealt with all the same.

~

While email may have been pointless, I was still a creature of habit. After spending much of the day crying, pacing, and mindlessly cleaning my house, I took a peek at my inbox.

It was an exercise in futility. Every message was a blur; whatever information I was able to glean flew out of my head as soon as I clicked on the next message.

The last email I opened was from Russ. He said he was sorry and wanted to see how I was doing. Nicer than usual—but then again, tragedy had a way of bringing out people's better angels, and I knew it wouldn't last. He wanted to let me know that he had nailed the presentation, but that George Blatner had requested a follow-up on a few particular items of business, and we would have to work together on a second proposal when I returned. I shouldn't worry about Yolanda, he assured me; he had placated her for the time being, and she was flying to Hong Kong with a team of researchers to meet with the Asian Pacific alumni board to discuss an upcoming genome project that required non-grant funding. I was about to attempt to respond when my phone began vibrating its way across the dining room table.

It was Matt. I took a deep breath and picked up.

"Hi," he said.

I paused, unsure what to say next. "Um, hi. How's Cecily?"

"Not well. I told her this morning. She hasn't left my side since, though she finally exhausted herself crying and is napping in our bed."

My eyes immediately filled with tears. "Can I help?"

"Yes, but not yet." He sniffed, or maybe it was a sigh or a small sneeze. "I'm calling to let you know we're going to have the funeral on Monday night at Barron's on Plymouth Road. Jenny will be cremated, so it's just a memorial service. Our families are flying in today and tomorrow . . ." His voice trailed off.

"Is it okay for me to begin telling people?"

"I don't know . . . yes. I guess people have to know. They'll find out." I could tell he was really talking to himself.

"Matt? I don't know what to say. About how Jenny died, I mean."

He didn't respond right away, and I wondered if I had crossed a line. Then he said, "I suppose you should probably keep it to the bare minimum."

And what was that? "Um."

"Tell them she accidentally overdosed on a prescription medication."

"You're . . ." I stopped and tried to compose myself. "You're positive? Did they run a toxicology report?"

"The full report takes weeks to come back, but I was told it was 'fairly clear.'" He laughed bitterly. "That's actually what the coroner said. He sees it all the time, he said. Jenny hadn't taken enough for it to be suicide, and there was no note or anything like that. Given her history . . ."

What history? I wanted to ask. But I said nothing.

He continued, "They said sometimes all it takes is one or two pills too many."

And then you're gone.

"She stopped breathing. That's how it happened," he added quietly. Then, louder: "It was an accident. It's important for people to know that. She didn't try to kill herself. She never wanted to die."

My stomach turned again, and though I hadn't eaten more than half a protein bar all day, I closed my laptop so I didn't throw up all over the keyboard. "No, of course not," I whispered.

"Thank you for understanding."

"Absolutely." I paused. "I had no idea she was even taking painkillers."

"I'm sure that part wasn't an accident," he said.

I felt stupid. As his comment implied, if Jenny had wanted me to know, she would have told me. But why had she wanted to keep me in the dark? I wouldn't have judged her. I wouldn't have spread it around town. I wouldn't have even told Sanjay, if that was what she had wanted.

"Penelope, about the other night."

"Yes?"

"No one else needs to know Jenny and I were having trouble or that she had a problem."

I was so numb, a needle to my skin would have barely made me flinch. "Right," I said.

"So, please," Matt continued, "if you and Sanjay could stick to saying it was a prescription error, it would mean a lot to me."

"Right," I said again.

"Thank you," he said. Then he added something that ended all discussion on the matter. "You understand that Cecily is my number-one priority. I don't want her to hear bad things about her mother before she's old enough to know the truth."

"Absolutely," I said. My voice sounded like a computerized message, or maybe a recording of someone who had lost the ability to emote. "I understand."

I hung up the phone feeling like a hollowed-out vessel of a person. *The truth.*

Which was fairly straightforward, wasn't it? Despite all evidence to the contrary, Jenny had not gotten along with her husband. She had turned to a terrible habit to cope with the secret pain hidden beneath the shiny surface of her marriage.

And she had chosen to hide all of it from me.

NINE

After much bargaining on Sanjay's part, Riya made the drive from suburban Chicago to help us with Stevie and Miles for a few days.

"Don't worry about me," I said, imitating Riya as Sanjay plopped down in the driver's seat of his car, which was slightly less battered than mine. "It would be *sooo* much easier if you had cable, but I'll be just fine. You two go have fun at your funeral."

"She came, Penny," said Sanjay, turning the key to start the car. He was wearing a gray suit, and though his shirt was too loose and his tie was longer than it should have been, he looked as good as I'd seen him in months. "I'm not sure what else we can ask for."

"We can ask your mother to not be a jerk," I said. "We shouldn't have to guilt her into spending time with her own grandchildren so we can go mourn my closest friend."

"Whoa," said Sanjay as he backed out of the driveway. "That's not like you. I know you're upset, but let's keep our eyes on the prize, okay? Mom's here and she's helping us."

Upset? Upset was realizing your best black dress was now several shades of maroon because you had entrusted the laundry to your husband, who had confirmed your long-standing suspicion that high standardized test scores had an inverse relationship to practical intelligence.

Upset was discovering that your son had peed the bed yet again and failed to disclose that he had done so, and then learning that no amount of odor-neutralizing spray could rid his room of the smell of two-day-old urea crystals.

I wasn't upset. I was irate.

"Maybe I'm *not* myself, because right now I'm thinking that if your mother makes one comment about Stevie not losing her baby fat, I will personally cut her," I said, smoothing the fabric of my black skirt. I wore it to work twice a week; it didn't seem right to be wearing it to Jenny's funeral. But since my favorite dress had been ruined, it was either that, another black dress that cut off all circulation south of my stomach, or the bank-teller pantsuit. If Jenny were still alive and I were attending someone else's funeral, she would have lent me a roomy yet stylish black shift and helped me put my hair up in a twist or braids that somehow didn't make me look like Heidi. She knew how to do things like that.

Damn it, Jenny, I thought as I turned to glare at my husband. *I need you right now.*

I'm here, she said back.

My head jerked back. I had just heard Jenny's voice clear as day—as though she, not my husband, were sitting beside me in the car.

Which could only mean one thing: I was officially losing it.

Sanjay, oblivious to my mental meltdown, sighed and gripped the steering wheel. "I'm going to remind myself that you're hurting. And maybe a little nervous about giving a eulogy."

Not nervous—just calmly watching my marbles roll right out of my head. Nothing to see here! "I'm fine," I said through gritted teeth.

I had wondered whether Matt would ask me to speak at Jenny's service. After all, he had just revealed that I didn't know his wife nearly as well as I thought I did. Which made memorializing her a mite tricky.

But it had been Jenny's mother, Kimber, who had called to ask me if I would give a eulogy. "I know you meant the world to Jenny," she had said. "She was always talking about you—how funny you were and what a good friend you were to her. It would really mean a lot to Paul and me if you might say a few words at the service."

Naturally, I agreed. Only afterward did I begin to panic about what I would say.

"Okay, you're not nervous," said Sanjay in a way that made it clear he didn't believe me.

"Would you like me to cut you, too?" I said. "The steak knives are dull, but I'm told that the vacuum shop on Fourth Street can sharpen the whole set for less than the cost of one new blade." I knew this because I had wanted to buy new knives last winter, but Sanjay had said he would bring our old ones to said vacuum place instead. I was still waiting to be able to slice through something tougher than butter.

"Self, she's struggling," he said.

"Now who's being a jerk?" I said, but I had just spotted the funeral home in the distance and my voice lacked conviction.

Sanjay pulled into the parking lot and turned off the engine. Then he put his hand on my leg and squeezed lightly. "I love you, Penny," he said.

When had he last said that? I looked out the window to hide my eyes, which were filled with tears. It had been a good long time.

"I want to thank you all for being here." Matt was standing at a lectern at the front of the funeral home. He had just replaced Jenny's father, Paul, who had spoken little but had shown a slideshow. The photos of the joyful, freckle-faced girl Jenny had once been had gutted me, and that was even before the Beatles' "In My Life" began playing.

"I'll never forget the day I saw Jenny through the window of a restaurant in San Francisco," said Matt. "They say when you know, you just know. And I knew. I went in and asked if she was waiting for someone. And she smiled and said she was waiting for me. We were together from that day on. Jenny was the love of my life."

Really? I thought. Their story, which I had heard many times, had all the makings of a *New York Times* Vows column. But Matt and Jenny's beginning sounded a lot less like a fairy tale now that I knew the ending.

"Jenny was an amazing mother to our little girl," said Matt, choking back a sob. "As fantastic as she was at connecting with people through writing, she always said her calling was being a mother. Cecily was her whole world."

That, at least, rang true. My swollen eyes focused on Cecily, who was sandwiched between Kimber and Paul. With her perfect posture and straight-ahead gaze, she was so self-possessed. Would she remember this day for the rest of her life? Would Jenny's death rob her of a normal childhood, if such a thing even existed?

"Jen brought joy to everything she did," continued Matt.

Except maybe your marriage. But as soon as I thought this, I felt terrible. Even if their relationship had been a disaster for years, as he claimed, he must have loved her—a person couldn't fake the way he had looked at Jenny.

Anyway, I reminded myself, the man had a right to grieve.

I glanced around as Matt continued, trying to muster up positive thoughts before I spoke. The funeral home made it almost impossible. The walls were decorated with cheesy nature paintings, and beneath my feet the carpet was a bland shade that Jenny had often referred to as greige. She would have hated this place. I hated Matt for choosing it.

In front of me, Kimber's shoulders were shaking. Instead of holding his wife, Paul was looking off in the distance. They were good parents but bad spouses, Jenny had once told me. Was that how she had felt about her own marriage? And had her parents been told the truth about their daughter's death? I wanted to assume so, but assumptions weren't working out so well for me lately.

"There was so much I should have said to her," said Matt, and now he was openly sobbing. "There was so much I should have done while I still had the chance."

I was glad to hear him say this. But if only he hadn't stopped there. I had been the one to call Sonia and Jael, and both conversations had been horribly painful—not only because of what I had to tell them, but also for all the things I could not say. I was glad I hadn't had time to chat with them before the memorial service, because I wasn't sure I was strong enough to lie directly to their faces.

Matt's skin was the color of the carpet, and he looked like he had lost fifteen pounds in four days. The gravity of his new identity brought a new wave of pain. He would be a single parent now. He would have to learn to do all the things that Jenny had done, and even half of that was a very long list.

I thought about his constant traveling. I had every intention of telling him that would have to change—and that conversation was one I would not allow him to dance around. The pain of my father's inability to talk about my mother's absence was still fresh, even after all these years. Instead of trying to fill the hole she left, he created another one by making himself scarce. Matt might not realize it yet, but that wasn't going to be an option for him. Cecily didn't have an older sister to care for her. And she deserved better.

"Penny." Sonia's hand was on my shoulder, and I realized that people were looking at me. Matt had finished speaking. It was my turn to go up.

"Thanks," I mumbled. I stood. I pulled down my skirt, which had hitched up around my hips. Then I walked to the front of the room. When I reached the lectern, I gulped and looked at the note card I was holding.

I had spent the past few days agonizing over what to say. How could I accurately portray my friend's life when I was not allowed to concede the circumstances of her death? Every passing was a tragedy. But Jenny's had shone a spotlight on the many things I thought I knew—and how very wrong I had been.

Borrowed wisdom seemed like a smart way to avoid flat-out lying or saying something inappropriate, but a Google search for "best funeral poems" left me wanting to scratch my inner ear with an ice pick. The titles alone were so clichéd that they verged on parody:

Gone but not forgotten.

We never said goodbye.

If you do one thing, remember me.

A life well lived.

Well, that last one had given me pause. Not the poem itself, which was a mélange of rhyming melodrama. But the idea had applied to Jenny . . . hadn't it? She enjoyed writing and beautiful things, and she had combined the two to create an incredibly successful career. While her marriage had turned out to be a myth, she adored Cecily and had a circle of friends and family who adored her.

I ultimately decided I did not believe that Jenny's problems had canceled out every good thing in her life or her ability to enjoy them. And so, while I would not recite the actual poem, I would steal its sentiment.

Except standing in front of more than a hundred people, many of them strangers who would stay that way, what I had written no longer seemed right at all. I could feel my underarms growing damp as my eyes darted back and forth over my note card. All I could see was what I had left out.

"Jenny loved life," I began.

But it was too much for me and I tried to escape.

My head shot up—her voice was in my head again. I commanded myself to stay calm; hearing her was just a manifestation of my grief. "Whether she was writing a post for her website, setting the table for one of her dinner parties, or just pointing out the good in someone, she brought beauty to everything she did."

Except death, she said. *Even I couldn't make that beautiful.*

"She loved her family and friends so much."

I looked at Matt. *But not my husband. At least not the way everyone thought I did.*

"As I'm sure everyone here can attest, she would give you the shirt off her back or all the cash in her wallet before you even realized you needed it." I looked at Cecily, who was back at Matt's side and watching me stoically, save her quivering bottom lip. "But more than anything, she loved Cecily. She was Jenny's entire life."

In the end, even my love for my daughter wasn't enough to save me.

My eyes landed on Sonia, who was weeping into her pashmina. "Jenny was my closest friend."

And yet you didn't really know me.

I had planned to say that Jenny had been a role model to me. But even if her voice *was* a hallucination, I still couldn't lie—not with her in my mind, taunting me with the truth.

I would always try to emulate her positive attitude and her zeal for gratitude. I would continue to channel her way of finding the best in every person. But I didn't envy her approach to marriage anymore. As for her seemingly perfect life—how could I possibly admire it now, when I knew it had required what must have been an enormous amount of effort to conceal what never should have been concealed in the first place?

Sanjay was watching me. As our eyes met, I thought of our conversation in the car and how surprised he was when I'd vented. He was used to me biting my tongue in the service of keeping the peace in our marriage.

I felt like the air had been snatched right out of my lungs. Jenny wasn't the only one who had been pretending.

I must have been quiet for a while, because everyone was looking somewhere other than at me, as if to allow me a private moment.

Inhaling deeply, I set my note card on the lectern and said what I believed Jenny would have wanted to hear. "Jenny taught me that kindness is a daily practice. Instead of simply accepting difficulty, she encouraged me to change my circumstances whenever I could and to help others do the same. She inspired me to be a better person, and I'll miss her every day for the rest of my life."

I returned to the pew-style benches, feeling as sorrowful and bone tired as I ever had. When I reached my seat, Sanjay extended his hand. I looked down at his long, elegant fingers—ideal for a surgeon, or so everyone said, though now I knew they were better suited for writing and playing the guitar.

I took Sanjay's hand and squeezed it tight as I sat down. He looked at me with surprise and then squeezed back. His gold wedding band, which I had chosen for him, shined up at me. We had once been wildly in love; we had once been partners in this life. I couldn't pinpoint the exact moment that had stopped being true, but pretending I was fine and our marriage would fix itself wouldn't get us back to that place.

Jenny's last text to me came ricocheting at me once again. This time, though, I heard her say it aloud in my head: *If you're not happy, make a change.*

How'd that work out for you? I shot back, maybe a bit more saucily than I would have under different circumstances. But she was dead, I reasoned (as much as one can reason while having a mental conversation with one's dead friend). She could handle it.

Before she could respond, it hit me: Jenny hadn't taken her own advice.

But I still could.

TEN

After the service, Sanjay and I had gone to the Sweets' house, where their extended family and a few close friends had gathered. Imaginary conversations and thoughts pertaining to my marriage were quickly forgotten as I exchanged empty words about my beloved friend. Painkillers were not mentioned, and neither was her secret pain, because as far as I knew no one knew about either. Such a lovely, kind person was Jenny: that's what everyone said, and I nodded because this, thankfully, was true.

But in the middle of a flimsy conversation with Jael and her husband, Tony, I suddenly couldn't do it anymore—not even for one minute. I knew it wasn't my place to reveal what happened, but I couldn't continue to sidestep the giant prescription bottle in the middle of the room while people made stupid speculations, like how perhaps a genetic mutation caused Jenny to have a severe allergic reaction to an otherwise harmless drug. I was seconds from barking that there was no such thing as a harmless drug when I spotted Sanjay serving himself a drink in the kitchen.

I excused myself and strode over to him. "I have to get out of here," I whispered.

"We can't leave yet," he whispered back. "We barely just got here."

"I know, but I can't do this. I'm on the verge of a breakdown." Technically I was already in full breakdown mode, but this would become evident in short order.

He looked at me. I must have looked as wild-eyed and desperate as I felt, because he said, "Okay, we'll tell people you're not feeling well. Let's go say our goodbyes."

While he headed off to find Matt, I went upstairs, which was where I had last seen Cecily. She was in her room, in her bed, hidden beneath a pile of blankets. Kimber was beside her, saying something soothing in a low voice. She and Jenny had often butted heads, but Jenny's mother always had a kind word for me, and she loved spending time with Cecily, whom she took for a week at a time during the summer and for school vacations. How terrible for her, I thought, to have had to live through the death of her daughter.

"Hi, Penelope," she said quietly. "Cecily's having a rough time."

"I can understand that. Cess?" I said, sitting at the end of the bed. "You there?"

She peeked out at me from under the covers.

"Today was hard, huh?" I said. Tomorrow would be hard, too. And next week, and next month, and two years from now. And while it would get easier at some point, Cecily might one day find herself wedding-dress shopping and suddenly burst into tears because several good friends could not take the place of the one woman who was not there.

Her blue eyes were glassy with tears. "I miss Mommy."

"Oh, love, I know. I do, too," I said. "So very much. I know I'm not your mommy, but I'll be here for you anytime you need me—and I mean that. I'm going to be around so much that you're going to get sick of me. You're going to say, 'Aunt Penny, please get out of my house, because I can't stand to look at you anymore.' But I'm going to come back anyway."

The corners of her lips turned up, and I smiled at her. "Your mommy loved you so much, Cess," I said. "And we all do, too. Your daddy, and Granny Kimber and Grandpa Paul and Nanna and Grandpa Joe and your aunts and uncles and Stevie and Miles and everyone else. This is going to be hard—I won't tell you it won't be. But we're going to surround you with so much love."

She sniffed.

I paused, considering what to say next. Yes, she could hear it, I decided. "Did I ever tell you my mommy went away when I was six?"

"Went away?" she said.

"She decided to leave my family," I said. "I didn't hear from her or see her after that."

When Cecily was much older, maybe I would tell her the whole story. Shortly after I graduated from high school, my mother attempted to reinsert herself into my life after more than a decade of being a nonentity. She seemed genuinely remorseful—a wretched childhood had led her to make a terrible decision, she claimed. But she was ready to be the mother she should have been all those years.

I fell for it. I fell so hard that two months later, when she moved to Arizona with a man she had just met and stopped taking my calls, I considered—for the first and only time—whether it was worth it to continue living. Because if my own mother could not love me, then who would?

Yet Cecily's situation was worse. Because she could never cling to the hope that Jenny would stride through the door one day. No, of the many possibilities in Cecily's future, one thing was certain: she would never have a mother again.

"My mommy would never do that," said Cecily indignantly.

"That's for sure," I agreed. "Your mother wanted to be with you more than anything else in the world." I had been aiming to comfort Cecily, but found that these words consoled me, too.

In spite of my plan to flee, I stayed with Cecily for more than an hour—telling her stories about Jenny, reading her books, and rubbing her back until she fell asleep. Then I told Kimber, who would be staying in town for at least the next week, to call me if she needed anything at all.

Sanjay had parked across the street from the Sweets'. I got into the car and stared out the window as he started the engine. Their lawn was freshly mowed, and there were ceramic pots filled with blossoming flowers on the porch. The front door was open, revealing a home full of people, all of whom Jenny had loved. Anyone who didn't know better would think she were throwing a celebration.

A familiar anger resurfaced in my gut. Intentional or not, Jenny *had* left Cecily, and that never should have happened. She was a highly intelligent person. Even if she had not known the danger of the medication she was taking, she had the resources to get help.

Why could she tell me to make a change, but not bring herself to admit she was due for one, too? Why couldn't she confess she was struggling?

Everyone expected me to be perfect, I heard her say. I spun around toward the backseat, half assuming I would find her there. But there were only a couple of crumb-covered car seats and a candy-bar wrapper.

Maybe she was right, I conceded. Many of her readers scrutinized her every word and photo, and she was routinely raked over the coals for the most innocuous things, like posting a makeup-free selfie that apparently made her skin look too good. The year before, she'd come across an online forum dedicated to making fun of bloggers and so-called "social media influencers"—including her. "They call me Sweet'N Low," she told me half-indignant, half-tearful. "They say I'm saccharine and artificial."

And now, of course, I wished to God I had not blown off her comments about Matt's high expectations for their home and life.

As Sanjay pulled away from the curb and the Sweets' picturesque house disappeared behind me, I wondered for the first time if Jenny had believed that I, too, expected her to be perfect.

Then I had an even more alarming thought.

What if that were true?

ELEVEN

Sanjay groaned. "Penny, you're hurting me."

I loosened my grip on his shoulder. "I need to talk to you."

"Now?" He squinted and glanced at the alarm clock. "It's two a.m."

"It's important."

"Can it wait? I can't have a conversation in the middle of the night."

The fact that his eyes were open and he was speaking indicated that in fact he could. If only I had tried violently shaking him awake years earlier, I could have spared myself dozens, maybe even hundreds, of linen changes after Miles wet the bed.

"You could have dislocated my shoulder, you know," he said, still lying there. "Is this about Jenny?"

"No. Well, sort of."

It was three days after Jenny's memorial service. As with the previous two nights, the few hours of sleep I had gotten had been fretful; I had tossed and turned, unable to staunch my thoughts. Had I given Jenny the impression she couldn't be real with me?

She had turned to me when she was overwhelmed with terrible, unfounded worries about something bad happening to Cecily. She had flung open her door and invited me in when she wasn't wearing a bra and hadn't covered up the bags under her eyes or the pimple on her chin. She confessed that she sometimes bought expensive items just for the rush, even though it lasted mere minutes and she knew it was a stupid financial move. These were not the habits of a woman posing as perfect.

Yet if she complained about Matt, I sometimes teased her and said most wives would give their left foot for a difficult spouse like him. Maybe that had kept her from opening up to me about their struggles. Or maybe she felt I was invested in the idea of him as a model husband—which was at least a little true, I had to admit—and didn't want to shatter that illusion.

I tried to think of other things I may have done. When she had discussed her endometriosis, which had sometimes left her incapacitated for days, perhaps I had made a disparaging remark about pain relievers. I couldn't remember having said anything of the sort, but I couldn't say with certainty that I hadn't, either.

And that was driving me nuts.

But even as I fretted over what I might have said or done, I kept coming back to the question of what I could still do—specifically within my own marriage. I had no doubt it was time to start being more honest with Sanjay. But what did that *mean*? Go to couples' counseling and talk it out? I knew he would cringe at that suggestion. Many of his parents' friends were psychologists or psychiatrists, and Sanjay said dinner parties at his house often felt like eating on Freud's couch. He would probably relent if I pushed hard enough, but I wasn't willing to do that. Not for something I didn't particularly want to do, either.

What, then? Make him sit through a litany of complaints and demands? Start spouting off the way I had in the car on the way to Jenny's service? Maybe, I thought, I should just let it go.

Not ten minutes before I woke Sanjay, I had gotten out of bed and gone to the kitchen for some water. I stood at the sink as I drained my glass. Through the small windows over the sink, the night sky was blinking at me spectacularly. I blinked back, and within seconds the stars were blurred and my face was wet.

Jenny and I had talked about the afterlife once or twice. We agreed it was more important to be a good person for the present moment than as a means of building up some sort of karmic credit. Neither of us believed in ghosts or spirits. Back then, though, it was all theoretical. The last person I knew who had died was a seventy-eight-year-old office clerk who worked down the hall.

But there Jenny was again, whispering in my ear: *Make a change.*

I wiped my eyes. Then I said aloud, "Okay." Because that, at least, I knew how to do.

When I was distressed about the extra twenty pounds I'd gained during college, I started walking three miles a day. The weight was gone in a couple of months. After realizing I was doing most of my old supervisor's job at *Hudson*, I wrote up a summary of my tasks and accomplishments and requested what should have been an outrageous promotion. I got it. And though it probably seemed to most people that I emerged from the womb as a type A, I had once been a tornado of a child who left a trail of mess in her wake. It was only after my mother left that I had, by necessity, learned to clean and cook and keep track of what had to be done and how that would happen.

It was simple: You set a goal. You devised a plan. Then—this was the kicker—you followed that plan. To steal a line from Yolanda, couldn't I apply that "skill set" to my marriage?

I had run back to the bedroom to share my revelation with Sanjay. Now he was propped on his elbows and squinting at me in the dim lamplight.

"I realized at Jenny's memorial service that things between you and me aren't right," I said, still a little breathless from dashing up the stairs. "They haven't been for some time now."

He was suddenly wide awake. "What?"

"We need to save our marriage," I said.

From the look on his face, you'd think I'd just suggested polygamy. "I wasn't aware that our marriage was in need of preservation."

"Don't attempt to redirect the conversation with your verbal gymnastics."

A smile formed on his lips.

"Sanjay," I said, "I'm being serious here."

Chastened, he pushed himself into a sitting position. The ice cream he had dripped on his T-shirt before bed was now a Rorschach stain. To me, it resembled a middle-aged man succumbing to his inner slob. "Oh, Penny," he said. "I know what Matt said to you about their marriage is probably eating at you. But they're not us. We're not them. You know that, right?"

I shook my head. "We have the same problem they did."

He regarded me warily. "And what's that?"

"We've been pretending everything's fine in our marriage. At the very least, I have been."

"Hey," he said. "I know things between us have been a little tense lately—"

"If by *lately* you mean at least the past three years, then yes."

"Jesus. I'm sorry I haven't been as attentive as I could be, but are you sure this isn't your grief talking?"

Then I wasn't the only one who was aware he found his phone at least 70 percent more interesting than me. Instead of relief, I felt even more irritated—because if he knew this, why didn't he do something about it? Or had I gone the way of many a wife before me, fading into the scenery while other more riveting pursuits moved to the foreground?

"I don't think it's a good time to be making big decisions," he said. "And for the record, our problems are ripples compared to the tidal wave that wiped out Jenny and Matt's marriage."

"I don't agree at all," I said firmly. "I think this is the exact right time to be addressing our issues. Things aren't great between us, and we need to be honest about it instead of sweeping it under the rug. We need to get real with each other. Jenny's death was the wake-up call I never wanted, but now it's happened and I can't pretend otherwise."

He glanced at the alarm clock. "Speaking of wake-up calls, you have to be up in less than five hours. Can't we discuss this in the morning?"

"See, that's what I'm talking about!"

He pulled his head back with surprise. "What did I do?"

"*I* have to be up in less than five hours? What about you?"

"Sheesh! I wasn't saying I didn't plan to get up! I was trying to be helpful. You're always worried about being late to work." His voice trailed off, and his eyes had moved south.

"What?" I glanced down and realized one of my nipples had decided to flee the confines of my tank top, which had been stretched beyond its limits by our decrepit washing machine. "You're such a child," I said, tugging my top back in place. I would go shopping for new sleepwear this week. Maybe next week. Soon.

"I didn't want to say anything," he said with a shrug. Then he put his hand on my knee, and I immediately felt myself soften. "Hey, same team, remember?" he said. It was something he'd picked up from Stevie's preschool soccer coach, who had hollered it at the girls when they stole the ball from each other.

"I know," I said quietly. "It's just . . . I want our marriage to be healthier. I know we're not Jenny and Matt, but we're not ourselves anymore, either."

"People change, Penny," he said. "We're not young and childless anymore. Are you really unhappy?"

Unhappy? Yes—at least more often than I wanted to be.

The bigger issue was that I was afraid. Because I had been spending way too much time thinking about how nice it would be to escape the ever-mounting pressures of our life. Before Jenny's death I told myself this was a normal fantasy for a woman under duress. But now the stakes had been revealed, and they were much higher than I had ever imagined. I could no longer pretend I was a normal woman. I was one whose mother had taken a permanent leave of absence from her family. And I didn't want to follow her lead—or Jenny's, for that matter.

If my father were to be believed, my mother had not suffered from mental illness. "She was selfish," he said by way of an explanation when I had been old enough to press him for a real answer about why she left. "End of story."

In truth, it was just a fraction of the story. In one of my clearest childhood memories, I am standing in our small kitchen shortly after my mother left, deeply unnerved by the silence. Where are my parents' yelling voices? Where are the sounds of slamming doors, stomping on stairs, screeching tires? As long as I had been conscious, I had been aware my parents disliked each other. I wasn't even sure they had ever loved each other—though at some point her wild-child soul must have been attracted to his workaholic ways, as they had chosen to marry and have two children.

Yet as bad as it had been when they were together, it was worse after my mother left. I had sworn to myself that if I ever had a family, things would be different for us. No one would be yelling. And no one—*no one*—would be leaving.

For all my thoughts of running away, I would never abandon my children (though it occurred to me that Jenny must have told herself that very thing). And Sanjay and I weren't my parents. We did love each other, even if we struggled at times to like each other, and we weren't yellers or prone to dramatics. Our arguments were more like a series of fissures.

But even a solid foundation could crumble from one too many cracks. I was willing to bet Jenny had not gone into her marriage thinking it would end up the way it did. Or that the first pill would lead to her last breath.

There were things that weren't right between me and Sanjay. And it was time to admit that before something terrible happened.

We sat in silence. The plan that had seemed so crisp and clear just a few minutes earlier was already shapeless. Was it really smart to tell Sanjay the truth? To ask—and expect—more of him? How would I do that, and what did I want, anyway?

"We can work out the details later," I finally said. "I guess I just needed you to know this is a priority, and I want to do something about it. And I hope you do, too."

"I do," said Sanjay, but then he said nothing for a very long time.

"Well, what is it?" I eventually asked. "What do you think?"

"What do I think?" He opened his mouth and shut it. Then he sighed deeply. At last he said, "To be honest with you, Penny, I worry that too much honesty might be a bad idea."

TWELVE

"Howdy!"

I had just poured myself a cup of coffee and walked into the living room when Lorrie came flying through the front door.

I startled, spilling hot coffee all over my pants. They were my last clean pair, and while they were at least black, I now would either have to walk around smelling like dark roast or spot-clean a dirty pair and hope a quick tumble in the dryer would remove the wrinkles.

I wiped my dripping mug with my free hand and turned to my neighbor. "Lorrie, what are you doing here? It's not even eight yet." This came out as a squeak, making me sound more nervous than irritated, which I was. It had taken me a good forty-five minutes to pass out again after talking to Sanjay, and I had barely been able to pull myself out of bed that morning. Our talk must have jolted Sanjay, because he had gotten up at the same time I did. But I was still running behind and needed to locate a clean cardigan to throw over my camisole before we finished getting the kids ready.

And now deal with my wet pants and pour myself a fresh cup of coffee.

"The door was open, and I saw the littles playing on the porch. Figured you were up and at 'em," said Lorrie, entirely too perky.

Lorrie had moved in across the street from us four years earlier. One morning soon after, she had come marching over with a basket of muffins. She was a chemistry professor at the university and a single mom to two-year-old Olive. She had smiled at Miles and said wouldn't it be nice if our kids could be friends?

She was an odd one—that was clear from the get-go. But she was smart and friendly, and I felt a little bad for her, which in retrospect is a lousy reason to invite someone into your life. When she crossed the street at the end of the day to chat with me, I welcomed her conversation. When she suggested we take our children to the park to play on Saturday mornings, I agreed—or at least I did in the beginning, before Olive began chomping on Miles like a teething biscuit every time I took my eyes off him for half a second.

But then I would come home from a long day at work and she would be waiting on the porch, waiting to yap my ear off for the next hour. She started knocking and then sticking her head in the door to call for me. More recently—maybe because I had stopped answering when I heard her yodeling—she had taken to walking straight into our house. I had made plenty of comments such as, "We're about to eat dinner," or "You scared me," but I could not bring myself to have the Talk with her.

I suspected this was because in my mind, such a conversation would prompt Lorrie to ask, "Do you still want to be friends?" and I would either have to lie to her and say yes, or admit that no, I did not, and in fact I deeply regretted not taking the advice I gave my children by accepting treats from someone I didn't know. Which would make it awfully awkward to be neighbors.

"Don't you need to get Olive ready for camp?" I asked.

"Oh, she's home, happy as a clam on the ol' iPad," said Lorrie, waving in the direction of her house. She was wearing a shirt that said, "Hos before bros." I started to smile because I knew I would text Jenny the minute I pushed Lorrie out the door to tell her about my latest home invasion.

Then reality set in, and it felt like a boulder had just fallen on my chest.

Lorrie prattled on, telling me all about how the good folks of Silicon Valley were helping Olive make major strides toward independence. (And thank God, since she had left the child home alone.) After a minute or two of this, she tilted her head. "You look tired. Is now a bad time?"

Yes. Now was a very bad time, and so was later on, and next week, and the rest of eternity. But Lorrie had started making this sad pouty face that apparently connected directly to my estrogen receptors, and I felt myself softening. "Yeah, I'm exhausted," I admitted. "And I have to get the kids to camp and get to work. So . . ."

She kept sitting there, so I did something I knew I'd regret later and shared more information about my life than I wanted to. "Also, my good friend just suddenly passed away. We're all reeling from it and could use some privacy."

Her pouting shifted to a sincere look of sympathy. "Oh, Penelope. I'm so sorry."

I was ready to forgive Lorrie her trespasses when she added, "As I'm sure you recall, my Mr. Pickles died last year. I'm still a real mess about it."

Her cat?

She was comparing the natural demise of her elderly cat to the untimely death of my closest friend?

I stared at her, unable to think of a response—any response—that didn't involve me coating her in catnip and stringing her up in the middle of the Humane Society.

"Lorrie? Mary and Joseph," exclaimed Sanjay, who had just come down the stairs in a pair of boxers and the same dirty T-shirt. "I'm not decent."

"Oops! It clearly is a bad time," she said as she rose from the sofa.

He turned to me, not bothering to lower his voice as Lorrie skittered outside. "Whatever happened to the eye hook on the front door?"

"It's still there. The kids unhooked it when they went out front to play."

"We're going to have to talk to them about stranger danger."

"Lorrie's not a stranger," I said.

"I cannot think of anyone stranger than Lorrie." His face grew serious. "You need to tell her to stop letting herself into our house."

"I know," I said.

I looked at Sanjay, who seemed awfully sprightly for what he usually referred to as an ungodly hour of the day. "Aren't you exhausted?"

"I wouldn't call myself well rested," he said. "But I'm up, which is a miracle given my two a.m. shake-awake."

My thigh was damp, and my hand was still dripping coffee. "About that . . . I hope you're not upset with me."

"Not at all," he said.

I eyed him suspiciously. "What happened to 'too much honesty might be a bad idea'?"

"You truly want to improve our marriage, right?"

I nodded.

"Well, I do, too. I'll admit, I was pretty surprised by you bringing it up. But then I was thinking about it this morning and maybe you're right. It couldn't hurt to try to make things better, could it?"

There was a lump in my throat. "No," I said. "I don't think it would hurt. And though I'm having a hard time about Jenny and probably will for a long time, I don't see an advantage to waiting to get started. The problem is, I don't know what we should *do* to make things better."

"As it happens, I have an idea."

"Really?"

"Yep." He looked awfully pleased with himself, which made me nervous. "The thing is, you're a list-maker."

"By necessity," I said.

"All the same, you like lists. They work. So why don't we give each other a list of what we want the other person to change?"

That *was* what I was asking for, wasn't it? So why was his suggestion making me clammy and nauseated? "You're serious," I said.

"Completely."

"Then that's it? I tell you what I want and you do it?"

"And vice versa," he said. "We're not mind readers. I mean, I know some of the things that irritate you, but I don't know what's most important to you or what you think would most improve our relationship."

This was a good point. But did I even know what was most important?

"I do think we should keep the lists fairly short," he added. "I don't want to get stuck in the weeds about stupid little things. Let's stick to what's important."

"Good call."

Sanjay smiled broadly, revealing the dimples that had first drawn me to him when I had spotted him on the other side of the *Hudson* newsroom. He was happy I was on board with his idea. "I even have my first request," he said.

"And what's that?"

"I would like for us to have sex more often."

~

Sex! We had sex. We did. Well, not as often as we used to. Maybe once a week—or at least once every other week. Looking back, I was forced to admit that January, February, and May had been particularly dry.

But that was what happened when two people decided to make two more tiny people.

Once upon a time, in a land before children, Sanjay and I had been very good at sex. That's probably what kept us together when we first started dating, because back then neither of us really knew how to have a healthy relationship. After all, I had never been in close proximity to one myself. Likewise, Sanjay's parents' marriage had been arranged, and rather than the story most people wanted to hear—that they fell deeply in love soon after their wedding—they didn't particularly care for each other and spent most of their time in separate rooms of their large home. Riya was happiest when she went to India for a month and a half every winter to see her extended family.

Sanjay and I had no relationship role models, but we had epic rolls in the hay. By the time we finally figured out how to mostly be decent partners after our breakup, our erotic encounters had slowed a little, but they were still hot enough that we didn't have to schedule sex like a dental cleaning, as the purported relationship experts in women's magazines always seemed to recommend.

Then came Stevie's birth and Sanjay's brief medical school tenure. Sex petered out.

And by petered out, I mean we basically stopped having it.

It's hard to bounce back from that kind of baseline—even Sanjay dropping out of medical school didn't help. Nowadays it happened when it happened, which I supposed wasn't particularly often. And when it did happen, it was usually in the dark or with my eyes closed, because I got distracted by Sanjay's ear tufts, which he had the barber trim and then promptly forgot about until his next appointment. Anyway, it was easier to get to where I was going when I couldn't see the laundry basket at the end of the bed.

Really, was it any surprise that when he came on to me—which was almost always at the end of the night when I was ready to pass out—I thought about how I would be awoken by my urine-soaked son in another two to four hours and said, "Maybe tomorrow"?

As I made my way into work, still clad in my coffee-stained pants, a comment Jenny made a few months earlier floated through my head. "Sex keeps our relationship going," she had said after I feigned disgust when she showed up late to a coffee date with flushed cheeks and an excuse that Matt had been frisky.

Was she being disingenuous—or had she been trying to tell me that sex was one of the few things she and he had shared?

It was one more thing I would never know.

When I walked into my office, a bouquet of white orchids was in the center of my desk. I had never seen so many orchids in a single arrangement—there must have been eight flowers to a single stem and a dozen stems to the lot. It was the nicest bouquet I had ever received, and the sight of it made me want to burst into tears. At any other time, I would have assumed Jenny had been the one to send it. She did things like that—gifting me a lipstick that she knew would look just right on me, or bringing me tulips after I secured a big donation.

This time the flowers were from my coworkers.

"Is white appropriate?" asked Russ, who had just stuck his head in my door. He looked kind of embarrassed, and I realized he must have been the one to pick them out. "Do you even like orchids?"

I could feel a sob coming on and had to look away. "Yes," I finally managed. "I like them very much."

"Good," he said. Then his head disappeared.

I composed myself and then called into the hallway, "What's on the agenda for today?"

This time, his whole body appeared in the doorway. "I put the final touches on Blatner's second proposal, so if you have time to look it over, that would be great. I'm meeting with Dean Willis at one thirty to discuss EOFY numbers."

"May I join you?" I said.

"I can cover if you want to catch up on other stuff."

I had been off work for several days, and he had come through for me on all counts. I appreciated that—but he was still Russ. The last thing I needed was for him to treat me with kid gloves, only to use this to unseat me as co-director or call in some massive favor later on. "I'll come with," I said.

He smiled, and then a strange thing happened. Semiobjectively, Russ was attractive—he had the kind of moody green eyes you didn't see very often, straight white teeth, and an almost uncannily symmetrical face. He also happened to be pale, stocky, and on the short side—which is to say the opposite of Sanjay. Yet as I looked at him, I realized . . .

No.

Except yes—I had just felt a twinge of attraction toward him. Was this some sort of inappropriate grieving response? A temporary spell cast by the sight of that beautiful bouquet he had chosen? Or had this been lurking in my subconscious, just waiting for the right time to wallop me?

My cheeks burned, but if Russ sensed my discomfort, he didn't let on. Instead, he just kept smiling and said, "Great. Swing by my office at one so we can prep."

~

"So," Russ said as we were walking across the medical campus to the dean's office several hours later. "How are you holding up?"

July was days away and the sun beat down hard, baking the morning's spilled coffee into my pants. And just as well, as that made it easier not to think about whether the attraction I'd felt toward Russ earlier was a one-off. "I'm fine."

He looked at me. "Really? Because your eyelid has been twitching for a solid five minutes now."

My lid had been fluttering off and on for days, in fact—not that I was about to share this. I *knew* it was stress related. But thank goodness Russ had pointed it out to me. That was guaranteed to make it better.

"I'm fine," I said.

"You know, it would be okay to take a break if you need to," he said.

So he could swoop in and become the sole director of our department? Not a chance.

"It's good to be at work," I said. "Keeping busy is better than doing nothing." Yes, to be in motion was to not have to think about anything other than the task at hand.

He gave me a skeptical look. "If you say so, Pen."

We had just reached the administrative building where the dean's office was located. A gust of icy air hit us as Russ pulled the door open for me. A question popped into my head, and I opened my mouth before I could second-guess whether to let it out. "Hey. What do you know about prescription painkillers?"

Russ had not been to medical school, but he was well versed in health issues ranging from the everyday to the obscure. He claimed this was because he had only ever worked in medical development, but I would not have been surprised to learn that he rose early each morning to peruse science journals before hitting the gym.

He glanced at me briefly as we began down a corridor. I was relieved that his eyes didn't unsettle me and he was back to looking like regular old Russ. "Do you want the politically correct answer, or my real answer?"

"The latter."

"Let's just say I only needed to pop one Vicodin to know I should never take another. It's different for different people, though. Some people fall asleep on painkillers. Others feel euphoric, like they can do anything, and that's usually what gets you hooked. If a doctor prescribes them to you—which, given what we know now, they probably shouldn't unless you're out of options—you'd better hope you're in the pass-out category." Now he was staring at me intently. "Tell me you're not doing that junk, Penny. It'll kill you."

My expression must have betrayed me, because Russ did a double take. "Whoa—wait a second. Is that what happened to your friend?"

I blinked several times to pull myself together. In less than two minutes I would be discussing a several-million-dollar endowment with the dean who had the power to make or break my career, and it would not behoove me to walk in on the verge of tears. Also, I had just revealed a major secret to a coworker with whom I had an uneven relationship. "Please don't say anything to anyone," I said.

We had just reached the dean's assistant's desk, and Russ reminded her we had an appointment. Then he turned back to me. "I won't," he said quietly. "But for the record, I don't think addiction should be a secret."

∼

Later that day, when only the janitor and I were left in the office, I sat at my desk and thought about the word Russ had used.

Addiction.

Matt hadn't used that word, but the facts spoke for themselves.

How long had Jenny been hooked? How had I not noticed *something* was amiss?

Pen, how long did you overlook what was wrong in your marriage? I heard Jenny ask. *You've had your head buried in the sand for years now.*

"Your point," I muttered.

As my imaginary friend had just reminded me, I needed to focus on my marriage. But what did I really want from Sanjay? And what did I want for us?

I could ask him to put his damn phone down once in a while, but would that really be enough to ease the underlying irritation I felt toward him?

No. But him doing more around the house and with the kids—without being asked to—would. So that would be my first request.

What else?

There was no question that he needed to begin bringing in more than a few hundred dollars here and there as well as the occasional check from his parents. I was grateful I had the ability to keep our family financially solvent, even if I did sometimes worry about what would happen if I, say, fell through an unsecured manhole cover and suffered a devastating brain injury. But our financial arrangement was looking permanent, and that kept me awake at night nearly as much as Miles' bedwetting. I had been telling Sanjay it was fine—he would be making more money soon enough.

Well, he still wasn't, and though I was loath to point this out, it *wasn't* fine. I had bitten my tongue because I was worried the truth would crush his self-esteem and stifle his ambition. When he had first sat me down one morning and told me he was dropping out of medical school—"Today, Penny. I literally can't do this for one more day"—I had mostly been relieved; he had been so damn miserable. "What are you going to do?" I had asked, and then he had confessed what I already knew to be true—he wanted to go back to writing.

I was so happy I could have danced. I imagined him fulfilled and even financially successful—after all, we knew plenty of writers who made a good living. Our friend Alex, for example, had left editing to pursue freelance writing and was now making six figures.

But then Sanjay said he wanted to write a book about jazz. I didn't remember exactly how the conversation went down, but at some point, I had pushed him to be realistic and think about more immediate and lucrative streams of income.

He never mentioned the book again.

Lesson learned. After Miles began full-day preschool, Sanjay turned his attention to freelancing, and I waved my invisible pom-poms in the air and cheered on any idea he mentioned, breathing a secret sigh of relief when none of them involved anything longer than a few thousand words.

In retrospect, maybe the cheerleading had been a mistake. Because over the past three years, he had published some—a couple of stories in an obscure music magazine, a few reviews in our local paper, and one feature, thrillingly, in the *Chicago Tribune*—but not nearly often enough for our bank account or his ego. And sometimes when I saw him bent over his computer, it seemed to me that so many hours with so little to show for it had frayed the best parts of the man I had married.

"It's time for Sanjay to get a job," Jenny had remarked when I confessed I was concerned about our family's finances. "Like, a regular nine-to-five job."

I had raised an eyebrow at her—this was amusing advice from someone who ran her own business. Then again, she and Sanjay were cut from different cloth.

"Maybe," I had said, knowing I would not demand this of him. At the time, the convenience of having one parent at home who could run to school to pick up a sick kid at the drop of a hat seemed invaluable. And I had done what I always said I would and avoided marrying the type of workaholic my father had been.

But now I understood Jenny had been right. It *was* time. We needed to contribute more to our meager retirement account and the kids' insufficient college funds. And wouldn't it be nice to do some of the umpteen things we had been putting off, like taking another family vacation this century or replacing the dishwasher, which no longer deserved its name? Most important, I needed to know that at some point soon I would not be shouldering my family's financial burden alone.

Then him making money would be request number two. Even a part-time job would be a start.

Sanjay had suggested we keep our lists short, and just as well—for all my dissatisfaction, I couldn't think of a third change to ask him for. I shut off my computer and told myself it was enough.

～

Later that night, I coaxed Stevie and Miles to tell me about their days. Stevie had just finished describing all the naughty things Miles had done at camp when I glanced over at my husband, who was chomping on a fish stick and staring into the living room. At once, I was hit with an unsettling realization.

All these years, I had been congratulating myself for marrying someone who wasn't like my father. But really, the two had plenty in common.

They were family men who didn't take off when the going got tough. There was no doubt this was admirable. But both had an uncanny ability to be there—and yet not be there at all. As a teenager, I sometimes told people I was an orphan because it felt like the truth. My father may have lived with me and Nick, but he was mostly disengaged. Sanjay hadn't reached that point, but as he studied the dust particles floating in the air or did edits in his head or whatever he was doing behind those vacant eyes, it seemed to me he was on his way.

When was the last time he and I had an engaging conversation? When we started dating, we never ran out of things to talk about. Now our hot topics included children, work, and our ever-growing domestic to-do list—all shared in thirty-second bursts on the way out the door or as we were falling asleep. No wonder he found his phone so riveting.

"What is it?" said Sanjay, looking at me suddenly. "You have a look on your face."

"Nothing," I said. I glanced down at my plate and speared a green bean. It was limp and joyless in my mouth, but I ate it anyway.

Could I really ask my husband to find me interesting again?

I looked at Sanjay, who had already returned his attention to the nothingness in the distance, and realized I was going to have to.

THIRTEEN

On Saturday I awoke early, intending to use the bathroom quickly and go back to bed. By the time I had reached the hallway, my mind was already abuzz with all that I needed to do that day. I sat on the toilet and put my head in my hands, ruing the sleep-deprivation hangover that would soon set in.

At my feet, the small hexagon tiles were cracked; a few were beginning to crumble. They had seemed so charming when Sanjay and I had bought this house almost seven years earlier. Everything about our town had seemed charming then. How nice the houses were, how spacious! How novel that the kitchens had dishwashers, and the basements had washers and dryers, and there were garages and attics for storing belongings we didn't actually own, as there had been no room in our Brooklyn apartment for items that did not fulfill an immediate need.

Now our attic was full (though of what I could not say for certain). The laundry sat in dirty, defiant piles in the basement. And the walk from the bathroom to the kitchen was so far, so very far as my head pounded and my veins pumped feebly as they awaited a caffeine infusion.

But the smell of coffee came wafting at me as I walked down the stairs. All was not lost.

I found Sanjay standing in front of the coffee maker. "Hello," he said.

"You're awake. And . . . dare I say cheerful?"

"Yup. I thought we could talk about our lists before the kids got up." My pulse quickened. "Great."

He took two mugs from the cupboard and filled them with coffee. He gave me one and then handed me the cream. "I feel like I should preface this conversation by saying I'm thinking about how to make more money. I know what I'm pulling in isn't nearly enough." I must have looked surprised because he said, "I'm not dense. I know it's time, and that it's been hard on you, being the breadwinner."

And you waited to tell me that because . . .

"I was probably trying not to think about how long it had been," he said. "Coasting has been easier than admitting that I'm failing. I'm sorry."

My bitterness instantly dissipated. "You're not failing. And you don't have to apologize."

He gave me a funny look. "I kind of am, though. And I *am* sorry."

I had been planning to tell him I expected him to find a job until he was able to make more from writing, but now that he was in front of me talking about how he had failed, the last thing I wanted to do was shine a spotlight on that. So I said, "Well, I was hoping you'd think about getting a part-time gig to supplement your writing."

He leaned against the counter. "That sounds fair."

"You don't have to agree to it if you don't want to do it," I added.

"I didn't say I didn't want to."

"But you don't."

He set his mug on the counter and sighed. "No, Penelope, I'm not geeked about trying to find a job again, since the last search didn't go so well. And to be honest, I like being at home. But if that's what you're asking me to do, then that's what I'm going to do. Besides, part-time is better than full-time. I would prefer to keep part of the day open, at least."

It couldn't be that easy . . . could it? Best not to look a gift husband in the mouth. "Thank you. Do you want to know the other things?"

His expression settled between a smile and a grimace. "Let me guess: you want me to look like less of a slob."

Well, if you want to have sex more often, it couldn't hurt. "No, I was hoping you would be more proactive at home. Help out more with cleaning and the kids without me asking you to."

Sanjay crossed his arms over his chest. "I'm not sure if you've noticed, but I've really been stepping it up the past week or so."

He meant since Jenny died.

"I've gone grocery shopping twice, and I'm making dinner most nights," he said. "I cleaned the kitchen and the upstairs bathroom a few days ago."

I had to try hard not to glance around—the sink was loaded with day-old dishes and the counters weren't much better. "Yes, and I really appreciate it. What I'm asking for is more of that on a regular basis. I feel . . ." I felt like he wasn't pulling his weight. But as he had pointed out, too much honesty was a bad idea. "I would just like to come home to a little less mess every day. And have fewer tasks to do on the weekend."

"I work all day, too, Penelope. I wish you wouldn't act like I'm watching soap operas."

I shook my head. "I was worried this would happen if we traded lists."

"No one said this was going to be easy," he said. "This is a tough conversation to have. But at least we're having it, right?"

Our eyes met, and I wondered if he was also wondering whether things would have been different if Matt and Jenny had a conversation like this, too.

"About the kids, though," he said. "Even though I spent all that time with them when they were little, they just don't care about me as much as they care about you."

I could see the hurt in his eyes. "Maybe you could schedule more of their activities and register them for camps and whatnot," I supplied.

"But you're . . ."

"The organized one?" I sounded defensive.

He nodded.

"I have to be," I said. I softened my tone. "I'd be perfectly happy if you took over. And for the record, when Miles has peed himself in the middle of the night, I guarantee he doesn't care whether it's me or you who's helping him into dry pajamas."

He sighed. "Okay. I'll try to help out more. But if I'm not doing enough, just tell me, all right? Because I know I'm going to forget something."

"I can do that, if you promise not to get upset if I ask for more."

"Deal." He took a sip of his coffee. "So, what's number three?"

"I, uh, was thinking . . . I . . ."

"Come on, Pen. Whatever it is couldn't be worse than telling me I'm a slouch around the house."

"I was hoping we could talk more, like we used to. I was hoping you could maybe, you know . . . stop acting like you'd rather be on your phone."

Now he looked irritated. "What does *that* mean?"

"It means I want you to be more engaged. I want you to be present when you're present."

"The way you were present when I was telling you about the story I'm thinking of writing last night?" he said.

I could all but hear the crickets chirping. "Which one?"

"About how Bob Dylan's 'Blowin' in the Wind' inspired Sam Cooke to write 'A Change Is Gonna Come.'"

My face burned. "Sorry. Obviously, I need to do some work on that, too. I still think we could be doing better in terms of conversation."

"Is that it for your list?" he asked.

I nodded.

"Okay," he said, looking relieved. "Can you email them to me?"

"You won't remember three things?"

"I just want to have a concrete reminder in front of me."

"Fine," I said. "Your turn. You expect me to turn into a sex kitten. What else?"

"Uh-uh, Pen. You don't get to pull that on me. You said we were supposed to be honest, and I agreed."

"Because you want to make me feel better after Jenny's death," I said.

"Yes and no." He rubbed his forehead, looking tired for the first time that morning. "I can't argue with the idea of trying to make our marriage better. We've been bickering too much."

My eyebrows shot up. Because I couldn't remember the last time Sanjay had complained about our relationship, I had assumed I was alone in my frustration.

He continued, "And like I said the other night, what happened to Jenny made me realize how it could all be over in a second. We should be enjoying life more. The past few years were harder than they should have been. Maybe it's stupid or overprivileged of me to think this, but even if we can't enjoy life more than we already are, there's got to be a way to make it less difficult."

I sighed. "I suppose that's true. And yeah, it wouldn't hurt for us to have sex more often."

He frowned. "Only if you're into it, though. I want us to have sex, but not if you don't want to."

Great, so going through the motions wasn't enough—I needed to resurrect my libido, too. How did one do that, exactly? Develop a porn habit? Stock up on the packs of horny goat weed they sold at the gas station? "I want to," I said. "What else do you want me to change?"

"That's it for now."

"Pardon me? One thing?"

"No, not one thing. One thing at a *time*. You've already got a lot on your plate."

"But we agreed to do this."

Sanjay tilted his head, almost like he was confused. "Penny. Your best friend just died. Your workload is crushing. You've got two kids, neither of whom is particularly easy. Your dad barely calls, and your brother isn't much better. And your bum of a husband isn't bringing in any cash."

I could feel the familiar swell of tears behind my eyes. While it was a relief to know he understood my life's load, it was overwhelming to have it recited to me. "You're not a bum," I said, sniffing.

"If you were me," he said, not acknowledging my rebuttal, "would you suggest a handful of changes at once, or just one?"

My many marital failings were suddenly lit up like a series of neon signs in my head. I was a nag. I always played good cop with the kids. I failed to protect us from Lorrie's home invasions. I broadcast my sexual disinterest with granny panties and gray bras that hadn't been white in years. "Wait a second. How many requests do you have?"

He looked up at the ceiling for a moment. "Three."

"Are you saying that just because I had three?"

"Does it matter? Three sounds fair. Since we're talking terms, how long are we giving this?"

I made a face. "I don't know. It was your idea."

"*Our* idea," he said.

"I was hoping the changes we make are permanent," I said. But as soon as I said it, I wished I hadn't. Because if all went well, we both had decades left to live. And if I had sex with Sanjay even twice a week, the lifetime sum of that was probably the equivalent of more than a year of extra sleep. Learning Mandarin suddenly seemed less daunting than being cheerfully intimate with my husband on a regular basis.

Whether I liked Sanjay's request or not, I had to give him credit for being honest. Wasn't that exactly what I had asked for?

He was about to say something when Miles, grumpy faced, appeared in the doorway of the kitchen. "Hi, Mommy."

"Hi, Daddy," said Sanjay pointedly.

"Hi," Miles mumbled in his direction. He walked over to me and buried his face in my shirt. Ah, he was still such a peanut that I wanted to cry. If Stevie's behavior was any indication, he would soon have little need for me.

"Sweetheart, it's early. Why don't you go back to bed?" I said.

"Can I watch a show?" he asked, ignoring my suggestion. "And can I have pancakes for breakfast? *Please?*"

I looked up at Sanjay. "We'll talk about this more later?"

"Sure. But I have to ask—at what point do we take a step back and assess whether this plan is damaging our marriage or actually working?"

"Damaging? This could only be good for us."

Sanjay was about to take another sip of coffee, but stopped short and looked at me over the rim of his mug.

"What?" I said.

"Nothing." Still staring at me, he took a drink, then said, "I just hope that's true."

FOURTEEN

When Stevie and Miles were very young, I remember thinking that the segmented, highly scheduled days coupled with sleepless nights turned time to molasses. The period following Jenny's death recalled that glacial pace; the week after her memorial service might as well have been six as I waited to hear from Matt. It was a fine line, respecting his privacy without letting Cecily drift too far. But my patience finally ran out, and I called to ask whether I could see her. Matt agreed and asked me to come by after work on Monday, two days after Sanjay and I had discussed our lists.

For all my anticipation, I stood there like Cecily was a spotlight beaming at me in the dark when she opened her front door. What did one say to a child who no longer had a mother? I had once been that child. Somehow this did not help me find the right words.

"Hi, Cess," I finally said. "How are you doing?"

Her face was a mask, static and unreadable. "Hi, Aunt Penny. I'm okay." She was wearing a pair of too-small cat-print leggings and a faded pink dress with a kitten wearing large sunglasses printed on the front. The outfit had been her instant favorite when Jenny had bought it for her two years earlier. That she was wearing it now said everything her expression had not.

Suddenly I *did* remember something. After my mother left, every-one treated me like a china doll that would shatter from the slightest jostle. All I wanted was for people to act like they used to—back before I had been left behind. This, at least, I could do for Cecily.

"It's great to see you," I said. "Can I come in?"

She nodded and led me to the kitchen, where Matt was pulling groceries out of a bag. He looked even more exhausted than the last time I'd seen him. When he saw me, he stopped and walked across the kitchen. He paused just before he reached me, almost like there was a force field between us. I leaned forward so he could air-kiss my cheek like he usually did.

He hesitated before taking my cue. "Hi, Penelope. Good to see you."

I couldn't tell if he meant it, but I couldn't fault him for that. I was still alive, which was probably another reminder that Jenny was not. "You, too," I said.

He turned back to the groceries and retrieved a bottle of maple syrup from a bag. "Where does this go?" he muttered, looking around with bewilderment.

Was he really so clueless, or had Jenny never let him help in the kitchen? "The fridge," I said. "Though the cupboard is fine, too, if you plan to use the whole thing in the next couple of months."

"Thank you. I guess I have a lot of things to learn now that . . ." He turned his attention to the groceries without finishing his sentence.

"Well, I've spent way too much time in your kitchen, so let me know if you want a hand," I said.

He was holding a box of instant oatmeal. Jenny used to put organic oats in a pot to soak in coconut milk overnight. In the morning, the Sweets would wake to a delicious, decidedly uninstant breakfast. Not that I was about to tell Matt this. At least he had gone grocery shop-ping rather than sent his daughter to the corner quick mart for bread and bologna. Of course, times had changed. Men were now lauded for cooking. I still somehow doubted modernity would have made my father more hands-on at home. He loved me, but he had loved my mother more, and for a long time the man couldn't see further than his own sorrow.

"I think I'm good," said Matt, stashing the box in a cupboard full of pots and pans.

I sat beside Cecily at the kitchen island as Matt finished emptying his bags. The counters were dusty, as were the knives in the knife block and the espresso maker. A stack of mail was strewn across the end of the marble island. Cecily's lunchbox was lying open beside the fridge; the glass containers in it had not been emptied of their food remnants. If it were my house, this all would have been normal. Clean, even, by our standards. Jenny, however, would have already had her sponge and disinfecting spray out and all traces of dirt and disorder would soon be erased.

You know I wasn't just relying on coffee to get it all done, whispered Jenny in my ear.

I shook my head vigorously. Jenny's voice was already gone, but her message lingered. A pristine home no longer seemed quite so aspirational.

"Cess, are you going back to camp this week?" I said.

"I don't know," she said, but she sounded like I'd just asked her if she wanted to play with a hornet's nest. Then, more loudly, she said, "Daddy, am I?"

Matt stopped wrestling with the empty paper bag he was trying to fold and looked at her. I was waiting for him to say, "I'll do whatever you want, love. If you want to stay home with me, let's do that." He could afford to take unpaid family medical leave. Even at a high-pressure firm, the death of a spouse bought time and goodwill.

Instead he said, "Well, pumpkin, Daddy has to work. I could pick you up early every day, though."

Her face fell.

"Miles and Stevie will be there all of the rest of this month, and most of August, too," I said, hoping to soften Matt's blow. "I know they're already missing you."

"Okay," she said softly.

"Want to color, or maybe play a game?" I asked. She hesitated before nodding. Then she slid off the stool and ran to her room.

"Do you really have to go back to work so soon?" I said to Matt once she was gone. "It might be good for the two of you to be together now."

He rested his elbows on the kitchen island and put his head in his hands. "Yeah, I do. I've already been away too long."

My eyebrows shot up, though they shouldn't have. I of all people knew this was what workaholics did: they worked, even when—or, one could argue, especially when—their family needed them.

"I remember wanting my dad around after my mom left. It was the loneliest time of my life," I told him. "And that was even with my brother there." Nick was a photographer now, and though he shared an apartment in LA with a couple other creative types, he was usually living out of a suitcase in some far-flung location. I rarely heard from him.

"It's not exactly the same," said Matt.

I wondered if anguish was occupying most of his neurons. Could he not see that what Cecily was dealing with was far worse? I took a deep breath. "No, it's not. I still hope you'll give it some thought."

"Sure," he said, in the tone people use when they plan to do the opposite.

"And what about you? How are you doing?" I asked, hoping to redirect.

"Me?" He seemed surprised I had asked. "I'm angry. I know it's not right, but I can't believe she left us."

"Yeah," I said. Along with frantic sobbing and sudden confusion, blind anger had become one of my go-to states. "I understand that."

"I'm going to start seeing a therapist. Cecily is, too."

"That sounds like a smart idea." I decided to take advantage of Cecily's absence. "Have you heard anything more from the medical office?"

He shook his head and looked toward the staircase. "It'll take weeks to get the report back. Though I'm not sure it matters."

It mattered to me. I understood it wasn't going to change what had happened, but I wanted to know just how much I didn't know. It wasn't right, but somehow that bit of information seemed like a friendship scorecard that would inform me just how off the mark I had been. Everyone has a secret or two, but hers had managed to cast our entire history in a hazy light.

I swallowed hard. "I know it's not my place to tell you what to share, but I'm having a really hard time making sense of what happened. Jenny didn't even mention she was taking painkillers, so this came as a really huge shock."

"I know, but what's left to say? She made a fatal mistake." He met my eye, almost daring me to push it further.

The sound of Cecily's feet slapping against the wood came echoing into the kitchen. She was holding a large puzzle. "Can we do this together, Aunt Penny?"

"I'm here for *you*, sweetie." It took every ounce of willpower for me not to give Matt *the look*, as my children called it, as I said this. "I'm happy to do whatever you'd like."

~

I stayed through Cecily's bedtime, even though I needed to get online and finish my annual self-evaluation, which was due in two days, and had just received an email from camp saying there was a lice outbreak and I would need to buy a special comb and go through my children's hair—and PS: backpacks, lunches, and extra clothes would have to be brought to camp in a trash bag each day until further notice. I reminded myself that asking Sanjay to handle it wasn't just a good idea; it was part of our deal. He must have been thinking about that, too, because when I sent him a quick message he texted back, **Already on it.**

"Thanks for having me over," I said to Matt as he walked me to the front door. Cecily had already hugged me goodbye and was upstairs getting ready for bed.

"I'm glad you came by. Cecily was happier than I've seen her since . . ." His voice trailed off. "Well, you know."

I knew. "We'd love to have her over in a few days, if you think that might be all right."

"Absolutely," he said.

I slipped my shoes on and regarded him. The tension from our earlier conversation was nearly gone, and I didn't want to ruin it by saying something. But as I reached for the doorknob, I realized I couldn't swallow my words. Not when it came to Cecily.

"Matt, you probably know this already, but Cecily's going to need more attention than she'll ever ask for," I said.

"Okay," he said. The word came out as a question. He looked at me, waiting for me to say more.

"That's all," I said to him. "I'll see you both soon."

I was no therapist, but Cecily would probably feel like she needed to act as though she were fine—just like Jenny had, I realized with a pang. Her sorrow would reveal itself from time to time, but she would likely seem calm and poised, and everyone would say she was so, so brave.

But while they were busy praising her, they might not notice that she was starting to fill in the daily holes left by her mother. That her grief followed her like a shadow.

That she was missing out on parts of her childhood that would haunt her long after they had passed.

~

That evening, I brought my laptop and a glass of wine up to bed. I had intended to finish my review, but when I looked at the dent in the sheets beside me, I was reminded that I still had not sent my list of changes to Sanjay, who was working downstairs. I should have emailed him after we talked two days earlier. Well, better late than never. I opened a blank email and began to type.

> Hi. Here's my list:
>
> Make more money. Maybe find a part-time job.
>
> Help out more around the house and with the kids.
>
> Be more present when you're with me.
>
> xo, Penny

But could I really sign with kisses and hugs after giving my husband a short list of his personal and marital deficiencies?

I erased the xo and wrote,

> I love you.

Then, for reasons I could not explain, I erased that, too, and replaced it with Love.

Then I quickly hit "Send" before I had a chance to continue to overthink it.

Good job, I heard Jenny say.

I was no longer worried about losing my mind—it had probably gone missing years earlier, anyway. But these chats I'd been having with Jenny seemed impossible, and not just because she was dead. Which person was I even speaking to? The friend I thought I'd known—or the woman who had been hidden beneath all that polish?

Impossible or not, I still felt compelled to answer. "Thank you," I said. "I'm trying."

"Who are you talking to?" Sanjay had appeared in the doorway, toothbrush in hand.

"Myself," I lied.

He raised an eyebrow. "Should I be worried?"

Probably? But radical honesty or not, I wasn't ready to tell him about the mental conversations Jenny and I had been having. "I'm fine," I said.

"You know it's okay if you're not, right?"

I frowned. "What does that mean?"

He sighed. "It means I love you, Penny."

Then he was gone. I heard his footsteps creaking down the hall, and then the sound of the bathroom door closing. I squeezed my eyes shut, waiting for Jenny's voice to return. Instead, I fell into a deep and dreamless sleep.

FIFTEEN

Most people say they want the truth. What they mean is that they want it if it's palatable. I was surprised to realize that the majority of our mutual friends and acquaintances were pacified by the explanation that Jenny had been the victim of an unspecified prescription error. ("It happens more often than you think," Sanjay's father, Arjun, had said, and since he wrote prescriptions, he would know.) I wondered if they believed this, or if they were worried additional information might soil Jenny's memory.

Jael was not most people. We met for a drink a few days after giving Sanjay my list. I'd wanted to see her but had been putting it off; our conversation at the memorial service led me to believe she would pepper me with questions about Jenny's death.

I wasn't wrong.

We'd barely sat down when she began asking: What kind of medication was it? Was the family suing the pharmacy that provided the prescription? What about her doctor or even the drug company? Weren't they at fault, too? Someone had to be held accountable.

I had some of these very questions myself, but all I could do was weakly reply that I didn't know. I hated lying and was pretty sure the omissions I was making were one and the same. In desperation, I had finally suggested she reach out to Matt to ask him herself. I was relieved when she said that she would.

"One down," said Jael. She waved her empty wineglass at our waiter. Then she looked at my glass, which was still nearly full. "At least grief isn't turning you into a lush."

"I'm just tired today." I took a small sip of my drink. If I hadn't had to keep my wits about me, I probably would have tossed the entire glass back like a shot and immediately repeated the process.

She gave me a sad smile. "I have so many regrets, you know? I hadn't seen Jenny in almost two months before she died. I'd been really bad about seeing anyone, really, since Caleb was born," she said, referring to her third child.

It wasn't just her. Our friendship circle had casually unraveled around the time Sonia had become part of the one percent. When I ran into Jael at Jenny's memorial service, it had been nearly half a year since she and I had last gotten together, and I'd almost not recognized her at first. She'd lost weight—a combination of nonstop nursing and no time to eat, she said apologetically, probably because motherhood had the opposite effect on me—and her black hair was streaked with gray. Her face was bare, and brambles of fine lines had formed around her eyes. She looked decades older than the last time we'd met up, as though the years of her life had all shown up at once.

"Listen, we've all been bad about getting together," I told Jael. "Don't beat yourself up."

"Yes, but I avoided Jenny for the wrong reason. I felt so guilty about getting pregnant with Caleb when she's had such a struggle because of her endometriosis. And you know, with forty just around the corner . . . it seemed like that chapter of her life was over. That must have been hard on her and Matt."

I paused, my wineglass halfway to my mouth, wondering how to respond. I knew Jenny had wanted another child, but she had also said she had come to love their family of three exactly as it was.

Now I had to wonder if that was the whole story.

"That's what it was, wasn't it?" Jael said suddenly. "The hormones she was taking. I read that they can cause fatal blood clots in women over thirty-five."

"It's possible," I fibbed.

"I bet it was," she said, nodding. "When I told Jenny I was pregnant again, she said they had moved past it a long time ago. But I don't know if that's something you can ever really move past, especially when it doesn't work out. My sister had secondary infertility, and it was really hard on her, even after she ended up having another child."

"At least Jenny and Matt didn't mind trying."

Jael gave me a funny look. "What do you mean?"

"They were like rabbits." I quickly amended myself: "Well, maybe not rabbits."

"Because rabbits make lots of babies."

"Sorry—that was me sticking my foot in my mouth," I said, embarrassed. "But you know how Jenny was always talking about how they did it every day when he was home—sometimes even twice a day. Sanjay and I haven't been like that since we were in our early twenties." I hesitated, then added, "He wants us to have sex more often."

Jael rolled her eyes. "Men. If I've learned one thing, though, it's that having to do it saps the joy right out of it. Tony and I only ever had to try with Rachel," she said, referring to her eldest. "But it was the *worst*. In my experience, the fastest way to murder your libido is to remove spontaneity from the equation."

My husband's direct request was hundreds of miles south of spontaneous—but that was my fault. "I can definitely see that," I said, staring into the red abyss of my wineglass.

~

"Sanjay," I whispered.

He was asleep on our bed, as straight and still as a log. I straddled him and leaned forward. I was wearing the tight White Sox T-shirt he loved and a pair of navy underwear. The underwear had a tiny tear where the polyester lace met the elastic band, but that was in the back and it was dark and hey, at least I was trying. "Hi," I whispered, trying to rouse him.

"Hi," he mumbled, opening an eye. Then the other one sprang open. "You smell like wine."

"It's my new perfume," I said saucily. Jael and I had chosen a restaurant within walking distance of both of our houses, so I'd decided to have a second glass, and, following Jael's lead, a third. Now my bedroom was swaying ever so slightly. But when I'd walked in the door, I'd had a spontaneous thought: tonight would be the night I would give it the old college try.

And damn it, I was *going* to enjoy it.

He pushed himself up on his elbows and looked at me. "You look really good."

I wanted to remark that this was because my T-shirt covered my stomach, but I was just clearheaded enough to curb my sarcasm. "Thank you," I said in a tone of voice I had not used in a long time.

Then I leaned forward and kissed him. At ten at night he already had morning breath. That didn't bother me nearly as much as his stubble, which felt like sandpaper against my chin. I would not be so easily thrown off course, though, so I adjusted my face and kissed him again. This time it wasn't nearly as irritating, and he now tasted a little like wine, too. Victory.

My hair fell around our heads, blocking out the pile of clothing next to the bed and the watchful eyes of Stevie's stuffed koala, which she had discarded on our dresser. There was only me and Sanjay, whose arms were soft yet taut beneath my fingers and whose skin smelled like soap, which had always turned me on. Maybe this list idea wasn't so ill conceived, after all.

"What did I do to deserve this?" he murmured.

Was this a trick question? The answer was nothing. It was also that he had agreed to sign on to the fix-our-marriage project. "Less talking," I whispered.

"Okay," he said.

"Still talking."

"Sorry."

"Shhh." I kissed him again. Then I pushed my hips into his and took his hands and placed them on my breasts. He lingered there, almost like he was reacquainting himself with my body (which I suppose he was). Then he tugged my shirt over my head. Happily, I was no longer thinking about what was jiggling or whether my underwear would rip more if I leaned in the wrong direction. This wasn't bad at all. In fact, I was on my way to liking it.

I realized Sanjay's eyes were on my face. He was looking at my forehead, probably wondering if the faint lines between my eyebrows indicated I was only going through the motions. His gaze drifted to my lips. Was my pursing a pucker—or evidence I was ready to get this over with?

A little of both. I wondered if he could tell.

Then he looked into my eyes, and somehow that made me feel as naked as I ever had. I didn't want him to read me; I didn't want to connect on a deeper level. Because one minute I'd be thinking about how I loved my husband, and the next, I'd be crying over my dead friend. No, what I wanted—what I *needed*—was surface-level intimacy. Hormones. Pheromones. Good old shut-eyed, emotion-free lust.

I rolled off of him.

"What is it?" he said, still lying beside me. He propped himself on an elbow. "Did I do something wrong?"

"Not at all. I just wanted to switch it up." I pulled him on top of me and then gently took his shoulder and pushed him down. I watched the top of his head make its way past my stomach and dip between my legs. Then I couldn't say anything else because my dead zone had just shocked me with a sign of life.

And then there was another sign and a wave of pleasure, at once familiar and surprising. Maybe the wine had been a good idea, because I didn't think about Sanjay's ten o'clock shadow chafing my thighs or that we were doing this, well, sort of because he had asked me to, or that I literally couldn't remember the last time he had done this particular thing to me. For a few minutes, I was able to let go of everything.

But then, out of nowhere, I began doing marital math in my head. I was making progress on Sanjay's request (finally). Which was fantastic, but I was still coming up short. He had been doing the dishes and making lunches—not well, but at least he was doing it. Just the day before I'd caught him wielding the minivacuum like he was on payroll at Molly Maid. And the same day we had traded lists, he had done the impossible: folded the laundry and put each piece into its correct drawer.

In a split second, my pleasure withered into nothingness.

"Hang on," I said to Sanjay. "I need a minute. Sorry."

His head surfaced. He looked confused.

"I was really enjoying it, but then I started thinking about the wrong thing and—I'm sorry. It's really not you."

"If it's not me, who were you thinking about?" he asked with a lopsided grin.

I couldn't help but laugh, and then I was glad that I did because the fog started to lift. I wasn't turned on anymore, but that didn't mean I was done making progress. "Where were we?" I said, guiding Sanjay up toward me.

I began pulling his boxers down, but he stopped me. "No, it's okay."

"Why not?" I said.

He made a face. "That was nice. Let's leave it at that and try again another time."

"Really?" I said. "Do you not want me to succeed?"

He pulled his head back. "Is that the only reason you wanted to do this?"

"No," I said. "I was trying to be spontaneous. But then I started thinking about how you're doing so well and I'm, um, not."

He turned off the lamp on his nightstand. "This isn't a contest, you know."

"I know," I said.

But what I really knew was that "This isn't a contest" was something winners said to make losers feel better.

~

The next morning, I stood in the kitchen surveying Sanjay's success. The dishes were done and the counters, while hardly sparkling, were cleaner than they'd been since Riya's last visit. In less than a week Sanjay had already aced one of my three requests. Granted, he had not secured a job yet—which was fine, I knew that took time—but if the man was willing to sanitize the sink, it was feasible that he could eventually solve world peace if he were so inclined.

He'd have the money thing figured out in no time.

"Miles, *stop!*" yelled Stevie from somewhere else in the house.

"No, you stop!" he yelled back.

My instinct was to intervene before one of them sent the other to urgent care, but Sanjay was awake—he could do it. I began going through the motions of making coffee as I waited for him to intervene.

"I'm telling Mommy!" Stevie hollered. *"Mommy!"*

Miles reacted by screeching like a chimpanzee. A passerby would have reasonably wondered whether he had just snapped his femur, but I knew better. This was his power play to Stevie's tattling.

I paused, then poured fresh water from the coffee carafe into the machine.

The screaming continued.

I measured coffee grounds and tapped them into the coffee maker's metal filter, trying to ignore my pounding head.

There was a sudden surge of silence. I smiled, thinking Sanjay had finally intercepted.

Then a heavy thud and a new cry—a real one. I pressed the "Start" button on the coffee maker and marched into the living room.

Stevie, clad in her nightgown, was sitting on Miles' chest. "What?" she said, like I was interrupting a private moment between them.

Miles' face was crimson, and he was gasping for breath. "Help!" he wheezed.

"Get off your brother before I spank you," I said to Stevie.

Still sitting, she glared at me like I had already swatted her. Then she began to berate me. "Our family rule is use your words! Hitting is *mean*, Mommy! Mean!"

"Oh, I'm sorry, were those your words sitting on your brother's chest suffocating him?" I pointed up the stairs. "Go up to your room and get dressed, or I'll show you *mean*."

Glowering, she lifted herself off of Miles.

"Go!" I yelled.

Miles' face was returning to its natural color, but he was still lying there crying. And as I looked at him more closely, I realized he was also looking at me as if I were the ghost of Joan Crawford. "Don't *spank* Stevie, Mommy!" he yelled.

The enemy of my son's enemy was his beloved sister. "Oh, come on, Miles. I'm not going to and you know it."

"Then why did you say it?" he wailed.

Desperation? Another occasion that felt like rock bottom but was actually a trapdoor to somewhere even lower? It was anyone's guess. "Go up to your room and get dressed," I told him. "Now."

Then I went to look for Sanjay. He wasn't in the living room, so I assumed he had fallen back asleep. But when I reached our room, I found him sitting up in bed on his laptop with a pair of headphones on.

"Hey," I said, though what I wanted to say was *Headphones or not, how the hell did you miss that racket?*

He pulled the headphones from his ears. "Hey."

"Didn't you hear the kids?" I said.

"No," he said, glancing at the screen. "Sorry. I was working."

I reminded myself not to scold him for doing what I asked him to. "That's great, but it's Friday. The kids have to be at camp in forty-five minutes, and I need to hop in the shower and get to work."

"I'm sorry." He seemed sincere. "I was just really caught up in this."

My head was throbbing. Three glasses of wine on a school night! Who did I think I was, Mick Jagger? "What are you working on?" I asked. Naturally, I was hoping he would say job applications.

He smiled shyly. "You know that jazz article I've been working on for the past several months?"

No. "Yes," I said.

"I was doing it on spec for the *Atlantic*," he said. "Remember?"

Now I remembered. Alex had put Sanjay in touch with someone at the publication, who had passed Sanjay's pitch to the web editor. He had liked the concept, but since Sanjay didn't have a lot of national credits to his name, the editor said he would have to write the entire piece before they bought it.

"It's the one about the lost history of jazz's impact on American politics," he added.

"Right—you were excited about that. How's it coming?"

He sat up and closed his computer. "It's done. I sent it in yesterday."

"You did?" I couldn't disguise my surprise. Sanjay had been a perfectly efficient worker at *Hudson*, but he had been a junior editor back then, writing little more than headlines and photo captions. As a journalist, however, I had known him to obsess over a single paragraph for a full week. Really, the more he cared about something, the less likely he was to finish it. As such, I had half assumed he'd still be working on the *Atlantic* article when the ball dropped in Times Square at the end of the year.

"Yes, and the editor already read it and just wrote to say she loved it. And I quote: 'No major edits needed.'"

"That's wonderful!"

"They're going to publish it in October. Online *and* in the magazine. Print triples my fee."

I walked over to him and kissed him. "I am so proud of you."

"Thank you," he said. "But there's more."

Dollar signs began dancing through my head. The *Atlantic* offered him another assignment! Or maybe even a column!

"My editor told me this story is the kind of project that they often see morph into a long-form piece," he said. "Or . . . even a book."

My excitement exploded into a million little pieces. A book? That could take years to write. The pay was usually lousy, and that was sure to be true for a tome on a semiobscure subject. Even if Sanjay sold it for a moderate amount, it would come in a lump sum that would not provide the sort of steady income we needed. I wondered whether he had considered this, or if he was still riding an early wave of enthusiasm.

Well, I wasn't about to bring it up. Not given that the last time he talked about writing a book, I had lit a match to his plans with a few discouraging if realistic words. Maybe in a few days I would broach the subject of finding a job that was compatible with his project. For now, I was going to support my husband.

He put the computer on the nightstand and pushed the covers off. Then he stood and stretched. "It's the early days, but I'm going to work on getting a proposal together so I have something ready when the story's published. And if that looks good, I'm going to go to New York and try to find an agent and sell the book. I mean, this is all if each step goes well. But I've been looking, and it seems to me there's a real market for an idea like this written in a way that's smart but commercial. It could be the start of something bigger."

"That's great, honey. I'm really happy for you." And I was. I just wished he would realize that his future dreams were a tad optimistic. Even if they did materialize, they wouldn't serve as a long-term solution to our financial woes. I could just imagine myself as a wrinkled old woman, hunched over a computer as an office cog. When would *I* get a turn to stay home and write?

The answer, I realized sadly, was never. Or at least not until well after both kids were done with college. Who was to say I'd even want to pen children's books then? Admittedly, I could have carved out a few minutes at night or on the weekends and returned to one of the stories that had been swirling around in my mind for years. But that would require forgetting I was exhausted and managing to get inspired and then *working even harder.*

And to be honest, I wasn't sure I had it in me to do that.

At some point Sanjay would probably get a job—I had asked him to, and he seemed serious about our project—but it was unlikely to provide a salary anywhere near mine. I was stuck, and no marriage project was going to change that simple truth.

Sanjay was grinning sheepishly again. "So . . . what do you think?"

I channeled Jenny and smiled with both my mouth and my eyes. "I think it's great, honey. I couldn't be happier for you if I tried."

SIXTEEN

That Saturday I took Cecily and the kids out to dinner and a movie while Sanjay stayed home to write. At first Cecily seemed withdrawn, but by the time we were in line for tickets, she, Stevie, and Miles were giggling about fart jokes. She was still smiling when I dropped her off.

I was thrilled to see her happy—but I also knew just how fleeting that happiness could be. The nights had been the hardest for me after my mother left. Monsters and bogeymen were lurking everywhere, and in my mind my father couldn't protect me the same way she could have (never mind that I couldn't actually remember my mother being all that maternal). Nick crawled into my bed one evening, and the two of us continued to sleep that way until long after it was socially acceptable to do so. That didn't stop me from staring at the dark corners of my room for hours before finally passing out from sheer exhaustion, or waking up covered in sweat in the middle of the night and calling out for someone who wasn't there.

"How do you think Cecily's doing?" I said to Matt after she ran inside the house.

He looked over his shoulder to make sure she was out of earshot. "I don't really know if I can tell."

"Why's that?"

He shrugged, almost resigned. "I mean, she's at camp all day during the week. Last weekend was the first weekend without Kimber, but I spent most of it filling out insurance forms." He sighed. "There is *so much paperwork*. No one ever tells you that about death."

"I'm sorry," I said.

"It is what it is."

Should I push it?

I didn't need Jenny's voice in my head to know the right answer.

I shifted my purse on my shoulder and took a deep breath. "I'm a little worried about Cecily. She was down in the mouth at dinner."

He was looking at me like I was dense. "Well, yeah. Her therapist said she's going to feel horrible for a long time. She might even get depressed." He shook his head. "Depressed, at six years old! I never thought that was something I'd have to worry about."

"But you and the therapist have a plan for dealing with that if it does happen?"

"Is there something you feel like I'm not doing, Penny?" His voice was even, but there was no mistaking the anger flashing in his eyes.

"I'm just worried about Cecily. As you know, I have some experience with this."

"Right, because your mom left," he deadpanned.

Although Sanjay and I had often had dinner with Matt and Jenny, our friendship had never really taken flight as a foursome. Which was fine—I didn't need my best friend's husband to be my friend, too. But up until that point, I had never actively disliked him.

"I am trying to do right by your daughter." My voice warbled, and I could feel myself getting shaky—confrontation wasn't really my thing. In fact, I would have preferred jogging down Fifth Avenue in my underwear to having this conversation.

"And you think that makes one of us," he said.

"Those are your words, not mine."

He sighed, looking suddenly deflated. "I'm doing the best I can, Penelope. I don't know what else to tell you."

"I know you are," I said. "And so am I. You're the last person I want to be arguing with right now."

He gave me a skeptical look. "If this is your idea of an argument . . ." I was about to respond when he glanced over his shoulder again. "Not to change the subject, but there's something I wanted to ask you." His tone had softened, and I felt myself relaxing.

"Anything."

"I've been getting a lot of emails from Jenny's readers. And you know Tiana, Jenny's assistant?"

I nodded.

"She says people on the internet are saying things. They want to know why Jenny hasn't been posting. People don't know she died, but they'll figure it out soon enough."

"Right."

"I was wondering if you could write something—like a final post explaining that she passed, maybe asking for privacy. Something that honors who she was but puts an end to the questions. Since the two of you were so close and you're a writer, I thought it would be nice if you were the one to do it."

Was I a writer? It had been so long since I'd thought of myself that way that I was surprised to hear him say it. "Of course, I'd be happy to." Well, I wouldn't necessarily be happy to write something completely vague and possibly untrue about Jenny's death. But if that's what I had to do to protect Cecily, then that's what I would do.

"Tiana sent me the log-in info and posting instructions, so after you write it, I can post it. It's no rush—maybe in the next couple of weeks if you can find the time."

I looked at him. "I'll find the time."

~

For months, I had been talking to a woman named Nancy Weingarten about donating millions of dollars to support women in medicine at the university. The following Monday it was finally time to seal the deal, which would be the biggest of my career. That was, if I could actually seal it.

As I walked Nancy to the conference room where we were meeting, I found myself thinking about my conversation with Matt. Had he asked me to write something on Jenny's website only so we'd stop arguing? Given his tendency to hit the road when he and Jenny were fighting, I knew I wasn't the only one who was conflict averse.

Still, what he had said—that he didn't know how Cecily was doing because she was at camp all day and he was spending his free time doing paperwork—was like a splinter wedged beneath my skin. I could only seem to ignore it for short bursts of time; sooner or later, it would have to be dealt with.

I sat at the long mahogany table, looked across at Nancy Weingarten, and began the talk I'd prepared.

But as I thanked her for her time and consideration, again my thoughts flitted back to Matt. He could change the subject all he wanted. He could try to avoid me all he wanted. My pushy questions and I were not going anywhere. I may have failed Jenny in myriad ways, but I would do this one thing for her.

"Penelope." Russ' voice sliced through my thoughts.

My eyes suddenly refocused. "I'm sorry, Russell, what was that?"

"Penelope," he said slowly, as if I were new to the English language, "Ms. Weingarten was asking us to confirm that we would use the Weingarten Family Fund verbiage on all materials relating to the scholarship. Can you weigh in?"

"Absolutely," I said, but my tone didn't exactly project confidence and competence.

Nancy Weingarten had been among the first women to graduate from the university's medical school, and had gone on to get her doctorate from Harvard before creating a new therapy for rheumatoid arthritis that had completely changed the way the disease was treated. Much of her life had been an uphill battle, she told me in an earlier meeting, and she suffered no fools.

Now she was across the conference table looking at me like I was insufferable. "Absolutely you can weigh in, or absolutely you'll use my name on all things related to the scholarship?" she rasped.

"We'll absolutely use your name on all materials," I said, sitting up straight in my chair.

"Good." She narrowed her eyes and lowered her bifocals to examine me. "And how will you promote the scholarship?"

I smiled—I knew this part like the back of my hand. "We plan to announce it via the university's news channels, and work with local, state, and national media to spread the word."

I had just opened my mouth to continue when Russ interjected: "We'll also include it in the materials we send to prospective and current students."

How had I *ever* been attracted to this underminer, even for a second? "As well as media outlets that cover health news and research," I said pointedly.

Russ smiled at Nancy. "As you may have guessed, we put all of this in the case statement for you to noodle over." He parroted Yolanda so expertly that I almost expected him to squawk. Beside Nancy, Yolanda was nodding with narrowed eyes, pleased.

"Penny," said Russ, like this wasn't my presentation. Maybe it wasn't anymore. "The case statement?"

I opened the folder I had put together that morning and retrieved a glossy, freshly printed brochure I had personalized for Nancy.

Except the document was the generic version we offered to anyone who donated more than five thousand dollars. I had grabbed the wrong document from my desk.

Tears began pooling behind my eyes, and I blinked in panic. In addition to abject humiliation, crying in front of my colleague, supervisor, and the biggest donor of my career was a guarantee I wouldn't have the opportunity to make the same mistake twice.

I took a deep breath. "I'm sorry," I said to Nancy. "I just realized that's not the document I prepared specifically for you."

"But we can get it to you today," said Russ.

"Thank you, Russell," said Yolanda, whose fire-starter stare was seconds away from igniting my eyebrows.

Nancy held up her hand. Then she looked at me expectantly. "I don't need a piece of paper. Ms. Ruiz-Kar, can you tell me about the type of students who will benefit from my scholarship?"

I could, I realized with relief. Better yet, I didn't need a brochure to do it. "Absolutely," I said. "Let me tell you about Leticia Alvarez, a first-generation college graduate whose family immigrated to the US from El Salvador when she was just five years old. Leticia, who will begin her first year at the medical school this fall, has been a stellar student her entire life. But she's not your everyday high achiever. You see, she and her family lived through the 2001 earthquakes that ravaged El Salvador. Leticia's mother was killed after being crushed by a building, but Leticia's family says she's the reason her younger brother, Eduardo, survived."

I paused and was pleased to see that Nancy had leaned forward to listen. "At just five years old, she managed to pull him out of the rubble and care for him until they were reunited with their father two days later. Leticia says the experience inspired her to pursue medicine. She hopes to practice emergency medicine, ideally working with a relief organization like Doctors Without Borders after her residency."

"Good," said Nancy. "Tell me more."

~

Yolanda's email was at the top of my inbox when I returned from walking Nancy Weingarten out of the building.

See me.

I sighed, knowing she would berate me for not batting it out of the park. When I reached her office, the door was open. She waved me in.

"Right. Well, let's talk that through. We want to ensure best practices . . ." It took me a moment to realize she was on the phone. She continued for another minute while I stood there, then hung up without saying goodbye. Her body remained facing her computer as her head swiveled to me. "What happened back there?" She didn't give me a chance to answer. "We discussed giving Nancy Weingarten the deep dive! We agreed to engage her on the granular level! That was . . ." Her head pivoted toward her computer, and she began to type. After a minute, she stopped as abruptly as she began and turned back to me. "Dean Willis was counting on this. You'll have to tell him yourself—I don't have the bandwidth for it this week."

"Nancy is ready to finalize the endowment," I said.

It was true. After everyone had filed out of the conference room, I had attempted to apologize to Nancy about the brochure and my uneven performance.

"Don't say you're sorry," she said, waving off my words.

"But I am," I stammered.

She eyed me from behind her glasses. "May I ask you a personal question?"

"Of course," I said.

"Do you have children?"

"Two. A daughter who's eight and a son who's six."

Nancy gave me a wan smile. She was short and lean, with narrowed, knowing eyes that gave her a wizard-like quality. I hadn't done the math, but I was fairly sure she was already well into her eighties.

"I had a feeling you might. I have three myself. I almost lost my mind until they went off to college. It's hard to work and have children, even if your husband helps. Which, unfortunately, mine did not. But as you know, things were different back then. I was the only woman on our block who had a job." She patted my arm. "Penelope, dear, can I give you a bit of advice?"

"Please do."

"Stop trying to make it look easy."

"Um . . . is that what I'm doing?" I knew the minute I said the words that it was.

"Do you see men acting like that?" She clucked her tongue. "Maybe it's changed for your generation. Judging from your colleague's behavior, I highly doubt it. Most men, they pretend to sweat over every single detail and then tell everyone it was even harder than they made it. If life is rough for you right now, act like it. You tripped back there, but you picked yourself back up and continued on, didn't you?"

"Yes," I said.

She laughed. "What you should be saying is, 'Yes, it was hard, but I did it anyway, and now I have the biggest female-generated endowment in the medical school's history to show for it.'"

"You mean—"

"God knows Harvard doesn't need my money."

The bit of hope I'd been clinging to blossomed into joy. "Thank you," I said. "That really means so much to me, and the medical school."

Nancy smiled at me. "Thank yourself."

Now Yolanda was arching a penciled eyebrow in disbelief. "You mean to say Weingarten agreed to the endowment."

"Yes." I sounded tired. But I *was* tired. Sanjay had been helping around the house more, but between my grief and confusion and the kids and Cecily and trying to make up for the work I didn't do after Jenny died, I was still so worn out I could crawl into a ball in Yolanda's leather lounge chair and wake up next year. "In addition to the scholarship, she's donating two hundred thousand to the General Fund." The General Fund was our most important campaign initiative, as donations could be used for almost any nonfacility purpose at the medical school, hospital, or research center. It also happened to be the area where we had the hardest time getting contributions of more than a few hundred dollars; turns out that people willing to part with large sums tend to want a say in where their money goes.

"This was a lucky break, Penelope," said Yolanda. "What if she hadn't asked you about the scholarship recipients? That was a great story you spun about Leticia, but if Nancy had quizzed you about how we would publicize the endowment, we would be having a different conversation right now."

I was ready to defer to her and say I was just glad it had worked out. But just as I opened my mouth, my conversation with Nancy Weingarten popped into my head.

"That was no spin—it was someone's life I was describing," I said, careful to make sure my tone was neutral. "And I don't think it was luck, either. I worked hard, and even though everything didn't go exactly as planned, it paid off."

She stared at me. Finally, she shook her head and said, "Let Dean Willis know."

My legs were shaking a little as I walked back to my desk—I had never stood up to Yolanda like that before. But I was smiling, too. Because I was already thinking about how I would tell Sanjay that maybe there was something to this radical honesty idea.

SEVENTEEN

I came home from work later that week to find Sanjay smiling so wide I could see his molars. He was wearing a nice pair of pants and a button-down that . . . could it be? Yes, it had actually been ironed!

"Did you have a job interview?" I asked, unable to disguise my delight.

His smile immediately wilted, but he quickly recovered. "No, but I'm skipping practice tonight."

"Okay . . ." I wasn't sure how band practice had anything to do with his attire.

"I hired a sitter and made reservations at Mario's," he explained, referring to our favorite Italian place.

"Oh," I said, because while this was a nice surprise and certainly more than what I had asked for, I also wished I'd stopped for a double espresso before coming home. It had been a marathon of a day and I was probably going to nod off into my tortellini.

"Oh?" he said.

I attempted to fix my face. "That sounds great—we haven't been out in ages."

"It's been a while," he said, sounding pacified. "I thought it would be a nice change of pace."

"It will be. Do you mind if I go change?"

"Of course not. Emma will be here at six forty-five. Our reservation is for seven."

"Perfect."

I went upstairs and slipped into a pair of jeans, which I immediately swapped for a skirt. If Sanjay was making an effort, then so would I. It had been months—maybe even nearly a year—since the two of us had gone out alone. Usually we went to Matt and Jenny's with the kids, because they had enough space that you could almost pretend the shrieking from down the hall was coming from another house.

As I replaced my melted makeup with fresh spackle, it occurred to me that in spite of my exhaustion, I was excited. Dinner alone would give us a chance to connect, like I'd told him I wanted to.

Except after we got to the restaurant and ordered and were looking at each other from across the small table where we'd been seated, it became painfully apparent how rusty we were at the art of adult conversation.

"How's the band going?" I asked.

He shrugged and took a piece of bread from the basket. "Don't know. Tonight makes three weeks that I've skipped."

"Really?" I said. How had I not realized that? "Why's that?"

He had just put an enormous chunk of bread in his mouth and finished chewing before answering. "I just needed a break."

I wasn't sure if he wanted me to push him for details or if he was being deliberately evasive. "Okay," I said.

"How's work?" he asked.

Riveting chat you're having, I heard Jenny say.

For once, I was able to curb my instinct to answer her aloud. *I'm trying,* I thought.

Try harder, she retorted.

"Penny?" asked Sanjay, not realizing I was more engaged in the conversation in my head than the one he and I were having.

I trained my eyes on him. "Work is going pretty well, if you can believe it," I said. "Do you remember me telling you about Nancy Weingarten?"

He nodded.

"Well, I landed the endowment. It's the biggest major gift from a woman in the medical school's history."

From the way he was beaming, you would have thought it was his victory. Or maybe he was just happy to have something to talk about. "That's fantastic! Why didn't you tell me that sooner?"

I wasn't sure. Most likely I'd been so busy with our evening routine that I'd forgotten, so I gave him a roundabout answer. "Well, it didn't go as smoothly as I would have liked. Yolanda tried to act like I'd screwed up the entire thing instead of making a few minor mistakes, but Nancy told me to stop making everything look easy."

He raised his eyebrows. "Did she?"

"Why are you giving me that look?"

"No look intended," he said. "It's good advice. I hope you'll take it."

This implied that I probably wouldn't. "Hmph," I said.

Sanjay reached across the table and squeezed my hand. "Penny, don't be like that. I'm really proud of you. Who would have thought back when you got that first development job that you'd practically be running the place seven years later?"

He'd meant it as a compliment, but I could feel my spirits sink. "Certainly not me." Eager to change the subject, I said, "Any news on the *Atlantic* piece?"

"I'm still waiting for it to go through another edit. But I'm making headway on the book."

Over dinner, he told me about how he had outlined the entire proposal and had started thinking through how he would begin the first chapter. I made sure to ask him questions and keep my eyes on him as he answered. But after he had finished telling me about his agent search and then looked at me like he wasn't sure what to say next, I drained my wine instead of speaking. Why did this have to be so much work? Shouldn't we—two people who had known each other for the better part of twenty years and had vowed to spend the rest of our natural lives as partners—be able to connect without so much effort, say nothing of a blasted list?

But these things took time. Just as Rome wasn't built in a day, my marriage would not be salvaged in a single date. I needed to believe that, because the alternative was more than I could bear.

Sanjay must not have shared my angst, because after we got to the garage where we'd parked the car, he put his hand on my thigh and gave it a squeeze. I stared straight ahead, because I knew exactly what that squeeze said: *Remember our project? We're supposed to be having sex.*

Well, yes, we were—but in a cramped sedan? In the middle of a parking garage?

"I had a nice time," said Sanjay.

"I did, too," I said. Especially the part where he paid the bill in cash—I hated to be so old-fashioned, but there was something romantic about knowing dinner wasn't going on our joint credit card.

He leaned over the gearshift to kiss me. His lips were soft but insistent, which was my kind of kissing.

A car, a car, a car, a car! I heard Jenny say. *Could you, would you in a car?*

I could not, would not, in a car. Because I couldn't stop thinking about where we were. Granted, it *was* dark, and no one appeared to be around. One could also argue that these same things made the garage an ideal location for a serial killer to prey on a couple midcoitus.

"I'm sorry," I said, pulling away from Sanjay. "I'm too anxious. Maybe at home?"

"No problem," he said.

"You're disappointed," I said.

He sighed. "No, I get it."

"But?"

"But I'm thinking that by the time we write the sitter a check and have a discussion with her about how we should really download one of those money-transfer apps and then peek in on Stevie and Miles and floss and brush away the garlic and Chianti and get into bed, I'm pretty sure neither of us is going to be in the mood."

"Well, when you put it like that . . ."

"It's fine," he said, but his straight-ahead stare on the drive home said otherwise.

"Sorry," I said again when we pulled up to the house. And I was. He had asked for one single thing, and I had repeatedly failed to deliver it.

"Don't be." He gave me a small smile. "It was nice to go out with you."

I put my hand on his. "It was," I said. "Let's not have the money-transfer app conversation with the sitter. And I'm okay with your garlic breath if you don't mind the taste of red wine."

He laughed lightly. "Deal."

When we got inside, our sitter, Emma, was slouched on the sofa. Her thumbs continued tapping on her phone as she addressed us. "Have a good time?"

"Yes," Sanjay and I said in unison, then smiled at each other. I knew what he was thinking: *Get out of here.*

"That's awesome?" said Emma, using intonation I suspected was intended for whomever she was texting, or whatever newfangled app she was using to communicate.

While Sanjay cut Emma a check and sent her on her way, I ran to the bathroom, feeling abuzz with nervous anticipation. Aside from our one aborted attempt the night I had drinks with Jael, Sanjay and I hadn't slept together since before Jenny's death. And the last time we had, it had been . . . well, it must have been rote, because I honestly couldn't remember it. But in spite of the parking garage incident, I was feeling optimistic. I could do this.

In front of the mirror, I dabbed concealer under my eyes and on the sides of my nose. Upon further inspection, I decided a bit of blush wouldn't hurt. Freshly rouged, I went to the bedroom and changed into the new camisole I had ordered online. It looked far better on the model than it did on me—as completely unshocking as this was, it never failed to disappoint—but it matched the underwear that I had purchased to go with it, which were cutting into my hips. Maybe they would stretch if I kept them on long enough. Worst-case scenario, I would swap them for cotton briefs before going to sleep.

I got into bed, draped my legs with the duvet, and waited for Sanjay while attempting to get in the mood.

In my mind, I was striding down a snowy street near Grand Central in Manhattan, just a few months after 9/11. I was still apprehensive about the state of the world, but I was excited to meet Sanjay, whom I had just started dating, for drinks. Then I was watching that no-longer-new boyfriend sleep as the early morning sun streamed through the bay windows in our Brooklyn apartment. I was introducing him as my husband at a coworker's wedding. I was putting a tiny, dozing Stevie into his arms for the first time. He was carrying me over the threshold of our first home.

It was odd—these were hardly the kind of thoughts that normally turned me on. But they made me remember that I loved my husband, which in turn made me crave the physical connection that once brought us together.

Except . . . where *was* he? At least fifteen minutes had passed since I'd gone upstairs. I grabbed my cellphone from the bedside table. After turning off a too-bright lamp and turning on another and then carefully positioning myself, I took a selfie from my best angle: from the neck down. The picture was suggestive without being graphic, and would hopefully get Sanjay upstairs before I fell asleep. I texted it to Sanjay.

My phone dinged back at me almost immediately.

Cute, wrote Sonia. Guessing this wasn't for me.

Ack! No, so sorry!

For your sidepiece? she wrote back with a winking emoji.

Um. Not a chance.

That is not a husband photo.

It is, actually.

God bless you, then. I'd rather get a two-hour bikini wax than send Grant a photo suggesting I want to sleep with him.

Ha—please step away from the hot wax. Let's catch up sometime this century.

Let's. Xo

What would make her think I was having an affair? But then, why wouldn't she? I was the naïve one who thought friends laid it all out on the table.

Sanjay walked in as I was putting the phone back on my nightstand. He whistled. "You look incredible."

"Thanks," I said. "Where were you?"

"Just sending a quick email."

"This late? When we're supposed to be having a sexy date night?"

"Sexy, huh?" he said, but even his wiggling eyebrows couldn't ease my irritation.

"You gave me a hard time in the car, but then you go send an email instead of coming to bed?" I said.

"I did not give you a hard time," he said quickly. "And if you must know, I was emailing myself. I had an idea I didn't want to forget."

"For your book."

"Yes," he said. There was an unapologetic tone to his voice. But then he softened. "I like your nightie thing," he said, motioning toward my camisole. "Is it new?"

I patted the bed beside me. "Yes."

He dropped his pants and his shirt in a pile on the floor. I tried not to think about how I would trip on them when I got up in the middle of the night to pee or deal with one of Miles' accidents. Then he crawled toward me like a tiger, baring his teeth playfully.

I laughed as he drew closer, and he lifted a finger to his lips. As our eyes met, I felt a flutter in my stomach. We were flirting! I couldn't remember the last time that had happened.

"How's this for a sexy date night?" he growled into my ear and I laughed. He lowered himself onto me, and I told myself not to think about the fact that his waist was significantly narrower than my own or that his hipbones were kind of hurting me (though maybe my too-tight underwear was making it worse). I shifted, still smiling, and then he began kissing my neck, which I loved but he almost never did.

I arched my back and began to melt as his lips made their way from my neck to my collarbone. All systems go.

He had just begun to gently tug at my camisole when he raised his head. "Did you buy the nightie thing because of the list?"

"What?" I murmured.

"The thing you're wearing," he said. "Is it because of the list?"

"I don't know." His question was pulling me right out of my libidinous state of mind. "Can we go back to what you were just doing?"

Above me, his chest heaved in a sigh. "Sure."

"I was really enjoying that," I said.

His mouth returned to my skin, but he wasn't aroused anymore, and after a few minutes it became clear that was not going to change. "Crap," he muttered. "Sorry."

"We could try something different," I suggested, trying to sound game about it. It happened, or so I had read; he wasn't twenty-five anymore.

"Don't worry about it. I should have come to bed sooner." His voice was flat. I looked up at him, then turned my head away because I felt like I might cry.

This was my fault. If I had been more attentive—if I had spent just one or two hours a month meeting what was probably the most basic need for the average married man—he never would have had to ask for sex. Now my failure had become his.

"Sorry," he said again. He rolled off me, turned off the light, and then slipped between the sheets. After a moment, he said, "Maybe I should give you the next item on the list soon."

"I think that's probably a good idea," I said.

I blinked into the darkness, listening to my husband deliberately slow his breathing just as I was doing. Then the two of us lay there pretending we were asleep.

I didn't know how much time had passed—at least ten minutes, or maybe it had been an hour—when a sudden revelation socked me in the stomach.

Our project wasn't working.

In fact, if this evening had been any indication, it was backfiring, and I was pretty sure Sanjay giving me the next item on his list wasn't going to change that. He may have been dust-busting like a maniac, but we weren't connecting as a couple. We still weren't sleeping together, either. And though I was incredibly hesitant to bring it up, not only was he not making more money, I had yet to get the sense he had a concrete plan for doing so.

No sooner did I process all of this when Jenny's voice echoed into my ears: *Then what, Penny? What if your marriage does fail?*

Unfortunately, I knew the answer to her question: Then my family fell apart. Then my children didn't have the happy home I had sworn I would give them. Then I would have broken all of the promises I made myself as a child.

I didn't know what might happen after that, but it couldn't possibly be good.

EIGHTEEN

I'd just pulled into our driveway when my brother called. "Nick?" I had picked Cecily and the kids up from camp on the way home, and they scrambled out of the car. "Is everything okay?"

"Very funny, Penny."

I hadn't been joking. The last time my brother had called was Christmas. He'd emailed maybe twice in the interim, even though I messaged him every few weeks and sent pictures of Stevie and Miles. I wedged the phone between my ear and shoulder as I opened the front door for the kids. The three of them went clambering into the house, leaving a trail of shoes and backpacks in their wake. "How are you?"

Sanjay was in the kitchen, arranging chicken nuggets on a baking tray. He cocked his head. "Nick," I mouthed.

"Great. Just got back from Namibia," Nick said.

"How nice," I said.

My sarcasm was lost on him. "Dude, it was one of the most beautiful places I've ever seen. Landscape like a mother-trucking watercolor painting, and the people were beyond friendly."

"Dude, I'm jealous."

"Ha-ha. You should come with me sometime."

I looked at the dining room table, which had a river of glue running down its center. "I'd love that."

"So, Pen-Pen," he said, using my childhood nickname, "have you talked to Dad lately?"

"Dad who?" I said.

Behind me, Sanjay snorted. In his mind, my father was but one small rung above my deadbeat mother. Which was fair—we barely heard from him. When I called he routinely took weeks to call back, so sometimes I just didn't bother. He had been to visit us exactly one time since we'd moved from Brooklyn. Still, he was my only parent. I couldn't just write him off.

"I'm serious," said Nick. "He's having a hard time."

Yeah, well, my best friend just died, I thought. Which Nick knew— he'd sent me a sad-emoji-embellished text message after I finally posted something about Jenny's death on Facebook. Maybe our shared DNA sent out some sort of distress signal, because he added, "Hey, speaking of, how are you doing? With your friend being gone?"

How was I doing? How long did he have? My heart broke at least five times a day, and that was when I was doing my damnedest to keep my focus entirely on work and family. I was desperate to get to the stage where the sight of Cecily—who was currently running through the backyard as Miles chased her and Stevie with a water gun—would not fill me with the kind of sadness that made me want to weep in bed for a week. And even though I was struggling with my marriage project, I felt guilty for the progress Sanjay and I were making. At least *we* still had a chance to fix our relationship.

"I don't know, Nick. I'm doing all right. The kids are happy and healthy, and I'm getting a chance to spend a lot of time with Cecily."

"Cecily?"

"Jenny's daughter."

"Right."

I sighed. "So, what's going on with Dad?"

"Well, he's having some health problems."

My heart lurched. "What kind of health problems?"

"That's probably something you should talk to him about."

"I don't get it. If he called to tell you, why couldn't he call me?"

Nick paused. "He didn't call me. I was flying through Florida a couple of weeks ago, and I stopped to see him. He looked like hell, so I pushed and found out he's got some stuff going on."

This admission stung more than his forgetting Cecily's name. Nick hadn't been out to see us in several years, but he had managed to see our father, who hadn't made enough time for him a day in his life. "I can't fly to Florida right now, Nick. Do you think he'll tell me if I call him?"

"Don't know, Pen-Pen," he said. "You know Dad—hard to get him to say much about anything other than the Orioles and the weather. But you should probably try."

Through the kitchen window, a pair of small brown birds watched me from their perch on the fence. One pecked at the other for a few seconds, then the other craned its neck and returned the favor. One of the birds flew into the sky and then disappeared from sight.

I thought about my brother diving out of his bedroom window in first grade to see if he could fly. Immediately after, he'd come running to me to say that his arms hurt but he was sure he'd caught air. "Nick?" I said.

"Yeah, sis?"

"I'll call Dad. Come see us sometime, okay?"

"Sure, Pen. That sounds great."

"Love you," I said to the dial tone.

When I set down the phone, Sanjay was looking at me.

"What?" I sounded as dispirited as I felt.

"What?" he repeated.

"You were staring at me like I made some unintentional gaffe. What did I say?"

Sanjay glanced at the timer on the microwave, which he'd set for the nuggets. Then he met my gaze. "What happened to 'stop making everything look easy'?"

"How was I doing *that*?"

"Pen, even after everything that's happened lately, you're still smoothing things over with your brother instead of telling him that he sucks for never coming to visit."

"Need I remind you that I'm the one who told you I wasn't happy with how our marriage was going? That's hardly smoothing things over. And what about what I said to Yolanda after she said Nancy's scholarship was a lucky break? I even told Matt that Cecily needed more attention. Nick already knows I'd like to see him more often, and I'd rather leave it at that. I don't want to be *that* woman."

He scrunched up his face. "What woman?"

"You know the type. You say hi, and she immediately launches into a laundry list of what's wrong with her life."

Sanjay put his hands on his head. "Penelope, I'm not asking you to turn into Debbie Downer. I just think you feel the need to make it seem like everything is fine, even when it's the exact opposite."

I was seething. Make it seem like everything was fine! I didn't do that—not anymore. That I was standing in my kitchen fighting with Sanjay was proof.

"Even when you're direct, you still manage to avoid confrontation," he added.

"Are we not in the middle of a confrontation this very second?"

"Same team, Pen. I'm trying to be honest with you." He walked over to me and put his arms around my waist, but I shook him off. He couldn't just stand there insulting me and think I'd want to cuddle. "Okay. But you said you were ready for the next thing on my list."

"And I am," I said defiantly.

"Good. I want you to be more honest with everyone—not just me. This project is a start, but you could be taking it further than our marriage."

Had he missed everything I told him about Yolanda and Matt? "How?" I said.

"Well, I wish you'd tell Nick and your dad that you feel like an afterthought to them."

An afterthought. That's what I was, wasn't it? My face was growing warm, and my throat was tightening.

"I'm not trying to hurt you," he said, but he sounded defensive. "All I'm saying is that if things aren't okay, then don't act like they are."

"Fine." I waited until I was sure I could speak without crying. Then I said, "Since we're being honest, I'd like to know how your job search is going. I'm glad you're doing so much around the house, and trying to be more engaged in our marriage. But money is still a major issue, and I don't think the book project is going to fix that."

He looked wounded. "I haven't had anything to tell you. I'm sending out application after application. Doesn't that count for something?"

"Sure," I said. "It counts for a lot."

"Thank you. I'll let you know if I get any bites." He leaned against the counter, looking like he was on the verge of defeat. But he couldn't raise a white flag yet—at least *one* of us needed to be all in on our project. "It's been nearly a month. Do you really feel like this is improving our marriage?"

He had just told me to stop faking it, and I had agreed. But there was honest—and then there was stupid. "Yes," I lied.

NINETEEN

I might not have known how to fix my marriage, but I knew how to be a good parent, and I threw myself into the task. I read to Stevie every single night. I woke even earlier so I had time to build elaborate Lego spaceships with Miles before leaving for work. I helped the kids and Cecily set up a lemonade stand one weekend. The next, I took them to a waterpark and let them shove cotton candy into their little mouths with abandon, then gently coaxed them out of their sugar-induced meltdowns an hour later.

July was nearly over, though I couldn't say where the time had gone. But around midmonth, Miles had stopped wetting the bed; one dry night became two, and suddenly all four of us were sleeping straight through until the morning.

Jenny often liked to say that success stuck when it came with a reward, so one Saturday afternoon while Sanjay took Stevie to dance class, I took Miles to buy a toy. I knew he would play with it for three hours before requesting a new one. Still, when we pulled up in front of the toy store, you'd think I had just given him the keys to the kingdom.

"Can I get anything I want?" Miles asked, looking up at me expectantly.

"Not anything, love," I said, tweaking his nose. "You can choose something that costs up to fifteen dollars, remember?"

His eyes grew even wider. "Fifteen is a lot, right?"

Not anymore it wasn't, but I wanted to bask in the role of Best Mom Ever for at least a few minutes. "Let's go see what we can find," I told him.

Miles tore through aisle after aisle with a joy that made my heart ache. I could not remember a time when my own father had let me pick out my own toy. Would my son ever realize how fortunate he was—to have parents who not only bought him presents, but who also loved him as much as we did?

My mind quickly turned to another six-year-old who would never again visit the toy store with her mother. Cecily's list of nevers would be excruciatingly long, and my being there for her simply could not fix that.

"This?" Miles was holding up an action figure in front of my face.

I examined it. "It's twenty dollars, which is five too many. And you said you were scared of that guy."

"Yeah," he said, placing it back on the shelf.

"This?" he said two minutes later, holding up a bright-orange pistol.

"Sorry, you know the rule. No guns."

He scowled but put the gun back.

He returned with a zombie figurine that was guaranteed to have him peeing the bed until he was seventeen. I winced and shook my head. Who had decided to put such a thing in a children's store? And why had I agreed to come here again?

I was sure our outing was seconds from going south when Miles ran down the aisle to where I was standing. He was clutching a dinosaur, which he presented to me. If the packaging was to be believed, four batteries would transform the plastic beast into a roaring relic.

"I want it but it's sixteen dollars," Miles said mournfully.

"It's fine."

"You'll buy it?"

I nodded. He dropped the dinosaur on the floor and threw his arms around me. "I love you, Mama."

I squeezed him back. Sixteen dollars for him to call me Mama like he had when he was a toddler? A steal.

When we got home, Stevie was sitting in the entryway, still dressed in her leotard and tights. Her arms were crossed and she was scowling. He held out his dinosaur toward her, which she regarded with disdain. "You know that's actually made of real dinosaurs."

"No, it's not," I said quickly.

Miles was regarding her quizzically. "Mommy?" he said.

"It *is*," Stevie insisted, still planted in the center of the floor. "It's plastic, right?"

I nodded as we stepped around her.

"Then it is too made of dinosaurs. Because plastic is made of petroleum, and petroleum is made of fossils. And old dinosaur bones are fossils," she said.

I stared at her with surprise. "How did you know that?"

A faint smile appeared on her lips. "I found a book about the environment at camp the other day."

"Cool," said Miles.

Though she had been attempting to goad Miles, she was just as pleased that she had astonished him instead. "Do you want to go play?" she asked. "I can find your old stuffed dinosaur, and we can make them a family."

"Okay, but you can't touch my new toy."

Stevie shrugged. "Fine."

They ran upstairs. I headed to the dining room, where Sanjay was at the table, tapping away on his laptop.

"Mission accomplished," I announced.

He looked up. "Any meltdowns?"

"Not a single one. More astoundingly, he and Stevie went off to play together. How's the book proposal going?"

"It's going well," he said. He stood from the table. "But I'm done for now. How about I pour us some wine and we go sit on the deck?"

"It's only four o'clock," I said.

"It's Saturday, we have nowhere to be for the rest of the day, and our children are playing quietly. This is the parenting equivalent of a triple rainbow."

Was this his way of trying to make up for our argument about his job search? I decided I didn't want to know. "You're right. Let's go."

It was nearly ninety degrees outside, and the glass of pale-pink wine Sanjay handed me was beaded with condensation. "When did you go wine shopping? And how did you know I was secretly craving rosé?" I asked.

He smiled. "I know what you like."

Did he? "Thank you," I said.

"Thank *you*," he said, clinking my glass against his. "I very much enjoyed not making the trek to the toy store."

I took a sip of my wine. It was dry and delicious and definitely not the cheap stuff we normally bought. "This is fantastic," I said to Sanjay. "Did you decide to raid our 401(k)? And the last time I checked, you weren't even a rosé fan."

"I got paid for a story yesterday and thought it would be nice to get a decent bottle of wine to celebrate."

"Which one?"

"The summer music roundup for the *Free Press*."

"That's great," I said, careful to make sure my voice conveyed enthusiasm.

He sniffed his glass. "Turns out I like rosé just fine when it doesn't come in a box."

I laughed and leaned back in my chair, which pitched precariously. Our deck was not level and would probably fall right off the house in another year or two. Before me, the backyard looked like a small swath of the Sahara. I had given up the idea of landscaping after one of our neighbors had mentioned how much he had spent resodding. Still, the dead grass gave me a pang. It seemed like further confirmation I would never have an emerald-green carpet my children ran barefoot on. I would not grow peonies or plant a vegetable garden where the tattered trampoline currently stood. That yard indicated my life would be just as it was for a very long time—and that was only if I had the good fortune of things not getting worse.

"So," said Sanjay, "I have some news." He was wearing sunglasses, and I couldn't get a read on whether his news was the good kind or the bad.

"I talked to Alex a few days ago."

"About the book idea?" I said.

He nodded. "She told me that it's never been more difficult to land a deal, especially if I don't have a platform. My lack of name recognition and nonexistent fancy degree is going to work against me."

I was preparing to say something comforting when he added, "But she does think this book idea has legs."

He had just taken off his sunglasses and was staring at me with a sort of excitement and intensity I had not seen since, well—since the last time we were talking about his book. "Alex thinks the clips I have are a solid start. I'm not coming out of nowhere."

"Your work is paying off," I said.

"Yes, and the proposal is practically writing itself. I'm aiming to have it done and ready to show agents by September."

Sanjay had a natural curiosity as well as an eye for unearthing fascinating information others overlooked. I had often thought the only thing standing between him and the career he wanted was the ability to see the big picture and plan for it. Now here he was, taking it all in and coming up with a strategy. I reached out and took his hand, which seemed to surprise him. "I'm really proud of you," I told him.

He squeezed my fingers. "Thank you—that means a lot to me, especially because I know the book isn't on your list."

I frowned. "You don't *only* have to do what's on my list. I'm glad you've got that."

"I've got some other news, though." Suddenly his smile was as genuine as a Rolex hanging in some guy's trench coat. "I have a job interview," he said.

"You do!" I immediately forgot about his fake expression and jumped up and hugged him. "Tell me more."

"It's for a communications associate at the College of Liberal Arts. They're looking for someone to write press releases and website content and stories for the alumni magazine. The office is less than a quarter mile from yours. I'm going in for an interview next Thursday."

"That sounds perfect for you." I searched his face, unsure why his smile remained so disingenuous. "I had no idea the university had part-time communications positions."

His face twisted. "That's the catch. It's a full-time job."

"But—"

He held a hand up. "I know it's not what we talked about. And I know it would complicate our schedule even more and I might have less time to chip in around the house, which we'd have to discuss. But literally no one else has called me back, and this job sounds right up my alley. The salary isn't posted, but I looked up similar positions, and it would be enough that we could really make a change in the way we're living."

"What about your writing? Your book?" I wanted him to make more money, but I didn't want his passion to be snatched from him in the process.

"At this point, it's just an interview. But if it's a good fit, I wouldn't just stop writing. Plenty of people have full-time jobs and manage to handle side projects, too. I mean, that's how Alex transitioned to freelancing."

This was true. It was also true that Alex shared a studio apartment with a couple of potted plants.

My heart sank as I realized what I had done. My husband was on his way to meeting another one of my requests. But to do so, he was going to give up his dreams. Which would cause him to resent me. Which would very likely spell disaster for our marriage—the old adage "Happy wife, happy life" missed half the equation.

There was a clamor in the kitchen. I was ready to tell Stevie and Miles to go away when Lorrie emerged from behind the screen door leading to the deck. "Hiya, Kars!" she said.

Her nose was so crooked that it looked like it was sliding from one side of her face to the other. There were so many things about other people that you weren't supposed to notice! And yet you could overlook crucial details—for example, that your neighbor wouldn't know a boundary if it zapped her like an electric fence—until it was already too late.

Sanjay turned toward me. I could tell he was thinking, *Are you ready to do something about this, or do I need to?*

I stood.

"Lorrie," I said, and maybe my voice was a tad loud. Later, it would occur to me that it wasn't Lorrie I was mad at. I was irritated with myself for sabotaging my husband's hopes and dreams. But in that moment, she was my target. "I'm going to need you to knock before coming into our house," I told her. "And when you knock, you are going to wait until Sanjay or I answers and asks you to enter. You *cannot* keep walking in like you live here, because it's terrifying. Okay?"

She looked confused. Maybe even a little hurt. Before she or I could say another word, Olive, who must have followed her mother into the house, pushed past Lorrie out the screen door. She stood in front of me, teeth bared. "You're a mean lady!" she spat. "Mean!"

"Oh, oh, oh," said Lorrie, tugging Olive back as if I were waving a knife at her. "Look what you've done. I thought we were *friends*, but friends don't scare friends' children. Poor Olive," she cooed, pulling her daughter into her arms. "Poor love, had to see her own mother being scolded like a schoolgirl. Shhh now, Mommy's here." She kissed her daughter's head, then glared at me. "You're not the person I thought you were, Penny."

"No one is the person everyone else thinks they are," I said.

Lorrie glared at me, pulling Olive by the hand.

When they were gone, I sighed and sat back down. Saying my piece may have offered instant gratification, but the aftermath was exhausting.

Sanjay, who had not moved since Lorrie appeared, was staring at me with a mix of disbelief and wonder.

"What?" I said. I tipped back the last of my wine, which was now warm. "You told me to be more honest."

He shook his head. "I'm not sure that's what I had in mind."

TWENTY

If writing a speech for Jenny's memorial service had been painful, penning the final post for her website was excruciating. I toiled for hours, ultimately settling on a short note explaining that she had passed away suddenly from an unknown health problem. I asked readers to honor Jenny's memory by sending good thoughts to her family, while also giving them privacy during this terrible time. I ended the post by quoting from something she had written less than a month before her death:

> *This is not a test. Life is messy and sometimes tragic and often just plain hard for a woman to weather. But when you step back for a moment, the whole of it is incredibly beautiful—and that is what we must choose to focus on.*
> *xo, Jenny*

I was giving the post a last look one morning when Matt texted to see how soon I could come over. I had started to panic, thinking something had happened to Cecily, when he sent a second text explaining that Jenny's autopsy report had come in.

I had been in the office an hour and still had approximately three hundred and twelve things to do before lunch, but not a single one of them was a fraction as important. I told Matt I'd be there in fifteen minutes.

"Meeting," I said to Sheryl, the receptionist, as I hurried past her desk. It was the first week of August and already the month felt like Augusts often do—both idle and rushed as everyone cashed in on unused vacation time and tried to enjoy what was left of a season that they had mostly spent indoors.

She raised an eyebrow. "Enjoy."

This was the problem with having a shared office calendar: everyone had access to everyone else's schedule. Sheryl knew full well that I didn't have a single meeting planned until two. I almost came up with an excuse, but then I thought about Sanjay's second request. If my eruption at Lorrie was any indication, I needed more practice. Well, no time like the present.

"I won't," I said, not turning to take in Sheryl's response. "And I'll be back when I'm back."

~

When Matt answered the door, I nearly did a double take. He was wearing a faded Cubs T-shirt and athletic shorts, and his chin was covered with days-old stubble. I'd seen him the previous week after dropping Cecily off, and he'd looked like his usual clean-cut self then. Had the autopsy sent him over the edge?

"Penny," he said. "Come in."

I glanced around. There were papers and toys everywhere, and an overflowing basket of laundry in the middle of the hallway. This did not assuage my fears about Matt's mental state.

"You took the morning off?" I asked as I followed him into the living room.

He ran a hand through his hair, which was as long as I had ever seen it. "I'm working from home today."

"Great that you have the option," I said.

Other than the din of air-conditioning, the house was still. Jenny's voice pierced the silence. *Too bad you're not using it to spend time with your daughter.*

I no longer startled when I heard her speaking to me; if anything, it had become a comfort. The Jenny in my head was sharper and more sarcastic than she had been when she was alive, and I was glad for that, too—it felt almost as though I was finally getting a glimpse of the person she had been hiding from me all those years.

Well, she wasn't wrong about Matt's priorities, I thought as I sat across from him on one of the gray velvet sofas. When I'd asked Cecily how she was doing last week, she'd flat-out told me she was lonely.

Matt leaned forward and handed me a sheet of paper that had been facedown on the coffee table. "I know you wanted answers, so here they are. You're welcome to tell Sanjay what's in this document, but otherwise please keep it to yourself."

"I understand." I glanced at the paper, then looked back at Matt for confirmation I should proceed. He nodded and I began to read.

Below Jenny's name and personal information, a box had been checked. Manner of death: accident.

Beneath that was her cause of death: opioid toxicity.

My eyes, already moist with tears, traveled down the page to the toxicology findings. I inhaled sharply as the words began to register. Jenny had had oxycodone, acetaminophen, hydrocodone, and kratom in her blood and urine at the time of her death.

"What is kratom?" I asked.

"It's an herb. It can make you feel euphoric and energized. It's not illegal," he added in a way that told me this was important to him.

But everything Jenny had been taking was legal. And all of it had proved to be lethal.

"Lots of people take kratom . . ." He looked away. "When they're trying to get off narcotics."

Then she had been well aware she had a problem. She might have even seen death lurking in the shadows.

"There are multiple painkillers listed here," I said to Matt.

His eyes met mine. "I know."

"Where was she getting them all? Was she buying them off the dark web or something?"

He looked away again. When he finally addressed me, there was a bitter edge to his voice. "You'd be surprised. She was seeing a couple different doctors, and apparently no one checked to see if anyone else was giving her the same thing. I mean, why would they? She *was* in pain, or at least she had been at one point. And she looked so . . . normal. I probably wouldn't have even found out the extent of it if one of the pharmacies hadn't called me on accident to confirm a prescription I knew she'd had filled the week before. I started looking for signs and suddenly it all added up."

"Then you knew it was serious."

He pressed his lids shut for several seconds. "In retrospect? Sure. But she said she was tapering off. She said she was getting better."

"And you believed her."

"Yes and no. We had been fighting about it the week before she died."

But he left town anyway, Jenny whispered in my ear.

Matt sighed and looked off in the distance. "The thing is, Penny, Jenny loved the idea of me. I checked off all the boxes for her perfect husband—she even told me that on our second date. But I don't know that the reality of me ever met her needs, which is probably why we had a hard time being together for more than an hour or two at a time without fighting. After a while I started to say yes every time I had a chance to be on the road because it seemed like it was easier on both of us. Still, I wouldn't have been gone all the time if I had known how bad it was." His eyes found mine again. "She flushed a bottle of pills in front of me and vowed it was over. I really thought she was getting better."

"Damn it," I muttered.

"I know it's a lot."

"It is, but I wanted answers. Except the one thing this report doesn't answer," I said, poking my finger at the paper, "is why Jenny would hide this from me."

He sighed, then said, "I don't know what to tell you, except that as my therapist keeps reminding me, addiction makes liars out of people."

Maybe. But didn't their lies quickly come to light? My mother's sister, Jo, had drunk herself into the grave, while a man I had dated briefly in college couldn't function without a steady stream of various drugs pumping through his veins. One of my old editors had let bourbon destroy his marriage and annihilate his relationship with his children before finally getting sober. The editor had seemed like a jolly, high-functioning drunk. Even so, in every case, I had known the person had been struggling. How had I missed it with Jenny?

"They don't start that way and they don't mean to do harm, but the need takes over," said Matt. "It was important to Jenny that you thought she was fine. She didn't want to hurt you."

Hurt me! Had I really seemed so fragile? Damn it, if only life came with a rewind button. I would do it all so very differently.

He stood. "I've got to get in the shower and get cleaned up."

I frowned. "I thought you were working from home today."

"Just for the morning. Our CEO is already having a conniption about how much I've been out of the office this summer."

"Really? After all you've been through?"

"Yeah, well, there's not much I can do about it," he said.

Sure there is, said a voice, and for once I couldn't say for certain whether it was my own or Jenny's.

My underarms were damp and my forehead was growing clammy. But I had to say something.

"Cecily's lonely," I said. "She told me herself last week."

He stared at me. "You know, Penny, I'm beginning to feel like you think I'm a shitty parent."

If by *shitty* he meant the kind of parent who wasn't making the best decisions for his daughter, then yes. But that wasn't the point. "It's not about what I think," I told him. "I love Cecily, and if I know she needs something, then I have an obligation to speak up."

He crossed his arms. "I'm her *father*. I know what she needs better than anyone else."

"I respect that. I'm not trying to cross any boundaries. I'm just passing on what I've observed."

"Fine," he said.

I stood from the sofa. "Thank you for having me over and sharing the report with me."

"No problem," he said stiffly.

"By the way, I'm done with the last post for Jenny's site," I said.

He looked at me blankly.

"The one you asked me to write?"

"Oh. Right." He had already started for the stairs. "Let's talk about that some other time." But his voice told me that we wouldn't be talking about anything anytime soon.

I got into my car, drove a few blocks from the Sweets' house, and pulled over to put my head against the steering wheel and sob. The last thing I wanted was to be on bad terms with Matt. What if our already tenuous relationship was destroyed? What if he took Cecily and moved across the country and I never saw her again? Was this the price of honesty? Because if so, it wasn't worth it.

I cried until I looked like I'd just gotten a facial from a swarm of yellow jackets. Then I wiped my eyes and continued my drive back to the office.

After ducking into the lobby bathroom to splash water on my face and reapply makeup, I returned to my desk to discover that during the hour I was away, Yolanda had emailed twice and left me a voicemail. She was on vacation for the week, but had met a potential donor while traveling and needed me to speak to him. Immediately.

I was about to call her back when the phone rang again.

"Where have you been?" It was Yolanda, of course. "Sheryl said you went to a meeting, but there's nothing on the books."

Naturally, she had checked our shared calendar. I wouldn't be surprised if she began requiring us to implant GPS chips into our forearms so she could have ops on us at all times.

"I'm here now," I said. "How is your vacation going?"

"The Lake Michigan shoreline is *teeming* with potential donors, Penelope. You should make the trip. The PD I want you to call is John Sterling. He's number three at Xerox. He got his MBA from Columbia but his daughter had a lifesaving aortic arch repair at the Children's Hospital. Obviously, *major* potential donor. Are you memo-ing this?"

My IM box popped up; it was Russ, who was confirming our meeting—an actual, on-the-group-calendar meeting with the graphic designer who was working on a new fundraising campaign—at two.

"Hello?"

"I'm still here, Yolanda."

"Good." She rattled off a number and an email address. "And Penelope? Don't blow this."

I stared at the phone. Sanjay told me to be direct. If this backfired and we had to take up residence at his parents' house, this was on him.

"Yolanda, if I had actually blown one opportunity in the past seven years, I'd feel that comment was warranted," I said. "But since I haven't, I'm going to assume you've confused me with someone else. I'll call Sterling today. And rest assured, I won't blow it. Talk soon." Then I hung up.

I could just barely make out my reflection on my computer monitor. Wavy hair, laugh lines, shoulders sloped from so many hours at a desk: these were features I recognized.

But if I hadn't known better, I would have sworn there was another woman looking back at me. And if I was honest—a practice I was starting to question—I was a little bit afraid of her.

TWENTY-ONE

A single secret is like a lone roach. You know there will be more—it's only a matter of when. After learning Jenny's marriage was a wreck, the revelation about her addiction was more an inevitability than a real surprise. And though I hated to think about it, I was pretty sure those weren't the only things she had hidden from me. Keeping secrets of that magnitude would have required too much maneuvering for her to be truthful all the time.

What I had not anticipated, however, was that one of the secrets that would shake me out of my stupor wasn't Jenny's.

It was Sanjay's.

"I'll pick up the kids tonight," I told him as I was getting dressed for work on Thursday. His job interview was later that afternoon.

He was sitting on the edge of the bed in the T-shirt and boxers he'd slept in. "No, I can get them. I can't imagine the interview would go past five, and it's only a couple of miles from camp."

"But you have band," I pointed out. "You'll need time to change and get to Christina's."

"I don't have band."

He had a weird look on his face. Which I told him.

"I'm not trying to be weird," he said, shrugging. "I quit."

"What? When?"

"A couple of weeks ago."

"When you took me out to dinner, you said you were just skipping a night."

"At that point, I was just taking a break. Last week I decided it was permanent."

I had a sinking feeling in my gut. "This is about the list, isn't it? And your job interview. You think you're not going to have time to write, so you're already cutting back on the stuff that makes you happy."

"It's not about that, Penny." His voice was flat.

"Then what's the problem?"

His pupils were so large they almost enveloped his irises. "Christina."

My pulse was whooshing in my ears. For all my evangelizing about honesty, the second Sanjay said the name of his band's keyboardist, it struck me that some things in life—many of them, really—are better left unsaid. "What do you mean, *Christina?*"

"There was . . . tension."

The look on his face made it clear said tension was not of the artistic variety. I felt sick. "Are you having an affair?" I whispered.

"No," he said.

"What is it then? If you let me sit here and speculate, I can assure you my mind is not going to go to happy places."

"She's too flirty."

Christina was the kind of woman who would bat her lashes at a blind man. "Yeah, so?" As I stared at him, the picture slowly became clear. Sanjay would not have quit if this was just about her giggling at him or him wondering what she was like in bed. "Were you *falling* for her?" I spat.

"No. But . . ."

"But what!" I erupted.

He looked nervous. "You're yelling at me. Didn't you say you wanted us to be honest with each other?"

I wasn't sure when, but I had begun to pace our bedroom. "I'm supposed to stop pretending things are fine when they're not, but I can only do that in specific ways that involve not raising my voice. Got it."

"Okay, okay, I'm sorry. Yell if you need to. But believe me, Penny— there's no affair. No touching, no shared secrets—nothing. I just felt like things between me and her were heading in the wrong direction."

My heart hurt so much that he may as well have confessed they'd been tearing off each other's clothes every Thursday night. Someone had been attracted to my husband. And he was attracted to her, too. Why wouldn't he be? She had curly blonde hair and dimples and was barely thirty. Even more than that, though, Christina oozed charisma. She laughed easily and complimented frequently and was one of those people who made every conversation more interesting.

Whereas stale, old wifey had to pedal her mental wheels hard in order to come up with something other than work and pee accidents to talk about. As for radiating wanton magnetism? That ship left the port the very hour my first pregnancy test came back positive.

"What do you mean, *wrong direction*?" He didn't need to tell me not to yell this time; my words were again a whisper.

He took a deep breath. "I felt like she was paying too much attention to me, and I was liking it too much. I didn't want to stick around to see if anything more developed. I mean, you and I are working on our marriage right now, and spending time with Christina seemed like . . . the opposite of that."

What Sanjay had done was the right thing to do. It was exactly how any woman who cared even an iota about her marriage would have wanted her husband to behave in similar circumstances. Yet his acknowledgment made me understand why he had so readily agreed to work on our marriage. We were in more danger than I had realized.

Which was why his first request had been for us to have sex.

"Please don't be upset with me, Penny," he said. "I would have preferred not to tell you, but we're supposed to be honest with each other, right?"

"I'm not upset with you," I said quietly. "You didn't do anything wrong."

No, I had been the one to screw this all up. Suggesting honesty to improve our relationship. Thinking we could resuscitate our erotic life with a few compulsory rolls in the hay.

Assuming the only cracks in my marriage were the ones I could see.

Sanjay crossed the bedroom to where I was still pacing. When he reached me, he hugged me. "Penny," he said softly. "I'm so sorry. Are you okay?"

My arms hung limp at my sides; I could not bring myself to embrace him. My husband had kept a secret from me. What else would he soon disclose? I didn't want to know.

"I'm fine," I said into his shirt. "And neither are you."

I was still feeling weepy and defeated when I sat down at my desk later that morning. When I turned on my computer, a notice informed me that Yolanda had scheduled an impromptu meeting with me in half an hour.

Fantastic, I thought, eyeing my to-do list. Couldn't whatever it was wait until our usual Tuesday meeting with me, her, and Russ? But she'd just gotten back from vacation and probably wanted to lecture me for snapping at her about John Sterling.

I passed Russ' office on the way to Yolanda's. His door was open but he wasn't at his desk. For whatever reason, I stopped and stepped inside.

Russ' walls were white, just like mine; his furniture was identical to the generic pieces I used. Like me, he had no window. The only real difference was that his space was free of personal items, whereas I had decorated with family photos and taped up Stevie's and Miles' artwork.

But upon further inspection, Russ' office *was* slightly larger than my own—maybe two feet wider in either direction. How had I not noticed this before? Or maybe I had, and had promptly tossed this information into the mental trash can where I put unfair things that I could not change.

It's not important, I told myself as I stepped back into the hall. More space wouldn't buy groceries or pay for car insurance. Besides, what I most needed from a work environment was the ability to generate cash for my family.

When I reached Yolanda's office, she was not on the phone or looking at her computer. Unless my eyes were deceiving me, she was not doing much of anything. Which was strange.

"Come in," she called. "Close the door behind you."

I sat in front of her, wondering what she would say. She leaned back in her Aeron chair and folded her arms. "You made contact with Sterling?" she said.

"Yes. We have a meeting scheduled for next week."

"Good. I was surprised at your response when I asked you to follow up."

Now we were getting down to business. "Well, I was surprised you doubted me," I said in what I hoped was an even tone of voice. "Especially on the heels of the Weingarten donation."

"You were rather vocal about that as well."

"I was only trying to highlight my contribution to the medical school and this team. It's come to my attention that I've been downplaying my role and contributions at my own expense."

She raised an eyebrow. "Penelope, I'm going to come right out and ask."

I held my breath, expecting her to ask if I wanted to keep my job.

"Are you happy here?"

"Ha-happy?" I stammered. "Why do you ask?"

"I get the impression that you're not pleased with the way things have been going lately."

I needed to sound like someone who wasn't begging to be pink-slipped. I didn't know how to do that, so I decided to channel Nancy Weingarten. "As you may know, Yolanda, I've been going through a period of immense personal stress. I'm sorry if that occasionally surfaces, but I am doing my best to go above and beyond at work, and I feel that I'm still managing to accomplish an awful lot."

She pursed her lips. "You don't do face time, which makes some question your commitment to being a team player."

"I may not go to happy hour very often." And by often, I meant never. "Still, I've been logging fifty hours most weeks, and that's not including the work I bring home. I'd say I'm very much a team player. For example, I fielded three of Adrian's donor drafts while he was out sick."

"You rarely travel."

"You rarely ask me to. I'm just as available to travel as anyone else on the team." This was a partial truth, which is known in some circles as a lie. But because Sanjay worked from home—at least for the time being—I *could* travel more than many working mothers. Not that our office employed them.

She said nothing, so I decided to continue. "I brought in two hundred and thirteen thousand more than anyone in medical development just in the last fiscal year alone."

Yolanda eyed me as though she was trying to decide what she thought of me. This time, I forced myself to sit with the discomfort instead of filling the space. Unfortunately, this meant I also had to sit with a rapid-fire string of anxious thoughts about how quickly I could get another job and what it would cost to pay for health insurance for four people.

When Yolanda finally spoke again, she sounded more tired than upset. "Is there something that would incentivize your commitment to the medical development team?"

My stomach flipped as I thought of my family rolling their suitcases into Sanjay's parents' basement. What incentivized me was keeping my family in our home. But if she was asking, she wasn't going to fire me—not yet. "Are you saying I'm not committed? Or that I'm underperforming? Because if so, I'm more than willing to work on that."

"Not at all. I'm trying to unpack your core competencies. There are changes in the works, even if I'm not at liberty to share them yet. For the present moment, I'm trying to pin down the moving pieces and ideate the next steps."

Yolanda had a corner office—lots of windows. She was good at what she did, and I did not begrudge her those windows. But as I looked out at the tree-filled nature reserve just beyond the building, it seemed to me that all of this—striving and providing and maybe the very act of caring about any of it—was largely pointless. As Jenny's death had so painfully reminded me, we were all going to die, and the money wouldn't come with us. Maybe that's why, as I looked back at my supervisor, I felt strangely calm. I wasn't being fired. For now, that was enough.

"Thank you," I said to her. "I'll work on face time and think about what my core competencies are. Please let me know if there's something you need from me."

~

"How did your interview go?" I had just walked in the door from work to find Sanjay in the kitchen, still dressed in a crisp button-down and tie. He looked relieved that the first thing I asked him wasn't about Christina. Well, soon enough he would see that I wasn't ever going to drill him about her. In fact, I was fairly certain I would never say her name aloud again. One confession might lead to another, then another; and before long one of us would be packing a bag, and our next conversation would be in front of a couple of lawyers.

"It went great," he said, breaking into a grin. "Brian, the guy who would be my supervisor, thought my writing samples were terrific, and I met two other people in the department who are really sharp." Sharp—this was practically the highest compliment Sanjay gave. "Brian already emailed to ask me to come in for a second interview next week."

In spite of our morning conversation about She Who Would Not Be Named, it was impossible not to be happy for him. "I'm thrilled for you," I said.

"Really? You were so hesitant when I told you about it before."

"I know. But I can tell you're excited, and that makes me excited, too. Plus, it would be a big relief if there was another steady paycheck coming in."

He looked pleased. "Thank you. What about you? How was your day?"

It was a simple question—one I hadn't heard in a while. I hoped he was asking spontaneously instead of because I'd asked him to be more present. "Not great," I confessed. I told him about my conversation with Yolanda.

"I hate to say it, but maybe telling you to be more honest wasn't the brightest idea," he said as he pulled off his tie.

"What do you mean?"

"Well, sounds like Yolanda feels like you're challenging her. I just worry . . ."

"That I'm going to get fired," I supplied.

He nodded. "Until I officially land this job, your being out of work would be pretty disastrous for us. I wish I'd realized that sooner. You never said anything, so . . ." He shrugged. "Anyway, it was stupid of me not to think about how much we rely on you."

I was glad to hear him admit it, but I suddenly felt aggravated. Because while he was luxuriating in the simple worry of how to stay faithful, I had been spinning my wheels to keep us solvent. To have and care for a family was a privilege. Recognizing that lightened the load, as Jenny had often said. But it hardly eliminated it.

It occurred to me, however, that my being direct was hardly the only reason why I might join the ranks of the unemployed. Half the department could be eliminated during budget cuts. We could get a new dean who wanted to bring in his own team. If I let my mind spin out, there were myriad possibilities, all ending in catastrophe.

Then what? Sanjay and I were not prepared for the worst, let alone for anything to change.

And things changed. They changed all the time.

"It *is* stressful. It's incredibly stressful—and scary, too." I waved my hands around. "All this could go away if I don't do my absolute best at all times. You know what the funniest thing is?" My voice was starting to raise, but I couldn't help it. "Now that I think about it, Yolanda's question was totally absurd."

Sanjay looked alarmed. "What do you mean?"

"Who *cares* if I'm happy at work?" I said. "If happiness was the goal, I wouldn't have taken the job in the first place. It was always about the money! Maybe if I had realized that sooner, then I actually *would* have been happier."

Stevie had walked in the kitchen. She put her hand on my arm and looked up at me pleadingly. "Mommy, don't fight with Daddy."

My heart hurt, hearing her say those words. Wasn't this marriage project about protecting my children and giving them a happy home?

Sure, but what about your *happiness, Penny?*

Jenny had a way of showing up at the darnedest times.

Instead of talking back to her in my mind, I zoned in on Stevie's face, which was folded into a frown. "I'm sorry, sweetheart. Daddy and

I aren't really fighting," I said. "Just having a discussion. Why don't you go put a show on?"

She narrowed her eyes, but the promise of television was too tempting. "Okay," she said and ran off to the living room.

"You know, it's all right for them to hear us fight once in a while," said Sanjay after Stevie was gone.

"I don't want them thinking we're going to end up divorced."

"Who said anything about divorce? This is about this morning, isn't it? I knew I shouldn't have told you that."

"Yes, you should have. That's not why I said it." Not consciously, at least—though now that I was thinking about it, I had to admit it was perhaps a possibility. Still. "My parents fought all the time before my mom left. And lately it seems like you and I may be heading in that direction."

"That's part of the whole honesty thing, Penny," he said with exasperation. "You didn't want to keep pretending that everything was okay, but now that we're saying it's not, you're backtracking and acting like that's what's going to destroy us. Marriage is hard work. I'm sorry I wasn't trying harder before. I know so much of this is on me. But I'm here now. I'm trying."

I stared at him, unsure how to respond. He wasn't wrong. But *why* was marriage so much work? It didn't used to be. And if it did require such effort, shouldn't the fruit of that labor be a stronger, more satisfying union?

Jenny was right. I wasn't happy at work, and my marriage wasn't making me a whole lot happier, either. Stevie and Miles were a source of happiness—always in theory, and at least much of the time in practice—but children alone could not fill every void.

I wanted to tell myself it didn't matter. Happiness was nothing but a fleeting state—a modern construct used to justify personal fulfillment over the greater good.

But deep down, I knew this wasn't true. To me, at least, the word *happy* was shorthand for a life with meaning. And as of late, I was coming up awfully short on that front. Worse, I had no vision for how that might change.

There were so many things I could have said to Sanjay. But I took one look at him—still in his dress shirt, only the slightest remnants of post-interview joy on his face—and swallowed my pain.

Our marriage may have been a mess, but I still loved my husband. There was no need to drag him down further than I had already pulled him.

TWENTY-TWO

My father called Friday evening as I was getting home from work. I had left a few messages for him since my conversation with Nick about his health, but more than a week had passed with no response and I had given up on hearing back. "Everything okay?" I asked.

"Can't a man call his own daughter?" he said.

"Well, yes, obviously," I said, wedging the phone between my ear and shoulder as I fumbled for the keys in my purse. I had left work early—and by early, I mean when everyone else was leaving—and Sanjay was still picking up the kids from camp. "I've been trying to get in touch with you. How have you been?"

"Busy. Anita and I threw a graduation party for Luis last weekend."

Anita was his girlfriend and Luis was her son. I was pretty sure my father secretly preferred Luis to me and Nick. But maybe that was because Luis didn't expect anything from him. Anita was the one who expected things, but she loved him and he adored her. My father deserved that after so many years of being alone. Still, sometimes it hurt to hear how he bent over backward for them.

"How are you doing, *niña*?" He sounded older than usual. Or maybe he, like me, was just tired.

"Things have been hard lately," I confessed. "One of my good friends died."

"I'm sorry to hear that. When?"

I hung my bag on the hook near the door and kicked off my shoes. "Thank you. It was six weeks ago."

"Sorry," he said again.

This was more than I had expected—yet I wished he would have said something else, like, "Six weeks! Why didn't you tell me sooner?" Even "How did it happen?" would have been a start. Nick claimed that our father didn't know how to relate to us because his own parents had alternated between abuse and neglect, and our mother had not stuck around to help him figure it out. My brother felt it was enough that our father had not followed in our grandparents' footsteps.

I wasn't looking for a perfect parent, though. All I wanted was effort. After thirty-nine years I was aware I'd be more likely to wish my way into winning a million dollars, but this didn't stop me from hoping for the impossible.

"How are the kids?" my father asked. "And what about you and Sanjay?"

I told him about how Miles had stopped wetting the bed, and how Stevie was reading chapter books above her grade level. And I said things between Sanjay and me were great—everything was fine.

It was only after my father responded that I understood why I had stuck to my standard, sanitized response rather than admitting that we had been struggling.

"Good. You two are lucky. A strong marriage is a gift," he said.

How had I never noticed this before? My marriage was easily the thing he most praised me for, and his compliment had filled me with pride, maybe even a feeling of victory. Because with a few words, he was assuring me I had met my heart's purest goal—I had avoided turning into my parents, and in the process avoided turning my children into me.

"Thank you," I said. "Dad, Nick said you were having some health problems. What's going on?"

He tsked. "It's nothing. I was having a little stomach pain, so the doctor ran a few tests."

"And?"

"Eh," he said.

"Eh?"

"Eh," he said again.

"Then something *is* wrong."

"Maybe. I'm having surgery next month."

I felt queasy. "Surgery? For what?"

"I have a little cancer," he said.

My father had only spoken Spanish until his family moved from Puerto Rico to Baltimore when he was seven. Even all these years later, he sometimes mangled English phrases or used the wrong word. But I had a strong feeling his command of our common language had nothing to do with the way he'd described his health problem. "A *little* cancer? In your stomach?"

"That's what they say. They caught it early, though. Don't worry about me—the doctor says I'm going to be just fine."

I wanted to weep. "Then what? You'll have chemo?"

"Probably so."

"How can we help?" I said. "Do you want to come here for a second opinion? The university has one of the top oncology centers in the country. I'm sure I could help you get an appointment."

"No, no, I'm happy where I am. Anita will take care of me," he said.

Of course she would. I didn't say anything.

"I should probably get going. I just wanted you to know. Penelope?"

"Yes?"

"I'm sorry about your friend."

I swallowed hard. "Thanks, Dad. Please keep me posted about your health, okay?"

"Love you," he said by way of an answer. Then he was gone.

I was still staring at the phone when the front door opened and my family's voices rang through the air. It might have been the most joyful clamor I'd ever heard, but I still felt myself sinking back into the dark space where I'd been spending so much time lately. My father may have been a lousy parent, but he was the only parent I had. He couldn't die.

Sanjay walked into the kitchen, took one look at me, and said, "What happened?"

"My father just called to say he has stomach cancer. He's having surgery next month."

"Oh, Pen, I'm sorry," he said. "When is it scheduled?"

"I don't know."

"Do you know what stage his cancer is?"

I shook my head. "You know my dad—when it comes to personal info, less is more."

Sanjay's expression had quicksilvered from concern to what looked an awful lot like anger. "He thinks this is only about him."

"Yes, but I'm not going to be the one to point out that it's not. I can't force him to share things with me."

He looked at me quizzically.

"What?" I said.

"I don't get it."

"You don't get what?"

"You've been pushing Matt to be present for Cecily. Which is great—someone needs to do it."

"What does that have to do with my father?" I asked.

He frowned at me, like I had just asked a stupid question. "I just wish that you'd advocate for yourself the way you do for Cecily."

I felt like I'd been slapped.

"Don't look at me like that, Penny," said Sanjay. "I'm only saying this because I love you."

"It's fine," I said, not meeting his eye. "You're right."

And he was. If the past few months had taught me anything, it was that I could be honest. Brutally honest, even. Except when it came to the things that hurt the most.

~

The following afternoon Matt dropped Cecily off for a playdate. She looked sullen when they arrived, but her face brightened when she saw the kids and me in the kitchen.

I knew the feeling. My mind had been on my father most of the morning, but seeing Cecily pulled me out of my mental fog. "Hey, you," I said, hugging her. "Happy to have you over."

"Thanks, Aunt Penny." She grinned up at me. "Are we going to have ice cream today?"

I turned to Matt. He was clean shaven and looked less distraught than the last time I'd seen him. But unless I was imagining it, a chill remained between us. He shrugged. "Okay with me."

"Yay! We're going to have ice cream!" Cecily announced to Miles and Stevie. The three of them started whooping, and before I could tell them to take it outside, they went tearing off into the backyard.

"If I didn't know better, I'd say she's happier here than at home," said Matt. He glanced around the kitchen. "Can't say I blame her. I forgot how inviting your place is."

"I don't know about that," I said. I had intended to clean up before Cecily came over, but I had just pulled out the cleaning spray when Miles was stung by a bee. It had more or less been downhill from there.

"What Penny means is thank you," said Sanjay from behind me.

Matt laughed, surprising me. I couldn't remember the last time I'd heard him laugh, let alone seen him smile, and I found myself smiling, too. "I definitely meant thank you," I said.

Through the window, Miles and Cecily were jumping as high as they could on the trampoline to try to get Stevie, balled up in the center, to bounce. Popcorn, they called this game of theirs, and every time they played it, I wondered what possessed me to set up an enormous accident machine in my backyard.

"Hey, what are you guys doing with the kids at the end of the summer?" asked Matt. "I'd been counting on camp running until Labor Day and just found out it closes the week before."

"I'm supposed to be watching them," said Sanjay, "but there's a slim chance I might be working that week. I've been interviewing for a communications position at the College of Liberal Arts."

Matt was visibly surprised. "Really? I thought the writing thing was going really well."

"It is and it isn't. I'm hoping to sell a book soon, but I'm not making enough freelancing. It's time to make a change."

"Good for you, Sanj. I'm impressed."

I snuck a glance at Sanjay to see if he looked regretful, but he just smiled. "Thanks, man," he said. "You want a beer?"

"Sure—that sounds like just the thing."

Sanjay opened a couple of bottles, and they went out back to sit on the deck. As I watched them and the kids through the window, there were a few seconds where it all seemed so normal that I forgot Jenny wasn't in the other room or on her way over.

Then Matt came back inside. I wanted to remind him that I had finished the post for Jenny's website, but the way he was approaching me said he had something else on his mind.

Sure enough. "Penny, if you or Sanjay do end up watching the kids the last week of August, do you think you could take Cecily, too? I haven't been able to line up a sitter. I was going to send her to my parents in Maine, but she doesn't want to go."

"I can," I said slowly. "But don't you think it would be more fun to take that week off and do something together? I bet she'd love to go to Maine if you went with her."

He glared at me. "Can we have one conversation where you don't tell me how I'm the worst father in the universe?"

"I'm pretty sure you know that wasn't my intention."

"And yet." He set the beer bottle, which was half full, on the counter. "I'm going to head out. I'll be back for Cecily in an hour."

Our plan had been for her to stay through dinner. There was no way he had forgotten that. I stared at him, wondering if he was really so hurt—or cruel—that he would cut Cecily's visit short just because he felt I had insulted him.

But he was right. He was Cecily's parent. Her only parent now. Like everything else regarding his daughter, when she left my house was ultimately his decision to make.

"We'll see you then," I said.

~

That evening, Stevie and Miles were cooling off in the living room watching *Planet Earth*.

"Is there room for one more?" I asked, plopping down between them on the sofa.

"Mommy!" said Miles, not taking his eyes off the screen.

Stevie was slightly more attentive. "Are you okay?" she asked, patting my leg.

"Yes, sweetie," I told her. "Why wouldn't I be?"

"Because you and Matt weren't getting along," she said.

The child didn't miss a thing. Matt had returned exactly when he said he would. Though he acted as though our conversation had never happened, Cecily howled in protest over having to leave early, which in turn left me in tears. He and I exchanged chilly goodbyes without making promises or plans to get together again. As I watched them drive off, I had to shake off the thought that I might not see Cecily again anytime soon.

"I guess we're not," I admitted. "But it will blow over."

She looked doubtful. "Really?"

"I don't know for sure, but I hope so," I said. I put my arm around her. "Which episode are you guys watching?"

"The one about mountains," said Stevie.

"Ooh, I haven't seen that one." I settled back into the sofa cushions. On the television, two snow leopards were traipsing across a mountainside. The narrator introduced them as a mother and her nearly grown cub. The pair wrestled playfully, and then the mother began to groom her daughter. Though the cub was nearly as large as her mother, said the narrator, she had more to learn before going off on her own.

The kids and I watched, rapt, as the older leopard protected her child from two male leopards during mating season. While successful, she was wounded in the process, and as she limped into a cave with her daughter behind her, the narrator speculated it was possible neither would survive; the cub still needed her guidance to navigate mountain life.

As Stevie gripped my arm, I found myself blinking back fresh tears.

Then the mother snow leopard appeared again. The video had been taken several months after her injury and, no longer wounded, she was crossing a cliffside with ease. In later footage, her daughter—healthy, alive, and now navigating the mountain alone—followed her mother's trail. Separated by just a few miles, the two would live parallel lives, said the narrator, but it was likely they would never see each other again.

"Mommy, why are you crying?" asked Miles as the credits began to roll.

"I'm not. I'm . . ." I sniffed. "Okay, I'm crying. Mommy's a little sad."

"Because of Auntie Jenny?" said Stevie.

"Yes," I said. Because of Jenny, and Matt and Cecily, and my father, and my marriage and—well, almost everything, I realized as the tears continued to fall.

Stevie and Miles were suddenly climbing on top of me, hugging me with their little arms.

"It's okay, Mommy," said Miles, wiping my face with his hand.

"Cecily still has her dad," said Stevie.

Funny how memories can come flying out of nowhere; I found myself thinking about the time in elementary school that Nick had beaten up an older student. The kid had been bullying him, along with practically everyone else. The principal called me to his office to get Nick because the school couldn't reach our father, and Nick had insisted he needed me.

I didn't remember what I'd said to the principal, but I must have made a convincing provisional parent because Nick hadn't been suspended. Our father never did find out about that day. We were relieved at the time. In hindsight, it seemed like less of a lucky break.

"You're right, peanut," I said to Stevie. "Cecily does still have her dad." And I still had mine.

If only that were enough.

TWENTY-THREE

I was putting the finishing touches on a report—which is to say I was combing through Christina's social media feeds, trying to deduce whether her selfies were a tiny bit sad now that she and Sanjay were no longer in contact—when Russ came barreling through my door.

I looked up from my computer. "Russell, I would greatly appreciate it if you would knock before barging in."

"Whew! Someone needs a drink. Lucky for you, happy hour started five minutes ago." He was referring to the outing our colleagues had planned. Monday was the new Friday, they said. Even if that was true, I didn't want to spend a fake Friday with my coworkers. I liked them just fine, but I would have liked them better if I didn't see them more often than my own family.

"Two drinks, then," said Russ, who had mistaken my silence for a refusal.

"You know how I feel about that stupid hot wings place," I said weakly. Yolanda's comment about face time was still fresh in my mind, and I already knew I would go. As she had pointed out, I needed to prove I was a team player—one tiny, flame-orange chicken wing at a time.

Russ lowered his voice. "You do know we're up for review next month. No one's forcing you to organize the white elephant party, but seriously, whether you go to these things makes a difference."

Netting millions in donations made more of a difference. Or at least it was supposed to. "I know, Russell. I'll go for a drink, but only one," I said, even though I hadn't cleared it with Sanjay. "Give me a minute."

Russ didn't budge from his perch on my desk, so I waved him away with my hand.

"I'm not a dog, Penny," he said as he exited my office. "You can't shoo me." Then he barked outside my door.

As much as I didn't want to encourage him, I couldn't help but laugh. I had just composed myself when Sanjay picked up the phone. "It's me," I said. "A bunch of my colleagues are going out for drinks at the wings place, and I need to be demonstrating that I'm a team player. Would you mind if I went out for an hour? I know we'd talked about prepping for your second interview."

"Of course not," he said. "I have two more days to get ready. I'll be fine."

"Great, thank you."

"Have fun. And Penny?"

"Yeah?"

He paused. "I love you."

"I love you, too," I said.

And I did. I just wished that things between us didn't feel so strained. I wished that I had figured out a subtle way of improving our marriage rather than asking him to commit to honesty.

Because as I closed my browser—which had been open to a photo of Christina, grinning seductively while sitting at a piano—I was pretty sure I couldn't handle one more truth.

I was thinking about Sanjay when Russ sidled up next to me at the bar. He raised his arm, and the bartender, whom I'd been trying to flag down for five minutes, sauntered over. "What can I get for you?" he asked Russ.

"I'm going to defer to the lady here, since she's been waiting," said Russ. "Penny? What can this fine fellow bring you?"

I wasn't in the mood to be rescued. However, I was in need of a drink. "Vodka tonic with lime, please," I said.

"And the IPA you have on tap," added Russ, handing the bartender his credit card. "Can you open a tab and put both on this?"

"Sure thing," said the bartender.

"Thanks," I said to Russ. "You didn't have to. By which I mean you shouldn't have."

He flashed me a broad white smile. "I'd say it's the least I can do for dragging you to this armpit of an establishment, but it's a business expense."

"Gee, thanks," I droned. As soon as I realized I was smiling, I pushed my lips back into a straight line. There had been tension between us for weeks now. On the one hand, he did things like undermine me in front of my boss and a major donor. On the other, he had come through for me several times since the day Jenny died. He bought me perfect flowers and talked to me about Jenny—and I liked it.

Did that make me as guilty as Sanjay?

The bartender returned with our drinks. Russ took a swig of his, then wiped his mouth with his hand. "How are you doing about your friend?" he asked. His eyes were searching my face, which felt too intimate, even in the middle of a crowded sports bar.

I looked up at the television. Beefy men in suits moved their mouths as footage of two baseball teams I could not identify played behind them. "I'm managing to get through the days." Then I took a long sip of my drink. So long that when I put it down, half of the glass was empty.

"I'm sorry," he said. "I bet this is even tougher than you're letting on, huh?"

I turned back to him with surprise. "Yeah. But if you knew that, why'd you interrupt me during the presentation with Nancy Weingarten?"

He squirmed. Good—let him. "I'm sorry about that," he said. "Being a jerk is kind of my default state, but I'm trying to work on it."

Men in fancy shorts were now doing hand-to-hand combat on the TV. Russ and I both watched them for a minute.

"Thanks for apologizing," I said.

"I should have earlier." He took another drink of his beer. "So what's next, Penny?"

For a second, I thought he was talking about that evening. I was about to tell him I planned to go home, have dinner, and tuck my kids in when he added, "You know. After this gig. You can't possibly want to do this for the rest of your life."

"Yolanda gave you the talk about whether you were happy in development, too?" I said.

He frowned. "No."

"Oh. Well, she and I had a meeting last week, and she asked me if I was happy and wanted to know what she could do to, quote, 'incentivize me.'" I eyed him. "You're not allowed to use that against me, by the way."

He held up his hands in a show of innocence. "I would never. But it's not a surprise she asked you that. She's probably worried you're going to leave, which would make her job a hell of a lot harder. And mine, if we're being honest."

"I'm not going anywhere, but even if I did, you could easily run the department yourself," I said.

"Not as well."

"I don't believe that, but the whole thing is beside the point. To answer your question, for the foreseeable future, *next* is just paying bills and saving for college and retirement and keeping my family afloat. It's lucky that I'm good at development—it pays better than a lot of things. So, I'll ask for a raise at my review. If Yolanda ever leaves I'll try for her job, even though it's more likely to go to you or some other white dude. The plan is to keep on keeping on." The drone of my voice was as riveting as the sound of highway traffic, but there was no way to make this admission remotely interesting.

Russ smirked. "You sound excited."

I looked down at my drink, wondering how to respond. Then I thought, *Why not just tell him the truth?* "I used to think I'd write books one day. Kids' books." It was strange to admit this dream, which I'd had stashed away for so long that it had practically begun to mildew. "So sometimes the idea of staying in development another five to ten years makes me want to stab myself with a ballpoint pen."

"Really? I didn't know that about you."

"Yup."

"When's the last time you wrote something? I mean a story, not a donor report."

"It's been a while," I confessed. "As in seven years."

His eyes widened. "That's not like you, Pen."

"I know, but I'm exhausted when I get home at the end of the day, and my kids completely dominate my weekends."

"Well, is there anything you can do about that? You probably don't have to work as hard as you do."

"Says the guy who tosses his own projects at me."

He shrugged. "You can say no, you know. You're already excelling."

Yes, I was. And suddenly I knew the answer to Yolanda's question about what would make me happier in my position. "Do you think there's any chance Yolanda would let me go down to 80 percent at some point?"

"Like take Fridays off?"

"Yeah. But that's probably insane, isn't it? Yolanda's constantly on me to perform better. Reducing my workload is the opposite of that."

"I have a feeling you're wrong about that. But you'd have your salary cut. Could you swing that?"

"I don't know," I admitted. If Sanjay landed the communications job, I might be able to, but I wasn't one to count my chickens while they were still in the shell.

I didn't have a chance to tell Russ that, because Minna, our alumni relations chair, had just popped up behind us. "Hey, you two! Whatcha doin'?"

I could drink two pots of French roast and still not be half as chipper as Minna. "Just talking shop," I said.

"You going to join us plebeians at some point?" she said, motioning toward the long table at the back of the bar where our coworkers had gathered.

"Yeah, we'll head over to you guys in a minute," said Russ.

As she bounced away on the balls of her feet, I turned to Russ. "What about you? What's next? Any secret dreams?"

"I only ever wanted to make good money without working too hard. The good news is, that's what I'm doing." He smiled self-consciously. "I'd like to get married one day, too. Maybe have some kids."

As my eyes met his, I felt it again—the uncomfortable realization that yes, I was attracted to him. He wasn't the kind of man I'd want to date, let alone procreate with, but I would probably go to bed with him if I weren't married.

Which was deeply unsettling. I wasn't worried about cheating—like Sanjay, that was simply off the table for me. But why was it so easy to think about sleeping with someone completely inappropriate instead of with the person I'd vowed to love for the rest of my natural life?

Really, Russ and I had nothing in common outside of work. Why had we just slipped into the kind of easy conversation I wanted to be having with my husband?

I broke Russ' gaze. "This has been fun," I said, "but I really need to get going."

He looked confused. "You're not going to go say hey to the minions?"

"Nope. It's been a long day." A long summer, really. "I want to make sure I have a chance to spend some time with Sanjay." Yes—I needed to get home and see if maybe we could somehow share the kind of moment I'd just had with another man.

~

When I got home, the kids were on the sofa watching a movie, and Sanjay was at the dining room table in front of his laptop. His headphones were on, and his fingers were drumming the table to the beat of whatever music he was playing. He probably missed his band.

He took off his headphones when he saw me. "How was it?" he said.

"Fine." I sat on the bench and took off my shoes, wondering if my face hinted at my guilty conscience. Nothing would ever happen between me and Russ; I knew that instinctively. But I would have felt a lot better if I were so incredibly attracted to and engaged by my husband that I couldn't even entertain the thought of being with someone else. "Happy hour's kind of an oxymoron when coworkers are involved. Russ and I had a nice chat, though."

"That's good." I waited for Sanjay to ask me what we'd chatted about, thinking maybe I could somehow tell him that now I sort of understood his situation with Christina. But the question never came. "Hey," he said, already looking back at his computer, "the kids are fed and bathed, lunches are made, and there's a plate wrapped up for you on the counter. Do you mind if I go back to working on this? I want to finish another page or two before I call it a night."

I sighed, feeling defeated. So much for connection. "Fine," I said. "I'll put the kids to sleep after their show. I'm going to go change."

I'd just put on a nightgown when my phone, which I'd left on the dresser, lit up.

It was Matt.

I have been thinking about our last conversation and have realized that I need some space. Unfortunately, this means that I'm going to have to put your visits with Cecily on hold for a while. I'll reach out when I'm ready.

I stared at my phone. I wasn't sure whether to scream or cry, so I pressed my hands to my face, which was already flushed.

I had done the right thing by being honest and direct.

And now I had to live with the consequences.

TWENTY-FOUR

"You should see a doctor," said Sanjay. It was the following morning, and he was standing over me with a thermometer in one hand and a bottle of ibuprofen in the other.

"Leave me," I croaked. I didn't need my temperature taken to know I didn't have the flu, or even a cold. I just . . . couldn't get out of bed.

"Mommy? Are you sick?" Stevie was peering at me from behind Sanjay. She looked worried.

Yes—heartsick, I thought. I didn't know when I'd be able to see Cecily again, and that was my fault. My father had cancer and didn't want me to be involved with his treatment—or really, any other part of his life. My husband was attracted to another woman and I was attracted to another man. My harebrained attempt to save our marriage was having the opposite effect.

I couldn't remember the last time I'd felt so hopeless.

Actually—yes, I could. It was the instant I realized Jenny was really and truly dead.

"I'm going to be fine," I told Stevie. My eyelids were so heavy that I might as well have been sick. "I'll feel better after I take a nap."

"You can't nap in the morning," said Miles. He looked as concerned as Stevie, and for a moment I wondered if they might be making a connection between my illness and Jenny's death. The thought flew out of my head as fast as it had landed.

"Watch me," I said, and fell fast asleep.

When I awoke it was noon and I was alone. I had emailed the office after I woke up that morning to say I wasn't feeling well and would be out for the day, so I didn't bother checking my phone. Instead, I drank the glass of water Sanjay had left for me on the bedside table. Then I lay back on my pillow. It was so nice and dark and calm behind my lids; maybe I could stay there for a little while longer.

When I opened my eyes again, Sanjay was stroking my head. "Pen? You okay? You've been asleep for hours."

"What time is it?" I muttered. It was dark out, and I was kind of woozy.

"Almost nine."

"At night?" I pushed myself into a seated position. "I slept *all day?*" I hadn't done that since—well, ever.

Sanjay nodded. "The kids are fine," he said, but for once I wasn't thinking about them. "I've been keeping them away from you, though, so they don't get whatever you have."

"I'm not sick," I said.

He grimaced. "Are you pregnant?"

"No, and given the look on your face, thank God."

"What is it, then?"

I sighed. "I just really don't feel like living my life right now." Sanjay looked alarmed, so I quickly added, "I'm not thinking of hurting myself or anything like that. Matt texted last night to say he needed space, and that we would be putting visits with Cecily on hold until he was ready to see me again."

Sanjay put his hand on my leg. "Oh Penny. I'm sorry. I wish you'd said something."

"I thought you'd come to bed before I fell asleep, and the next thing I knew, I was passed out." I pushed myself into a sitting position. "I don't know what you could have said or done to make it better. I'm . . . depressed, I guess."

"Oh," he said. "I've kind of been waiting for that."

"You were *waiting* for me to get depressed?"

"Not clinically, necessarily."

"You sound like your father right now."

"Maybe I do. Point being, you haven't really dealt with your grief, have you?"

"This isn't about Jenny."

He raised an eyebrow. "No?"

"No," I said firmly. "I just told you about Matt. It's about you and me, too. It's about my dad. And the fact that everyone keeps asking me what I need to be happy and the truth is I have no idea."

But this wasn't true, exactly. I did have an idea. A couple, in fact. And every single one seemed utterly impossible.

"Do you want to talk about it?" he said.

Now he asked me.

"No," I said. "I want to sleep."

He looked at me with resignation, but I was too exhausted to try to fix how he was feeling. "Sweet dreams, then."

"Sanjay," I called weakly, but he was already gone.

∼

I did not go to work the following day, either, though I did get out of bed before lunch because my stomach was beginning to self-digest and I had a wicked caffeine-withdrawal headache.

When I came downstairs Sanjay was in the kitchen, running a sponge over the counter. He was dressed in another dress shirt and a pair of freshly pressed pants, and it took me a few seconds to remember he had his second interview today.

"Why are you cleaning?" I looked around. "You're going to get your clothes dirty, and the kitchen is already nearly spotless." I sounded disappointed, and maybe I was, because it almost felt as if his success were an indication of an unspecified failure on my part.

He tilted his head. "I'm just trying to stay on top of things. Anyway, I already went in for the interview."

"You did? When?"

"At nine, right after I dropped the kids off."

"And? How did it go?" I asked.

He broke into a huge grin. "I'm almost afraid to say it out loud, but I think it went really well."

I tried to smile, but I couldn't. My husband had done what I had asked. He was trying to make more money, and it looked like he was incredibly close to doing that. He was succeeding.

"What is it?" he said. "Isn't this exactly what you asked me to do?"

"Well, yes."

"Then why don't you look happy? I know you've got a lot going on, but this is a big break for us."

I stared at him blankly. I wanted to admit that I was truly worried that the minute he started a full-time job, he would no longer have the mental energy to work on his book and he would quickly come to resent me for that.

I wished I could tell him that the ease with which he had tackled his list only highlighted how much I had struggled to do the two lousy things he had asked of me. How could I be the one to say that we should fix our marriage—but not be able to do the work?

I was even tempted to say I was superstitious and secretly believed that if I let myself get excited about no longer carrying the financial load for four people, the job would never materialize and we'd be right back to square one.

Instead, I said, "I'm sorry. Like I said last night, I'm not feeling like myself right now." And I wasn't sure when I ever would again.

~

That night, I sat on the deck sipping a glass of wine. The sky had just begun to grow dark, and fireflies were hovering over the grass in our yard, lit up and ready for love.

As I looked at the trees and the clear, deep-blue sky marbled between their branches, I could feel sorrow rushing through me, as fast and steady as a stream. As much as I missed Jenny, the ache of Cecily's absence was even more acute. It seemed so obvious that Matt was punishing me for pushing him. What if he took it one step further and took Cecily out of our lives?

"Over here," yelled Miles to Stevie.

They should have been in bed, but Sanjay was having drinks with an old college friend, and I had decided to let the kids join me for this golden hour. I had given each of them a jar with a lid with holes punched in it, and they were running back and forth across the lawn catching fireflies. "Here!" they kept yelling to each other, sprinting from one spot to the next and squealing with delight as they cupped a new bug in their hands. "Here, here!"

Miles' jar was nearly full when he ran up to me and held it up for me to admire. As soon as I started to *ooh* and *ahh*, he began shaking the jar. "Watch this, Mama!" he said. "Electricity!"

I'd enjoyed my moment of pretending to have Hallmark children— at the very least, it took my mind off Jenny. Now it was back to reality, in which my son, mad scientist of the animal kingdom, gave no thought to the cost of his curiosity.

"Sweetie," I said, "you're going to kill all the fireflies if you keep shaking them."

He stopped abruptly and peered through the glass. It was apparent that several of the bugs had not survived their encounter with his human centrifuge. "Oh," he said.

Then he uncapped the jar, held it upside down, and shook it again, this time gently. Those who could, escaped. He scooped out the rest with his hand and threw their dark, motionless bodies onto the grass. "Goodbye, bugs," he said solemnly. "You had a good time and so did I. Now I release you."

He glanced up at me and smiled shyly, suddenly aware that he had an audience. I could feel my sorrow lifting, and I smiled back.

As I watched my own six-year-old gallop across the grass, Jenny's voice came vaulting through the dusk. *You can't just give up now,* she said. *Look at all you have to fight for.*

I'd been wondering where she'd been the past few days. I'd missed her. *You're not six years old anymore,* she added.

What does that mean? I thought. I waited for an answer, but none came.

As I watched Stevie cup a firefly with her hands, I suddenly understood what Jenny had been trying to tell me, even if her presence was nothing more than a mirage I'd made out of grief.

As a girl, I couldn't make my mother stay or make my father be more caring, and that inability had been the hardest reality of my childhood.

I still couldn't make anyone other than myself do anything. But I was no longer a child hindered by her own powerlessness. I was a grown woman with the tools to fight for the people I loved. I didn't know how to convey to my father that I wanted to become a part of his life now, before it was too late. Nor did I have any idea how to put an end to the animosity between me and Matt. Honesty hadn't been enough to make Sanjay and me true partners again, and I wasn't sure why or how to fix that, either.

But if I knew one thing, it was how to keep trying. And damn it, that's just what I was going to do.

TWENTY-FIVE

I rose early the next morning, surprised Sanjay with a kiss in bed, ignoring his shocked response, then rushed through my routine. When I arrived at my office, I sat at my desk but didn't turn on my computer. Before the day was swallowed by emails, meetings, and assignments, I needed to cross the most important thing off my to-do list. I reached for the phone. In spite of my plan, I had a split-second instinct to call Matt. But he had asked for space, and that's what I was going to give him. So I dialed the number I had intended to all along. "Dad?"

"Niña? What is it?" My father's voice was muffled.

"I'm sorry. Did I wake you?"

"No, no, I needed to be up."

"Sorry," I said again.

"It's fine. Is everything okay?"

"No, in fact, it's not." I looked over my monitor at a picture of Stevie and Miles I'd hung on the wall. Miles, then a sturdy infant, was sitting on Stevie's lap; they were both laughing, though I never did find out why. The photo was one of the many Sanjay had snapped while I was at work. At the time, I remember feeling jealous that he'd had that moment with them. Now I felt thankful that he'd been able to have it.

How lucky my children were to know their father—to have experienced the kind of love that three words just can't fully convey.

"Are you and Sanjay all right?" my father asked.

"We're fine," I said. "Well, actually, we've been having a rough go of it lately. Nothing catastrophic, but things have been strained."

"Rough times can be worked out," he said. "Maybe if your mother had understood that . . ."

"I know. I think so, too," I said. "But that's not why I'm calling."

"It's my stomach, then," he said.

"No. Well, sort of." I'd been thinking through this all morning. But as these things go, the conversation had been so much easier in my head. "Dad, I know you don't want me to worry about your health, but I'm your daughter. I'm going to worry. And the more you keep me out of what's going on, the more worried I'm going to be."

"I see."

I waited for him to say something else. And after a few seconds, he did. "I wasn't really thinking about it that way. You and Nick are so busy, I don't want to take up all your time."

"I *want* you to take up my time," I said, and suddenly tears were welling in my eyes. "That's what I'm trying to tell you. What I've been trying to tell you for years now, though maybe I just wasn't direct enough. I know you're a private person—"

"I'm not," he protested.

"You *are*. That's okay. I'm not asking you to be someone you're not. I don't want to drag you to family therapy or make you tell me all your secrets or whatever. I just want you to call me sometimes—"

"I call," he said.

"No, Dad," I said quietly. "You really don't. Even on the kids' birthdays. And I know Sanjay called you last year to remind you about mine."

"Hmm."

I wiped the corners of my eyes. "I know you like your life in Florida. I'm glad you and Anita are happy. But it would be nice if you invited us down there sometime. Or came here. Or anything—we could even video chat, so the kids can get to know you a little better." A tear splashed on my desk. "So *I* can get to know you better."

"Penelope," he said gruffly.

I sniffed. "I'm here, Dad."

He said nothing for a very long time. Then he said, "It's going to be a hard couple of months for me, now that I'm coming up on treatment. Surgery's next month."

"I know."

"I don't know that I can go anywhere or have visitors."

"I understand."

"But maybe I can call you more often."

"I'd like that," I whispered, because it was getting hard to speak.

"And maybe when you call, I'll call you back sooner."

Now I said nothing, because I was really crying. When I was finally able, I said, "Thank you."

"No, niña," he said. "Thank you."

~

Sanjay was sitting on the porch when I got home from work. I had planned to tell him about my father, but I took one look at his eager expression and said, "You got the job."

He broke into a grin. "I got the job."

This time I didn't have to force a smile. I threw my arms around him. "I'm so happy for you."

He pulled back slightly and looked at me with surprise. "Really? Don't you want to know about the salary or the hours?"

"Well, yes, obviously. But I can tell you're thrilled—aren't you?"

"I am," he said. "I think I'll like it there, and it feels good to be wanted."

"Then that's enough."

He looked skeptical. "The salary's so-so," he said. "But I can probably negotiate it a little, and so-so is still better than sporadic."

"I agree."

"I get three weeks of paid vacation each year, which is a lot more than I was expecting."

"That's really good. And how are the hours?" I said.

"Same as yours, though if Brian is to be trusted, it's not the kind of job where I'll have to take work home with me."

"Lucky you," I said, but not unkindly—I meant it.

He looked at me. "I know this might complicate the kids' drop-offs and pick-ups, but I think we could figure something out with a sitter or the aftercare program at school."

"You've thought this through." I sounded impressed, because I was. Sanjay wasn't usually a planner, but maybe this opportunity had brought out some secret organizational ability he hadn't yet tapped into.

"I thought it through when I first sent in my résumé."

"I'm proud of you. But . . ."

He knew what I was thinking. "Stop worrying about my writing, Penny. I've had almost six years to make it happen, and as we both know, it didn't happen. This is the right next step. Maybe having less time will help me write the book faster."

I really hoped that was true. "When do you start?"

"In two weeks." His eyes were shining.

"What is it?" I said.

"My poker face gave me away again?" As a child, Riya once told me, Sanjay had vomited all over their front lawn minutes after stealing a toy from his neighbor. I had known he wanted to quit medical school from the day he mailed in a check confirming his enrollment.

It made me wonder how he had managed not to tell me about Christina sooner.

"You're an open book in large print."

"Darn it," he said, pretending to be upset. "I was wondering if you would mind if I went to New York before I started work. Malcolm and I were emailing back and forth. He and Jon are going to London for a couple weeks and I could stay at their place. I wasn't planning on going so soon, and I don't know if I'll even have my proposal ready, but I feel like I should take the opportunity to try to meet some agents and get the ball rolling while I can. We'd have to hire a sitter since there's no camp that week. But I'll drive instead of fly, so between that and staying at Malcolm's, I'll keep the costs as low as possible."

I nodded. "You should go."

"Really?"

"Really."

He kissed the top of my head, then said, "Thank you, Penny. I feel like things are finally coming together for me, and I know it's because you pushed me. I'm sorry you had to do that, but I'm glad you did."

"You're welcome," I said.

Things *were* coming together for him, and I was happy about that. But what about *us*? Would the boost in his self-esteem be the glue that kept us together? It would help, but I couldn't believe it would fix everything.

And why did I feel so envious of his trip? We hadn't been to New York together in years, let alone anywhere else. I missed it—not even the city, but how I felt when I was there. Sure, now that Sanjay was working we might finally be able to afford a family vacation. But who knew how soon that would be—or what shape our marriage would be in then?

That was when I had another idea. But unlike my revelation about our marriage, I wasn't going to blurt this one out to Sanjay. This time I was going to make sure everything was in place before I revealed a single thing.

～

The following morning, I ran into Russ in the break room. He was making a cup of coffee with the fancy machine that had recently been installed.

"Hey, Russ," I said.

"Russell," he said.

"Sorry," I said, opening the fridge. I set the peanut-butter-and-jelly sandwich I had brought for lunch on a shelf and closed the door again. "You were Russ for more than four years, so I still forget sometimes. But do you really care what I call you?"

"I guess not," he admitted, mixing the cream into his coffee with a wooden stirring stick. "You can call me whatever you want."

"Thanks, Russ."

He laughed.

"I actually have a favor to ask you," I said.

"Hit me."

"Remember when you first proposed us being co-directors two years ago? How you said if one of us had to travel or be away from the office for something like family medical leave, there would never be a gap in the way the department ran? Well . . . I know it's short notice, but I was wondering if you'd cover for me next week."

He frowned. "You're not leaving, are you? Is this about our conversation the other night at the bar?"

I shook my head. "Nope, it's not that. It's . . ." For a split second, I considered feeding him a white lie. But weird vibes or not, we were friends, weren't we? "It's about my marriage."

"Well, then, sure," he said, like all I'd asked was whether he could grab me a cup of coffee while he was getting one for himself. "That's important. And you deserve a break."

"Thank you," I said. "Now I just need to convince my mother-in-law to watch my children and Yolanda to let me take the time off."

To my surprise, Riya quickly agreed to watch the kids. Yolanda was a harder sell. "Not possible," she wrote after I emailed her to request a week of vacation. "The team needs more notice than that, especially with so few people in the office at the end of August."

Her response wasn't a surprise, per se, but it still made me angry—I was the only one on the senior management team who had not taken a full week off that summer.

But what could I do? I couldn't quit. I wouldn't throw a fit, and I wouldn't retaliate by underperforming, because then I would mostly be punishing myself.

I thought about Sanjay's request, and what he had said about me avoiding confrontation even when I was direct.

He was right—but not for long.

I closed the email and marched over to Yolanda's office. When I got there an elderly couple was seated in front of her desk. They were immaculately dressed, and the woman was clutching a designer bag, which suggested they were major donors.

I may have been angry, but I wasn't a complete imbecile; I continued past her door like I had never intended to stop and circled back around to my own. When I got to my desk, I emailed her to say I wanted to meet at her earliest possible convenience. Almost an hour later, Yolanda stepped into my office.

"There are policies and procedures," she said in lieu of a greeting. "If you want to take a full week off, you need to follow them."

I tilted my head up. "You asked what would incentivize my commitment to this department. And I finally figured it out. I could really—*really*—use a break."

She stood in front of my desk with her hands resting on her hips. She was like a gazelle, her long, lean limbs quivering in anticipation of wherever she would dart off to next. "What about your work? You were recently out sick, and you've taken other time off this summer."

After Jenny's death—we both knew what she was referring to. "I can't imagine you're caught up."

"Actually, I have no donations in limbo, I'm up-to-date on all stewardship processes for previous donations, and Russell has already confirmed that he can cover for me while I'm away."

"It's a big ask," she said.

If she thought this was a big ask, then my chances of switching to an 80 percent schedule were nil. I sighed and leaned back in my chair. Well, at least now I knew. I closed my eyes for a moment, thinking about what she'd said about my future in development.

When I opened my eyes again, she was still staring at me. "Yolanda," I said as evenly as I could manage, "you're a good supervisor, and I'm a good employee. A great employee, some would say. And because of that, we've always gotten along, and together we've done excellent work. But if I'm going to keep doing excellent work, I need to hit pause for more than two days." I looked at her, amazed she was still listening and seemed to have no plans to interject.

I continued. "As you may recall, I'm still dealing with the death of my closest friend, and I never really gave myself time to grieve. In fact, aside from major holidays when the office is down, I haven't been out for more than three concurrent days since my last maternity leave. So I'm asking if you will please overlook policies and procedures this one time and let me take a week of my month of unused vacation time so I can go get my head on straight."

"I expect a full update before you leave," she said, still doing the wide-stance Superwoman pose she was so fond of.

"Really?!" I said, unable to hide my glee.

She eyed me knowingly. "Yes, Penelope. I'd tell you to get your head on straight, but I'm not sure that's what you need. Go enjoy your time off."

As soon as Yolanda was gone, I let out the breath I hadn't realized I'd been holding. Then I reached for my phone and sent a message to Sanjay. How would you feel about some company in New York?

TWENTY-SIX

The nine-hour drive was time enough for every doubt in my mind to ferment and rise. After four nights with Riya, my children's blood would turn to corn syrup. Yolanda would realize the position Russ and I shared was better suited for one person. And—most frightening of my many worries—this trip would change nothing for Sanjay and me.

This latter fear seemed particularly likely. On the way, we chatted about work and the kids and even Matt. But mostly I gazed out the window while he drummed his fingers on the steering wheel and sang along to the playlists he'd prepared for the trip. These were not the sparks of connection I had been hoping for.

But fresh excitement bloomed within me as soon as I saw the skyline's jagged edge. New York was where I had started my career. It was where I had stopped being the child whose mother had abandoned her and had become an adult with her own story. It was the place where Sanjay and I began—on a day that remained in the memory of every New Yorker who had been there.

We were at the office together that morning; Sanjay had been working at *Hudson* for only a few weeks, whereas I had already been there a year. I remember walking to the cubicle maze where my desk was located and realizing most of my coworkers were conspicuously missing, then wandering over to the break room, where I found every-one crowded around a television.

"What's happening?" I asked Alex as I watched the footage of the North Tower burning.

"They think it was a propeller plane or maybe a charter flight," she said. "A freak accident."

But barely a minute had passed when a stricken newscaster announced that the South Tower had also been hit.

It was not an accident.

Our editor-in-chief instructed us to stay calm as we awaited instructions from the mayor or the federal government or someone who could tell us what to do next. Our offices were in Midtown, which was probably another target, we all agreed, but who knew what or where was safe? At any rate, no one had to be reminded to stay calm—we were all preternaturally sedate as we called our loved ones to let them know we were alive, at least for the time being, then returned to the television and desk radios to try to make sense of what was happening.

Then the South Tower fell.

Malcolm immediately announced he was leaving—off to an aunt who promised to get him in a car and off to Rhode Island. Then Alex kissed me on each cheek and asked me again if I would come with her and a group of her friends who were going to try to head to New Jersey. I wouldn't, though I couldn't say why. I had already called my father and brother, who had both urged me to flee, but with the subways and trains already down, I wasn't sure that was even possible.

Then the phone lines at our office went out, and it became clear that waiting around in a building two blocks from Times Square was no longer a calm choice.

I quickly gathered my things and started for the elevator, wondering what the odds were that the entire island of Manhattan would be eviscerated and whether it was best to go to my apartment on the

Upper East Side or . . . somewhere else that I had not identified. When I reached the elevator bank, Sanjay was standing there.

"We should take the stairs," he said.

"Pardon me?" I said.

The initial attraction I had felt when we met had not disappeared, but I had muted any mating instinct—while romance wasn't prohibited in our newsroom, it wasn't exactly best practice to date a coworker. But that morning, decorum was the last thing on my mind. When Sanjay's eyes met mine, a sudden, overwhelming desire reared within me.

"The stairs," he said again. He was still looking at me. "We should take them. In case the power goes out."

"Good point."

A senior editor had jogged up behind us, and he disappeared into the stairwell without acknowledging us.

"Where are you heading?" I asked Sanjay as we began to descend the twenty flights leading to the lobby.

"North."

"As in Harlem, the Bronx, Vermont, or Canada?"

"If all goes well, Canada. But for right now, to my apartment in Harlem."

He actually lived in Harlem? It had been a guess on my part.

"I'm apartment-sitting for an old professor of mine until next year," he explained. "Where are you going?"

"I don't know yet," I confessed. I was still in shock, but fear was starting to break through. "I have no idea what's safe or smart right now."

I didn't know how to describe the look in Sanjay's eyes, except to say it matched my own. "Me neither," he admitted.

We had paused at a platform between stairwells, and Sanjay put his hand on my back. His touch was light, yet I still remember the shiver of possibility it sent up my spine. "Why don't you come with me?" he said quietly.

I didn't hesitate before answering. "Yes."

Now, sixteen years later, the man who had been a whim was my husband. As the Holland Tunnel spit us out into the city, he reached for my hand.

"I'm glad you're here," he said.

I wondered if he, like me, had just been thinking about our beginning. "I am, too," I said.

~

Malcolm and Jon had stacks of the *New Yorker*. The copies were wrinkled and dog-eared, which suggested that unlike the subscription Sanjay and I had canceled years earlier to save cash and a few trees, they had been read.

"Maybe this is what life would have been like for us if we hadn't had kids," I remarked to Sanjay as I riffled through a recent issue. Our friends' loft had high vaulted ceilings and a floor made of broad mahogany planks. The south wall was comprised entirely of windows; the other walls, like most of the furniture, were white. The few decorations were glass or otherwise fragile and expensive. Stevie and Miles would have laid waste to the lot of it within an hour.

Sanjay was staring out the windows. Three floors below, our old Brooklyn neighborhood had become a new place. Such was life. I could still remember Roger, the editor who had destroyed his marriage with whiskey, complaining that the last of the smutty theaters in Times Square had been shut down. He didn't care for those sorts of establishments himself, he said; it was the principle of the matter, that money took every tarnished thing and coated it in plastic.

"Maybe. I'm not sure I'd want to live someplace like this," Sanjay said. "But I'll take four days without children."

I already missed Stevie and Miles, but the honking cabs and wailing sirens were a symphony compared to their bickering. I walked to the window, and Sanjay put his arms around me, then kissed me lightly. I kissed him back and was relieved to realize it felt normal and right. "This is going to be good for us, don't you think?" I said.

"I do. I'm still impressed you told Yolanda you were taking the week off."

"*Asked* her."

"Still," he said. "You spoke up. You've come a long way when it comes to letting people know when things aren't okay."

"Thank you," I said. "But that's only one thing. We still haven't . . . you know."

"I do know." He hugged me tighter, surprising me. "But much of that's on me. And your supporting my book idea means more to me than sex."

"Oh," I said. This had not occurred to me. "But it wasn't one of the things you asked for."

"No, but I didn't realize how much I cared until I did, if that makes any sense." He frowned slightly. "You're sure you don't mind that I'm going to meetings while I'm here?"

"Not at all," I said. "I'm proud of you for finishing the proposal so quickly." I had read parts of it on the car ride to New York, and it was excellent—smart, often funny, and surprisingly engaging, particularly considering I wasn't exactly his target audience.

Now he was trying not to smile; I could tell. "I wouldn't say it's finished, per se. I'm still obsessively editing."

"But for all intents and purposes, it's done."

"Yes, I guess that's true," he said. "We have an hour to kill before you head to dinner with the girls. Do you want to go walk around?"

I wondered if he was hoping I would say, *No, let's go make love.* In the past that was exactly what we would have done after arriving at our destination—at least, it was before we had children. The conversation we'd just had left me feeling warmer toward him. Connected, even— though I hated to admit it for fear of jinxing us. Still, I couldn't shake

Christina from my mind. Had he been attracted to her before Jenny's death, back when we were still at least sporadically sleeping together? If so, was he longing for her as he reached for me? Oh, how I wished I hadn't always turned the lights off all the time. How easy it must have been to imagine—if not her curves, then her face, when mine was shrouded in darkness.

At any rate, you didn't just turn off attraction like a switch. Try as he might, there was no way she wouldn't be in his thoughts if we made love. Maybe he would even say her name when he came. I would rather not sleep with him than risk having that happen.

"Sure," I said. "Let's go for a walk."

~

"Oh my God, look at you!" The minute Harue saw me, she got up from her seat at the bar and began jumping up and down, glass still in hand. She was wearing bright-red glasses and a denim romper that would have made people think I was a farmhand. She looked fantastic.

I laughed as I leaned away from her. "I'm happy to see you, too, but not so happy I want to take a wine bath."

Alex had risen from her barstool, but not before glancing at the couple hovering behind her, daring either of them to try taking her spot. She wore black on black, and her mouth was a gash of magenta. "Darling, so good to see you," she said, hugging us both. "You'll love this place. You *must* try the pork belly."

"You're back on meat?" I said with surprise.

"Vegetarianism was impractical." She leaned in and said in a pretend whisper, "And I'm thinner when I up my protein."

Harue sniffed. "Traitor."

I laughed. "You guys are the exact same."

"Nothing stays the same," said Alex. "It just doesn't change all at one time, thank God. So, how is your loved-up trip away from your perfect children?" She looked at Harue and rolled her eyes.

"Goals, Alex," said Harue. "I can't manage to stay married for more than two years, but Penny and Sanjay—" She looked me. "How long has it been now? Three decades?"

I swatted at her. "Very funny. Eleven years."

"What's your better half up to tonight?" asked Alex.

"He's grabbing takeout and putting the finishing touches on his proposal. Thank you again for your help with that," I added.

"My total pleasure."

The hostess appeared and told us our table was ready. Once we were seated, Alex said, "I'm thrilled about Sanjay's project, but to be blunt, Pen, I thought you'd be the one I'd be talking about book deals with. Remember that story you wrote? About the little girl who loved dumplings?" she said, referring to a draft I'd written right before Stevie was born.

"It needed work," I said lamely, because it, like so many other things in my post-childfree life, had been abandoned for more pressing matters.

"Still, it was great."

"Thank you," I said shyly.

"Remember those funny poems you used to write about us at *Hudson*? 'Harue, Harue! The animals adore you—shunning bacon and burgers, too. Because you know what they do: Meat is murder!'" She laughed as she recited my ditty in a sing-song voice.

I couldn't help but laugh with her. "I can't believe you remember that. That was literally fifteen years ago."

"It was catchy! What are you working on lately?" she said.

"My marriage," I said.

"Ha-ha."

"No, seriously. Sanjay and I have had some tough times lately. We've been working through it, but it hasn't been fun. We're trying to be more honest about what we need and what we want each other to change." Maybe because honesty had become my new norm, this confession came easy.

"I'm glad, because if you two don't make it, then love is dead," said Harue.

Funny—I could imagine myself saying something just like that to Jenny before I knew what I did now. "Marriage is hard," I said. "At least, mine is."

"You're telling me! If it weren't, maybe I wouldn't have gotten divorced twice," said Harue. "But what about work? Alex is right—I'm glad you're doing so well at the university, but we all thought that was a short-term gig."

A waitress appeared to get our drink order. I was relieved—I didn't want to talk about my job. But the minute she disappeared, Harue pressed on. "What's your plan? Are you going to stay there?"

I thought about my conversation with Russ. "It pays well, and I'm up for another raise in September. So yeah, I'll probably be at the university for a while."

"Are you happy, though?" said Alex. "Or at the very least, do you have some sort of creative outlet outside of work?"

They were both looking at me, probably with disappointment. I shrugged. "Not really."

"Then it isn't really a surprise you and Sanjay are having a hard time," said Harue.

"What do you mean?"

"Darling," said Alex, "even *I* know the saying 'If a mother isn't happy, no one's happy.'"

Harue snorted. "I'm pretty sure it's, 'If mama ain't happy, ain't nobody happy.'"

"Exactly," said Alex.

I must have looked as shell-shocked as I felt, because Harue quickly apologized. "I'm not trying to make you feel bad. I'm just . . . surprised. If you would have asked me ten years ago, even five, I never would have predicted you'd still be living in the Midwest and working a job you don't feel passionately about."

I accepted the glass of wine the waiter had just handed me. "Me neither, but life with kids isn't exactly what the brochure promised, you know? And Sanjay had a really hard time getting back on his feet after dropping out of school. Instead of pushing him to do more, I more or less enabled his coasting. Things are getting better, with his book proposal and the new job, but I still feel kind of stuck." I hadn't thought about how much of a brave front I'd been putting up in email and on the phone until I was face-to-face with my friends. It was a relief to be frank.

"You need a change," said Harue.

"You're not the first person to point that out," I said, thinking of Jenny's text. "But I don't know that I have a choice." Hell, I had not had a choice since . . . if not when two tiny cells cozied up in my uterus and decided to multiply at lightning speed, then at least since Sanjay had dropped out of medical school.

"It's not like making yourself a priority is going to suddenly unravel your family," said Alex. She smiled kindly. "You know that, don't you, darling?"

She's not wrong, said a voice in my head—and this time, I was pretty sure it was my own.

At once I understood that I had been looking at things with the right intention but from the wrong angle. My marriage was imperfect and my job lacked meaning, but I had been searching for complicated solutions instead of addressing the common denominator in both equations—me.

Moreover, I'd been approaching my life as a zero-sum game. As Alex had just pointed out, meeting my own needs for a change didn't mean my family would collapse or sink into bankruptcy-level debt. There were certain parts of my marriage that might never be fixed—wasn't that what "for better or for worse" was all about?—but that wouldn't necessarily put Sanjay and me on a one-way dinghy to divorce island. And even if we *did* split, that wouldn't be the end of everything. It would hurt like hell, but it wouldn't erase the good times we'd had. My children would still have two parents who loved them and who would not opt out of their lives just because things were hard.

I sat back in my chair, nearly breathless from these realizations.

"Are you all right, Penny?" said Alex.

"I'd say I'm fine, but I'm not," I admitted. "But I just realized why, and that's almost the next best thing."

~

When I got home, Sanjay was sprawled on the sofa. His computer was resting on the coffee table in front of him, but his eyes were at half-mast.

"Hey," I said. "Did I wake you?"

He gave me a sleepy smile. "Yes, but I'm glad you did. How was it?"

"Really good," I said. Later I would tell him about my conversation with Alex and Harue. But right now, I had other things on my mind. I walked over to the sofa, straddled him, and buried my face in his neck.

"I probably taste like curry," he said in a muffled voice, but his lips were already on mine.

"I don't care," I said as he continued to kiss me. My sudden longing wasn't lust driven. What I really wanted was to feel his skin against my own—to share the thing that had brought us together, and maybe could again.

"Do you want me to get the lights?" he said, already reaching for the lamp next to the sofa.

"No," I said in a low voice. "Leave them on."

And then we were a tangle of limbs, our lips and fingers in places familiar and yet seemingly foreign. Admittedly it was strange—almost like sleeping with a friend for the first time. But I didn't have long to think about it, because before I knew it Sanjay was apologizing for finishing nearly as soon as he had begun.

I laughed and kissed him again, overcome with a sudden lightness. "I don't mind," I said, and it was true. I had finally met his request—but I hadn't once thought about how I was doing that, or even Christina, until we were lying there panting.

It felt, finally, like the start of something new. Or maybe not new at all—just better.

TWENTY-SEVEN

The next day, Sanjay set off for meetings. Alex had connected him with a few literary agents, and he was having lunch with a college friend who was now an editor at a publishing house. While he was out, I decided to take the opportunity to roam around the city, which had once been my favorite way to spend an afternoon.

How nice it was to be alone for a change, I thought as I sat at a coffee shop reading the paper. As I strolled through Gramercy Park and headed into Union Square, I felt almost like the woman I had been before having Stevie and Miles. I was no longer so young, but the world again seemed brimming with possibilities. I had not felt that way in a very long time.

But as I watched a woman roughly my age push an elderly man down the street in a wheelchair, my thoughts turned to my father. Our last conversation had begun to close the distance between us, but already I felt it widening again. I had said my piece; it was entirely possible that the only thing I could do now was to accept our relationship for what it was. I wondered if I could manage that. That was the thing about being honest—once you began, it was hard to go back to sanitizing life with white lies.

Sanjay, too, was on my mind as I window-shopped. Our lovemaking could be nothing but a one-time thing. The minute we got home, we might return to our staid, sexless routine.

I hoped not. Because in spite of the brevity of our encounter, something was stirring in me, and damned if it didn't feel at least a little like desire. I'd forgotten how enlivening it was to make love, to want and be wanted. Because yes—lights on, my husband's eyes locked with my own, I knew that just as I hadn't been thinking about Christina, he hadn't been, either.

Sanjay was still on my mind as I walked to a park a few blocks from Malcolm and Jon's apartment. It was just after five, and he was waiting for me on a weathered wood bench. He was dressed up, and as I dodged running toddlers and school-age kids on scooters to make my way across the park to him, I felt a rush of longing. *Of course* Christina had been attracted to him. When he wasn't wearing the demands of everyday life all over his face, he was incredibly attractive.

When he saw me, he stood and waved. I smiled and waved back.

"Does this mean it went well?" I said as I approached.

He leaned forward and kissed me. "It went *great*."

"That's wonderful," I said, sitting next to him. "What happened?"

"Well, I have an agent."

I scooted over to him and hugged him. "You are amazing! Is it Josh?" I said, referring to someone Alex had put him in touch with.

"Josh said my proposal was promising but he wasn't sure he had the right editors to pitch the book to. But you remember Naomi Goldberg, who I had queried cold?"

"Yes," I said, and for once I meant it—I had truly been paying attention when he told me about her.

"She's taking me on. She loves the proposal and wants to give a first look to an editor at Yale University Press."

"Oh my gosh! That's a big deal, right?" I said. I was a little jealous—he had found a way to do what I had never managed to. But my pride and delight were far greater than any envy I was feeling.

He smiled. "Sounds like a big deal to me. And there are several other editors she thinks might be interested."

"That's wonderful. We should celebrate," I said.

"Really? Even though it's just the first step?"

"No, the first step was you deciding you wanted to write a book. This is a milestone," I said.

As we strolled over to a restaurant not far from the park, I reached for my phone. But as I stuck my hand in my purse, I remembered yet again that I couldn't text Jenny to share Sanjay's good news. And maybe, just this one time, that was for the best. Because instead of diverting my attention to my phone, I linked my arm through Sanjay's. "I am so happy for you," I told him.

He glanced over at me. "That means the world to me. I hope you know that."

I thought of the way I had discouraged him the last time he'd wanted to write a book. How easy it was to accidentally go off course and stay there instead of getting back on track. But we were on the right path now; I felt it in my gut. "I do now," I said.

∼

That night, as I raised a glass of champagne to my husband's success, it felt almost like old times—except unlike when I cheered his acceptance into medical school, this time his enthusiasm wasn't feigned, and neither was mine.

One round of drinks became two as he chatted animatedly about the book and his new agent. Though I was content to listen to him, he asked me about my writing, and I told him about dinner with Alex and Harue. I was in the middle of telling him about what Russ and I had discussed about possibly reducing my schedule when it occurred to me we were finally having the kind of conversation I had been longing for.

Then it hit me—it was the kind of conversation I would have normally had with Jenny. It was impossible not to wonder if her absence had created a vacuum that Sanjay had wanted to fill long before she was gone.

Once again, I was faced with the very real possibility that I'd had far more to do with the issues in our marriage than I had ever considered.

~

"We need to call Stevie and Miles," I said a few hours later as we let ourselves into Malcolm and Jon's apartment.

"You mean check in on my mother," said Sanjay.

I laughed. "And that."

"I'm still impressed you convinced her to watch the kids for four whole days."

"It's amazing how easy it is to be persuasive when you threaten not to show up for Christmas."

Now he laughed and pulled out his phone as I locked the door behind us. "Hi, Mom," he said. "Yes. Yes. Okay." He passed me the phone. "Here, talk to your children."

"Hi, Mommy," said Miles as I pressed my ear to the receiver. He sounded so grown-up. "When are you coming home?"

"In two days, sweetheart. Which will be here sooner than you can imagine. How's it going with Cookie?"

He giggled, which I interpreted as "We're having candy for breakfast and cake for lunch." "Are you and Daddy having fun?" he asked.

I glanced over at Sanjay, who was stretched out on the sofa. "We are, but I miss you guys."

"I miss you, too."

"How's—"

"Here's Stevie the booger-face!" interrupted Miles.

There was a fumbling. Then Stevie's voice came through the receiver. "Mommy, Miles is being a big jerk!"

"Watch your language, love, and hi to you, too. I hear that your brother's having a hard time, but hopefully he'll go to bed soon. Are you being good for Cookie?"

"She's been wonderful!" called Riya, who I now knew was listening in.

"I'm glad to hear that," I said. "Stevie? You still there?"

"Yes," said my daughter. "Mommy, where are you again?"

"New York, remember?"

"Yeah. But where are you staying?"

"At our friends' apartment in Brooklyn. Not too far from where we lived when you were a baby."

She was quiet for a moment. "Are we moving back?"

I laughed. "To New York? Not unless Mommy wins the lottery."

"Sorry," she said.

"No need to be sorry."

I sat beside Sanjay on the sofa. I had just started to tuck my feet under me when it occurred to me that I might have dirt on my soles, which would end up on the white upholstery. The coffee table's glass top was pristine and I didn't want to get toe smudges all over it, either, so I let my feet dangle off the edge of the sofa, which was quite stiff, really. It made me miss my comfy living room, with its marker-scribbled but welcoming sofa and a coffee table that could withstand far more than a pair of feet.

"But you said you miss it," said Stevie. "If we moved back, we could live like Eloise."

Through the loft windows before me, downtown Brooklyn was twinkling. At another time in my life, every one of those lights would have looked like an opportunity.

Now they were just lights. "We couldn't even live like Eloise's nanny, sweetheart, but that's fine with me. I don't want to live in a hotel."

"Why not?"

"Because I want to live in our home." I stood from the sofa and walked over to the windows. It had just begun to rain, and the city's blinking lights were blurring in the glass. "That's where you and Daddy and Miles live. That's where my life is."

After we'd hung up, I looked at Sanjay. "I'm going to shower."

"Okay," he said.

"Why don't you join me?" I said.

He didn't try to disguise his surprise. "Is this about the list?"

I shook my head. "No. It's about you and me and some tough-to-clean places I need help with."

He grinned. "Okay, then."

Once again, I made love to my husband—in the shower with the lights on, no less. This time it wasn't over nearly as soon as it began. In fact, it was so languorous and lovely that we did it again the next morning.

As the city disappeared behind me as Sanjay and I began our drive home, a sense of anticipatory loss came over me. It had been such a wonderful few days—almost like early in our marriage—that I wished we could have stayed longer, if only to hold on to that magic.

"Things feel different now, don't they?" I said as we crossed the border from New Jersey to Pennsylvania.

"They do," he said.

"Do you think it will last?"

It was beginning to rain, and he kept his eyes on the road as he responded. "I don't know. I hope so. What do you think?"

"I don't know, either. Are we still doing the list project? You haven't given me your third item yet. Are you planning to?"

He paused. "Honestly? I've been debating it."

The sky was nearly charcoal, and the rain was now making it hard to see more than a car's length in front of us; the semitrailer ahead was visible mostly by its taillights. I held my breath as it fishtailed while trying to merge from the center lane into the right lane. "Maybe we should pull over until the rain slows a little," I said to Sanjay.

I expected him to say he was fine. Instead, he guided us onto a wide right shoulder beside a field. Then he put the car in park and turned toward me. We stared at each other, wordlessly asking the same question: Now what?

"Okay," he finally said. "I'll tell you."

I had to stop myself from shuddering—it never did get easier, finding out how you were coming up short.

"I need you to stop worrying I'm going to leave you."

"I don't think that," I said quickly.

He shook his head. "You do. I think that's why you haven't been more critical of me all these years, and I'm sorry I took advantage of that and coasted. Our life has been way harder than it needed to be and that's on me. I knew I wasn't bringing in enough money and that you felt trapped."

"I didn't feel trapped," I heard myself lying. "Trapped is a strong word. Stuck, maybe."

"Exactly. You gave up so much to care for our family while I played ostrich. Is it any surprise you didn't really want to sleep with me? Hell, I wouldn't have wanted to sleep with myself."

"Still, I could have done more. As you yourself pointed out, marriage is hard work, and I was buying the lie that it should have come easy."

"We both could have done more. But I need you to know that I'm not going anywhere, Penny—not unless you want me to. That's not going to change just because you tell me you need more from me."

"Oh," I said quietly. "Is that why you sailed through my list? You've been acing one request after another."

He nodded. "I hate to bring up Christina, but that scared me, Penny. That, plus Jenny's death—I knew something needed to change."

"But why didn't you give me all three items sooner? Why the mystery?"

"No mystery," he said, shaking his head. "It seemed like you and I both needed to tackle a lot of other issues before we came to that . . ."

"My fear of being abandoned."

"Yes," he said without hesitation. "And I wanted to give you more time to heal after Jenny's death. To be honest, I wasn't sure I'd ever bring it up. But after your conversation with your dad, I felt like maybe you were ready."

I had turned to the windshield. Outside, the world was such a blur that it took me a moment to realize my eyes were filled with tears. "You could change your mind," I said quietly. "It happens all the time."

"Penelope." He put his finger under my chin and gently turned my face toward him. "You left *me* all those years ago, remember? You were afraid of the same thing then, and you wanted to beat me to the punch. I don't fault you for it—I can't begin to imagine how hard it was to have lost your mother the way you did. But in spite of your fear, you came back to me."

"Yes," I admitted.

"You were probably still terrified when we started dating again. But you did it anyway, and you married me, and we started a life and a family together. Why was that?"

The storm was so strong that I could no longer see through the glass. I unbuckled my seatbelt and crawled onto his lap.

"Because love was worth the risk," I whispered.

"It was." He pulled back so he could look at me. "I want us to be *us* again, Penny. Don't you?"

"More than anything."

"Good," he said. Then he pressed his mouth to mine and kissed me tenderly, the way he used to.

The way he did now.

TWENTY-EIGHT

Matt called me the night after Sanjay and I returned from New York. "Hi," he said stiffly.

"Hi," I said. I was so relieved I could have fainted. "I'm sorry about our last conversation."

"I am, too."

"How's Cecily?"

"She's good. I took her to Maine, like you suggested. It . . . it was a really good trip."

"Oh." That he had taken my advice almost made up for the heartbreak of thinking he was going to keep Cecily from me for the foreseeable future. "I'm so glad to hear that."

"Would you like to see her?"

"You know I would."

"Great," he said. He sounded tired. "Do you think you might come over soon—say, tomorrow night?"

"I'd be happy to."

"When you do, could you spare an extra fifteen minutes?"

"Sure. Why?"

"I was hoping you could put up the post we talked about. I could send you the link and the log-in info, but I thought it might be easier if I just logged you onto the site on Jenny's computer when you're here."

"Sure—that sounds great."

"Thanks, Penny," he said. "We'll see you soon."

~

When I walked into the Sweets' house, Cecily came flying at me and I hugged her tight. When I was sure I wouldn't cry, I held her out to look at her. Her hair was a bird's nest, and her outfit was filthy, but she was smiling. In fact, there was a buoyancy to her that hadn't been there the last time I saw her.

"How was Maine?" I asked.

"Good." She grinned up at me. "I ate a whole lobster."

"A big one, too," said Matt. I could tell he was trying to act normal— but then again, so was I. "She surprises me sometimes."

"I'll say. Cess, anything you want to do tonight? We could go out to dinner."

"I'm not hungry."

"No problem," I said. "How about a puzzle? Or coloring?"

She shook her head.

I eyed her. "What do you say about writing a book?"

"Us?"

"Why not?"

"Okay!" she said.

We decamped to the craft station Jenny had set up in Cecily's play-room. After I had spread out paper and handed Cecily a box full of markers and colored pencils, I said, "So. Where should we start?"

She gave me a funny look. "At the beginning."

I laughed. "Right."

We decided we would write a book about a little girl who accidentally finds herself in a magical forest and has to learn to speak to animals to survive. One page became three. Then five, then ten. As we worked—Cecily dictating as I wrote at the bottom, occasionally making suggestions, then handing her the page so she could illustrate it—I felt like a young girl myself, escaping troubles real and imagined as I slipped into another world.

"What do you think?" I asked as I stapled our finished pages together.

"Good. I'm going to show my mommy." She looked up at me with embarrassment as she realized what she had just said, then quickly glanced down at the book.

"It's okay, Cess," I said. "Happens to me all the time."

"What do you do?" she said quietly. "When that happens?"

"Well . . . sometimes I'm just sad. But sometimes I send your mama a little message. Sort of like a prayer. Sometimes she even talks back to me."

Her lower lip quivered. "I'm going to tell her I might write a book about her one day."

I smiled. "I think she'd really like that. I've always wanted to write books one day, too. Your mommy knew that about me."

"Really?"

"Yep. I wrote lots of stories before Stevie was born."

"You don't anymore?"

I shook my head.

"Why not?" she asked.

It was a damn good question, and my usual excuse-filled answers weren't going to fly with her. "Well, sweetie, sometimes I tell myself I don't have the time or I'm too tired, but now that I'm thinking about it, the truth is that I haven't made it a priority."

She ran a finger over the cover page. With her dark bob and rosebud of a mouth, she looked so much like Jenny that I could have cried. I found myself hoping to God she would have all of her mother's strengths and none of her struggles. "You still can, right?" Her eyes were lit up, and she was regarding me with the kind of hope that spreads on contact.

I laughed and gave her a squeeze. "I still can," I said. "And I'm not about to take that for granted."

~

Matt turned on a television show for Cecily, then led me upstairs. I hesitated before walking through the door of Jenny's office; I had not set foot there since finding her in her armchair. I was relieved to see Matt had removed the chair. But the rest of the room was exactly as it had been before that day, and a chill went up my spine.

"I got Jenny's log-in info from Tiana, and she walked me through how to post on the site," said Matt, opening the laptop on the clear Lucite desk where Jenny had worked. "You said you emailed yourself what you wanted to write?"

"Yes," I said. "Did you want to read it first?"

"No, I trust you," he said.

Did he? I couldn't read him.

"Once you copy it, you can paste it into this area," he said, pointing to the blog dashboard he had just pulled up. He glanced at me quickly. "I'll give you some space."

Despite my mixed feelings about Matt, I didn't want to be left alone in Jenny's office. But he was already gone. I would just have to work quickly.

I had just pasted my post when a folder on the left side of the screen caught my eye.

Drafts (1)

I shouldn't, I told myself, but my hand was already moving the mouse to the folder. I hovered the cursor over it for a second, then clicked.

The draft could have been a snippet of a previous post, a random thought she had decided not to publish—anything, really. There was no real reason for me to feel nervous, but my hand was shaking as I clicked on the lone draft in the folder.

As I began to read, I understood why.

> I want you to know this website isn't a lie. It's really my life. But it's only the parts I've chosen to share with you. And I love sharing it. I truly do. Every time I write a post, I remember all that is so wonderful about family and friendship and the countless blessings God has given me. Sharing that with you is like a daily meditation in gratitude. And your comments make my days brighter. They make me feel that I have a bigger purpose.
>
> But some of you have written here and elsewhere online to say that what I show you here makes you feel bad about yourself. And oh, how that hurts me—more than you may ever know, because it was never my intention to make it seem as though you, dear reader, weren't enough.
>
> You are more than enough.
>
> But if you're feeling lacking or sometimes wish you could run far away from the demands of being a woman in this world, know that I understand that, too. I may not convey it adequately, but I do feel that way sometimes. Most of the time, if I'm honest.

I don't always deal with being overwhelmed and feeling inadequate the way I should, and maybe that's why I don't show you that side of my life. Maybe I'm not ready to fully face reality—not in the manner that some of you wish I would, even if you couldn't possibly know what that might entail.

Know that I am making an effort to be braver.

I am trying to change.

I'm sorry to be vague, but I guess what I want you to know is that however you're feeling, you're not alone.

The woman passing you in the supermarket who's dressed like she just stepped out of a magazine?

The old friend who sends you a holiday card featuring her three perfect children, her hot husband, and her hypoallergenic dog who never eats underwear?

Or the blogger whose life seems too good to be true?

Odds are, she feels a whole lot like you do.

So be gentle on her—and yourself.

With so much love,

xo, Jenny

By the time I was done reading, tears were spilling onto my lap. It wasn't painkillers that killed Jenny—not truly. It was that she was afraid to admit anything was wrong.

It was an instinct I knew all too well.

I wiped my eyes and read the post again. Then I went downstairs to get Matt to show him what I had found.

"This should be her last post—not what I wrote," I said once he was finished reading.

His eyes glinted with anger. "Absolutely not."

"But why? Don't you think if she had known how her life would end, she would have wanted this to be published? You know Jenny would have wanted to help other women, even if she couldn't help herself."

"What she would have wanted was to be alive," he said.

Yes, well, that was one thing we could agree on.

"I won't even consider it," he added, "so please don't ask again."

My sorrow was starting to take a sharp edge. "Did you even read what she said?"

"Of course I read it, and anyone with one eye can see what she's really saying. People will know what happened."

I shook my head. "I disagree—she could have been talking about any issue. The point isn't what she was struggling with. It was *that* she was struggling."

"If the point isn't her pill problem, then why bother putting this up? It doesn't even say she died."

"We can add that at the end," I said.

"Then we're back to this," he muttered.

I leaned against the wall, regarding him. "If by *this* you mean doing the right thing, then yes."

Matt stood from her desk and flipped the laptop closed. I wanted to dash past him and copy Jenny's letter to send to myself. If he wouldn't publish it, I wanted to at least preserve it so that one day, when she was ready, Cecily could read her mother's own words about what she was going through.

"Penelope," he said, "you were my wife's best friend, and believe me, I am not downplaying your grief or your place in her life. But this is not your call to make, and I need you to respect that."

"I do respect that. Otherwise I wouldn't have asked you for permission. But, Matt—" I waited for Jenny's voice, maybe hoping she would tell me to be brave, but it didn't come. "I'm tired of lying," I said. "It isn't right."

"I'm not asking you to *lie*. I'm asking you not to overshare."

I shook my head sadly. "One day Cecily will learn the truth. You know that, right? What will you tell her then? That you continued to make the same mistake Jenny made by pretending everything was fine?"

Matt startled. "Good Lord, Penelope. That's not like you. Maybe you should see a therapist, too."

"Probably," I admitted. "But you're wrong—this *is* like me. If Jenny were here, she would have fought for what's best for her daughter. But since she's not, I will. I'm sorry you and I can't seem to see eye-to-eye these days, but I'm not going to let the fear of losing Cecily keep me from speaking up. My post and Jenny's are in the drafts folder now; you can publish whatever you want." I looked at him one more time. "But you don't actually need my input, Matt—you already know what you should do. You and Jenny may have had your troubles, but she would not have chosen to spend her life with a man who wouldn't do right by his daughter."

TWENTY-NINE

"That's a nice shirt on you," I said to Sanjay as he put on a pale-blue button-down he'd purchased for his first day of work.

He looked down at himself. "It beats scrubs."

My conversation with Matt was still weighing on me, but I managed a laugh. "I hope so. Thank you for doing this."

"Don't thank me. Believe it or not, I'm excited. I think it's going to be a good place to work, and I'll still spend most of my day writing."

"I'm happy to see you happy," I said.

He grinned at me. "How could I not be after last night?" We'd made love again for the first time since returning from New York. I hadn't been expecting much, since we were back home and faced with all the usual stressors. But maybe the key to good sex was low expectations, because it had been even better than our best vacation encounter.

"Don't get too comfortable," I warned, and he laughed.

When we went downstairs, Miles was sitting at the table, dressed in his pajamas. He was watching us with a worried expression on his face.

"Sweetie, what is it?" I asked.

His bottom lip popped out. "If Daddy's working away from home, who will get me if I'm sick?" The kids had started school the day before, as had Cecily. I'd hoped to catch Matt at drop-off that morning, but he had hustled in the opposite direction before I could even manage a wave.

"Do you feel sick?" I asked Miles.

"No."

"Good. But if you did get sick, the school has Daddy's cell phone number and mine, too. He can leave. I can also come get you, you know."

Miles pushed his empty cereal bowl toward the center of the table. "Cookie told Grandpa Arjun that you're glued to your desk."

"She said that, did she?" I looked at Sanjay, who made an exaggerated grimace. "I hope you know that's not true."

"How could Mommy work if she was stuck to her desk?" said Stevie, looking up from a book.

"I'm pretty sure Cookie was implying that Mommy works too much," I told them. "But I've been working less these days."

"Is that why Daddy's going to work now?" said Stevie.

"No," I said at the same time Sanjay said, "Yes."

"Sort of," I conceded. "But you're big kids now. You're in school all day, and things are changing a little for our family."

"Like things changed for Cecily?" said Miles quietly.

His comment shredded me. "No, sweetheart, not at all like that," I told him. "I can't promise nothing bad will ever happen to Mommy or Daddy, but I don't think you need to worry about us dying." I would have to find some wood to knock on, and maybe say a prayer before crossing the street. All the same, there was no need to prime my children to be paranoid—not when I was perfectly happy to fret for all of us. "Listen, you two, it's Daddy's first day and we all need to get moving. We'll talk more about this later, okay?"

Miles' worries were fast forgotten. "Since it's Daddy's first day, can we get ice cream tonight?" he said, giving me his best puppy-dog eyes.

"Please?" Stevie chimed in. "Because you went to New York and didn't even bring us a gift?"

"I never promised to bring gifts, but be good this morning and we'll think about it, okay?"

I'd forgotten that translated as "yes," and they nearly knocked me over hugging me. "You enormous children," I said, kissing each of their heads. "It's a good thing I love you way too much."

"What about your husband?" said Sanjay with mock indignation.

I walked over and kissed him. "I love you the exact right amount," I said. "Break a leg today."

~

When I arrived at work, I opened an email Yolanda had sent me at six that morning. She wanted me to come to her office as soon as I got in, which was completely nerve-wracking. Wasn't that what happened to people who were about to be fired? I told myself to stay cool, but my stomach knotted at the thought of losing my job the same day my husband started his. We still had no idea if his job would work out, and his salary alone couldn't support us.

She was at her desk, swiveled sideways in her chair; her long legs were twisted around each other. "Did you enjoy your time off?" she said.

"I did," I said. My voice warbled, so I swallowed before adding, "I haven't been to New York in a long time, and it was good to be back."

"I find traveling opens my mind in a way that doesn't happen at home or in the office."

"I agree with that."

"Now that you've had a chance to think, I'd like to ask: Are you planning to stay in development?"

Was this a segue to her firing me? Or as Russ had suggested, did she think I was going to quit? I sat up a little straighter in my chair. "I have no plans to leave."

"I'm glad to hear that." She clasped her hands and leaned forward. "Because as it happens, I do."

"You're . . . leaving?"

I had never seen her smile so wide. "I accepted the top development position at UCLA's school of medicine."

"Wow. Congratulations, Yolanda. They'll be lucky to have you." I meant it, even if I wondered why she had scheduled a one-on-one meeting to tell me this.

Yolanda being Yolanda, she had already anticipated my next mental step. She tilted her head and regarded me. "I wanted to meet with you privately so I could ask you about applying for my position."

I couldn't hide my surprise. "Really?"

"Yes. In the interest of transparency, I encouraged Russell to apply, too. But Dean Willis and I both think you have a lot of potential."

"I'm incredibly flattered . . . but I'm also flabbergasted," I admitted. "I thought you were disappointed in me for asking for time off."

Her eyebrows shot up. "No, I said there were procedures to be followed."

"But you've also expressed concern about my work over the past few months."

"And in each instance, you've been able to prove me wrong. That's ultimately why I decided to ask you to come forward as a candidate. This position involves having hard talks and making your presence known. I didn't think you had it in you, but you do, Penelope."

This was a big compliment. I wondered why it didn't make me feel better. "Thank you," I said.

"You're welcome. Needless to say, if you take my position, your salary would be considerably higher. Granted, you'll have to ace the interview." She regarded me, and I glanced down at my dress, which was a plain navy shift. "You'll need to dress sharper. That's doubly true if you take the job. I may be the only person who will say that to you point-blank, but that's only because it's absolutely true."

I nodded.

"You'll also have to acquaint yourself with some of the nuances of working with . . ." She pursed her lips. "The ultrarich. I know you do a stellar job with our wealthiest donors, but I'm specifically referring to the select few I don't hand off to you and Russell, as they're a very particular type, if you get my gist. And you'll need to get used to being on the road several times a month. But I'm not leaving until the end of October. We would have a couple of months to noodle the details together. So, what do you say? Would you like to interview for VP of development?"

"Yolanda, I'm flattered," I said slowly.

"But?" she said.

But I wanted to reduce my schedule—not expand it. Still, I knew it was the biggest opportunity of my career. "Could I see a write-up of the responsibilities the position entails? There's a lot to your job that I don't know about. I'm also curious to know what my salary range might be."

Yolanda narrowed her eyes, and I steadied myself for some sort of reprimand. "I'll inbox you that and the job link today. Dean Willis and I would like your application by next Monday."

"Absolutely." I stood. "Thank you. This means a lot to me."

"Thank yourself, Penelope. You've been doing the work, and you told me to pay attention to that. This is all you." As she stood and gave me a knowing smile, I took a minute to appreciate her preternatural poise and commanding presence. I wondered if I would ever be able to fill her shoes.

I wondered if I wanted to.

～

When I got back to my office, Russ was sitting in my desk chair. He grinned at me. "So, Yolanda tell you about your new job?"

I eyed him. "How did you know about that?"

"She talked to me last Friday."

"Right. Then you know it's hardly *mine*," I said.

"Oh, come on, Pen." He spun in a full circle, then made a grand gesture indicating I could have my chair back. "Obviously I'm dying for the gig, but everyone knows you deserve it. Why don't you look more excited?"

"Don't I?" I said. There was no window to see my reflection in, but maybe I would put a mirror in my office. Or I could just take Yolanda's.

"You're going to apply, aren't you?" he asked.

"I'm not sure yet."

"You'll have that sweet office, a massive corporate expense account, and a legitimate reason to be free of the ol' ball and kids several times a month." He grinned. "No offense, but you could get a new set of wheels, too."

And a house with smooth ceilings and a bathroom on the first floor. We could sock away more than a few dollars for the kids' college funds and max out our retirement contributions.

I knew I was supposed to be leaning in—these were important years in my career, and I wasn't getting any younger. If what I'd read was to be believed, opportunities to vault myself to the next level would be few and far between.

But . . . I wasn't so sure I wanted to upgrade my wardrobe and get a haircut that said business and perfect my ability to hobnob with the ultrarich.

I was equally unenthused about the possibility of working *even harder*, at least at this particular job at this particular juncture, and regularly being away from my husband and children. Because now I knew—really and truly knew in a way I hadn't before—that it could all end in an instant. And if, God forbid, that happened, would I take my dying breaths feeling glad for getting a chance to fly business class?

Anyway, there were other things I wanted to do. Since Cecily and I had written the book about the girl in the magical forest, I had begun spinning another tale. It was still a glimmer of an idea, but I knew it would be about a child who had lost something dear to her. I needed the time—and yes, the mental space—to write it. And what about having evenings to read Sanjay's book and being able to pick my kids up after school—especially given that I had just told them I wasn't glued to my desk anymore?

"You'll apply, yes?" I asked Russ.

"Obviously."

"Good."

"What about you?"

"I'm not sure," I admitted. "Remember when we talked about how I wanted to be a writer?"

"Of course I do."

"Well, I thought about that a lot while I was in New York. I need this job, but I need to make my own writing a priority again, too. Plus, I've still got a lot of stuff to work through."

"By *stuff*, you mean your marriage and Jenny's death."

"Yes," I said. "And I'm pretty sure moving up the ladder will make that more difficult than it needs to be."

Russ was leaning in the doorway now. "Well, good for you, Penny. You've got guts to admit all that."

I thought of Jenny's letter. She seemed to be so close to finding her way out of that dark hole. Once again, it occurred to me how incredibly fortunate I was. "A couple months ago, I would have responded to that compliment with a self-deprecating comment," I told Russ. "But now I've got to agree with you. It takes courage to be yourself when everyone expects you to be someone else. I'm just glad I still have the opportunity to make that decision."

THIRTY

I visited Jenny's website frequently after her death, and each time I wondered the same thing: if she had never started her blog, or maybe if it had not become the sensation that it had, would she have found it easier to admit she was struggling and seek help?

Because sharing her life online meant strangers—and even loved ones, me included—came to think of her in the particular way she presented herself online. People had expectations about how she should look and what she should say and do. And the more everyone expected of her, the harder it must have been to disappoint us by deviating from the image we had already bought into.

Perhaps Jenny wanted to unshackle herself from the golden hand-cuffs of internet fame. I would never know now. The draft I had discovered on her computer didn't hold that answer. Nor did it provide closure, though it was close.

Still, that letter was the last thing I expected to see when I clicked on her site before shutting down my computer at the end of the day. It took me several seconds to process what had popped up on my monitor.

A new photo of Jenny and Cecily had been posted at the top of the page. They were sitting under the enormous oak tree in her backyard;

Cecily was in Jenny's lap, looking up at her as Jenny gazed down at her adoringly.

Below the photo, Jenny's letter had been published in full, followed by a brief note saying she had accidentally died of a prescription painkiller overdose on June 26. Just beneath the note was a list of resources for people struggling with addiction.

A sob flew out of my mouth.

Matt had done the right thing.

After I had composed myself, I picked up the phone to call him, but it went straight to voicemail. I glanced at the clock and saw that I needed to pick up Stevie and Miles from their school's aftercare program. I would have to try him again later.

Fifteen minutes later I pulled into the school parking lot. I was itching to see my kids, to put my arms around them and let their hugs lighten what had turned out to be an incredibly heavy day. I had just closed my car door when someone called out my name.

I spun around and saw a man jogging across the asphalt. As he got closer, I realized it was Matt. No wonder I hadn't recognized him—he was wearing a Jimi Hendrix T-shirt and jeans and had grown a short beard.

"I called you earlier," I said. "I saw the post."

"Good," he said. He kicked at the ground with his sneaker, the way Miles often did when he was bothered by something. I expected him to explain why he'd made the decision he had. Instead he said, "You should probably know that I left my job."

I stared at him with disbelief. Jenny often said she wished Matt would quit. She always followed this remark with a disclaimer that she was joking—but there was truth in most jokes. If only she were there to learn her wish had come true. "Wow. When did you do that?"

"Last week," he said. "The job isn't important. *Wasn't* important. We'll be fine for money for a while, and I need to be with Cecily. She's my focus. And dealing with Jenny's death."

An old instinct surfaced, and I almost blurted out that I hoped his decision had nothing to do with me. But that wasn't true at all. I wanted what I had said to have influenced him. Wasn't that the entire point of saying it? "That's great, Matt. How wonderful that you can make that choice."

"Yeah." He shoved his hands into his pockets. "I'm making some changes. I already told Cecily that Jenny accidentally died from taking too many pills, and for the time being that's where we'll leave it. Later, I'll tell her the rest. I'd appreciate it if you took the same approach with Stevie and Miles. But otherwise use your judgment with whoever needs to know."

"Sonia and Jael?" I said.

He shook his head. "That shouldn't fall to you. I'll call them myself tonight."

"Thank you." I had to take a few deep breaths before I could find the courage to speak again. "Are we going to be okay? You and me, I mean?"

The lines in his forehead deepened. "I don't know, Penny. You're probably not out of line to call me on the stuff I've done wrong, but it's hard to be around you sometimes."

"I know that. It hasn't been my intention to make you feel bad. But I know Jenny would have wanted me to say what I did."

"Yeah, I get that. But like I said, it's still tough to hear."

I swallowed hard. "I'll choose my words carefully. But please, Matt—don't punish me by keeping Cecily away from me. It's bad enough to have lost Jenny. I don't think I can handle losing her, too."

He ran a hand through his hair. "I know. And believe me, she can't handle losing you, either. Whatever differences you and I have, they're not as important as what Cecily needs. That's one thing I'm clear on."

I blinked furiously. "Thank you."

"Welcome. Well," he said, looking away, "we should probably get the kids."

"Right."

We were about to walk into the school when I stopped. "Hey, Matt?"

He turned to me. "Yeah?"

"Jenny would have been so proud of you."

Maybe it was just the light, but I was pretty sure there were tears in his eyes, too. "I believe you, Penelope. Because no one knew Jenny better than you."

When the kids and I got home, Lorrie and Olive were sitting on their front porch. I expected Lorrie to scurry away, the way she had been lately whenever she saw me. But she stayed where she was. I hesitated, then lifted my hand. Olive scowled in my direction, but Lorrie waved and then smiled faintly. I almost didn't return it—what if she took it as an invitation? Then I realized even if that happened, it would be fine. I smiled back.

Inside, I found Sanjay in Miles' bedroom. The usually cluttered bookshelf was in perfect order, and the floor was free of toys and stuffed animals.

"I was going to ask how your first day went, but now I just want to know what on earth you're up to," I said.

He was still dressed in his work clothes. He smoothed Miles' comforter and looked up at me. "Were you expecting me to turn into a slug around the house just because I have a 'real job'?" he said, making air quotes around the last two words. "And today went great. Mostly training, but I met the entire department and got set up on my computer."

"I'm glad. But you have two real jobs now. Who cares if Miles' room is clean?" He was staring at me. "Why are you looking at me like that?"

"Honey, do you have another fever? Because if you think it's okay for Miles' room to be a mess . . . well, I'm worried about you."

"Don't make me pinch you," I warned.

He laughed. "Let's go relax before the kids start hollering for dinner. I got more of that wine you like."

"Are you trying to butter me up?"

"Is it working?"

I grinned. "Yes."

"Then yes," he said, grinning back at me.

Ten minutes later we were on opposite ends of the sofa, our legs tangled together in the center. He had just told me about his first day, and in turn, I told him about my conversation with Yolanda.

"Will you apply?" he asked, watching me intently.

"I really don't want to," I said. As soon as I heard the words come out of my mouth, I knew them to be true. "But I feel bad about that. It's probably the best opportunity I've ever had, and another one like it won't come along anytime soon. Don't you think?"

"No," he said, shaking his head. "I think the best opportunity is the one you're excited about and truly want to take. The timing isn't right for this one. Maybe you'll never want a job like that. That's okay, too."

I took a sip of my wine and thought about what he'd said. "Thank you. I know it's early still, but you taking that job makes me feel less guilty about not springing for this opportunity. There's less weight on me now."

"You're most welcome—I'm just sorry I didn't do something sooner." He smiled at me. "Can we officially retire our lists? I feel like we're in a better place these days, don't you?"

"I do, but I'm not sure we can credit the lists for that."

"Well, yes and no. If you hadn't said you wanted things to change, I might not have gotten this job, and you would feel pressure to apply for Yolanda's, and then things would be a whole lot harder right now."

He lifted his glass, and I leaned forward and clinked my own against his. "So, here's to you and your crazy idea."

"*Our* crazy idea," I said.

"Yes," he said. "Here's to us."

As I looked at him—with those brown eyes, which I had been looking at for nearly two decades but could still take me by surprise—I thought about what might come next for us. If I had learned anything from our project, it was that our marriage was not strengthened during good times, or even during the bad. It was working together toward a common goal that cemented our bond.

A knock at the door broke through my thoughts.

I sighed. While I was glad Lorrie had finally taken my advice, her timing had hardly improved. "Ignore it," I said to Sanjay.

"You should probably see who it is."

I looked at him, puzzled. Had he ordered me flowers? A singing telegram?

But when I opened the front door, a face I knew as well as my own was staring back at me. *"Mi vida,"* said my father. *My life.*

"Dad," I said. Then I broke into tears. I could feel my father's ribs as he hugged me, and his hair was too gray, and—well, he didn't look particularly healthy. But when we finally pulled apart, he was smiling.

More important, he was *here*.

"I'm sorry it took so long for me to visit."

"It's okay," I said, not even bothering to try to stop crying. "Come in, come in."

"Thank you," he said. He glanced around. "What a nice place you have."

"Thank you. I like it, too."

Sanjay had come to the hallway. After he took my father's suitcase, he embraced him.

"You knew about this, didn't you?" I said.

He grinned. "Your dad wanted to come visit, so I told him to come as soon as he could. All I did was get Miles' room ready so he had a place to sleep."

My heart swelled. He knew how much this meant to me, and he had helped make it happen.

"Kids! Your grandfather is here!" Sanjay yelled.

Miles and Stevie came running down the stairs.

"Grandpa?" said Miles, looking at my father questioningly. And no surprise—he hadn't seen him since he was four. We had photos up, but it wasn't the same.

My father knelt and extended a hand. "Hello, Miles. You can call me *Abuelo*. It's nice to see you again."

"Abuelo," repeated Miles.

"Hi," said Stevie quietly.

He turned to her. "Stevie! You're the spitting image of your beautiful mother." She flushed and smiled shyly.

"Hey, kids? Can you give your grandfather a tour of the house?" I said. I didn't have to ask twice—they grabbed him by the hand and yanked him into the living room. "Gentle!" I called after them.

"I'm fine, Penelope!" he called back.

The screen door slammed as they pulled my father into the backyard.

"Thank you for doing this," I said to Sanjay.

"I didn't do anything except take your father's call. He's here because of you. Because you told him what you needed from him."

"I did, didn't I?" I gave him a teary smile, but Sanjay wiped my face with the sleeve of his new shirt and kissed me. "I'm going to go make sure the kids aren't making your father jump on the trampoline, okay?"

"I love you, you know."

He held my gaze. "I love you, too. More than ever."

After he left, I went into the kitchen to pour a glass of water for my father, who was wiping his brow and talking to Sanjay as the kids ran circles around them. As I regarded my family through the window, I was reminded of the night Jenny's voice first came to me, and what a comfort that had been.

It occurred to me that it had been several weeks since I had heard her. Somehow I knew I wouldn't again.

If Jenny were still alive—or even if we were still just having chats in my head—I would have told her how happy I was to be building a new bond with my father. I would have shared that I was finally making space for my own dreams. I would have confessed I was doing what had once seemed impossible and falling in love with my husband again.

And in spite of her pain, she would have been happy for me.

Close female friendships are built one secret at a time. What Jenny had concealed did not undo all we had shared; I would miss her for the rest of my life. But as I watched my husband gesturing animatedly to my father, I was profoundly grateful that I still had one person with whom I could share these thoughts, and the many ideas and experiences—and, yes, mistakes—that would follow.

Above my family, the sun was beaming in the cloudless blue sky. I wondered if Jenny was up there somewhere, or in the air around me, or at least a part of the universe somehow. Wherever she was, I only hoped she knew I had received her parting gift—the ability to look beyond what was missing and be thankful for all that remained.

AUTHOR'S NOTE

If you've read the news recently, you probably know the US is in the midst of an opioid epidemic. Addiction—including opioid addiction—has affected my friends and family, their loved ones, and so many others. With that in mind, I did not take writing about this topic lightly. Though I consulted medical literature, physicians, emergency medical technicians, and paramedics about the situations depicted in this novel, this novel is a work of fiction and should not be used for reference purposes. If you or someone you know is dealing with substance abuse, visit www.samhsa.gov/find-help/national-helpline for more information.

ACKNOWLEDGMENTS

Every novel begins with an idea. The idea for this one was sparked by the many conversations about marriage, parenting, and life that I had with my Burns Park friends—specifically Stefanie and Craig Galban, Jennifer and Jeff Lamb, Anna and Vince Massey, Stevany and Tim Peters, Nate and Mara Richardson, Nicole and Matt Sampson, and Michelle and Mike Stone, as well as my better half, JP Pagán. It takes a village; I'm so glad you guys are mine.

Elisabeth Weed, your enthusiasm for this story fueled me every step of the way. I'm honored to continue to call you my agent after all these years.

My deep gratitude to my editor at Lake Union, Jodi Warshaw, for believing in this book and helping me transform it into the story it was meant to be. Tiffany Yates Martin, your ability to help polish a rock into a diamond continues to amaze me; thank you for your wise editorial input. And many thanks to Danielle Marshall, Gabriella Dumpit, Dennelle Catlett, and the rest of the Lake Union team, as well as to Kathleen Carter Zrelak of Kathleen Carter Communications and Michelle Weiner of Creative Artists Agency, for championing my work.

Thanks to the dear friends and family who continue to cheer me on as I write, especially Shannon Callahan, Lauren Bauser, Laurel, Joe, and Jacob Lambert, Alex Ralph, Sara Reistad-Long, Janette Sunadhar, Pam Sullivan, and Darci Swisher.

Writing can be lonely work, but my fellow Tall Poppy Writers, especially Ann Garvin, make it less so. Thanks to the community of Bloom with Tall Poppy Writers, Jennifer O'Regan of Confessions of a Bookaholic, Andrea Peskind Katz and Great Thoughts Great Readers (especially the amazing Ninja crew!), Barbara Khan of Baer Books, and Kristy Barrett of A Novel Bee—your support means the world to me.

And of course, my love to Indira and Xavi, who inspire so much of my work and light up my life.

READING QUESTIONS FOR
BOOK CLUBS

1. Do you think Penny's friendship with Jenny hurt her marriage with Sanjay? If so, how?

2. Penny notes that "A single secret is like a lone roach. You know there will be more—it's only a matter of when." Do you think that's true?

3. In what ways did Penny's childhood parallel Cecily's? How did it differ?

4. Why did Penny have an easier time sticking up for Cecily than for herself?

5. At one point Penny notes that "close female friendships are built one secret at a time." If that's true, did what Jenny conceal from Penny mean the two women's friendship wasn't as close as she thought?

6. Nancy Weingarten tells Penny to stop making everything look easy, and notes that most men act like things are harder than they are. Do you agree?

7. Penny is rocked by the revelation that Sanjay has been attracted to another woman—even though she knows he handled the situation in what she feels is the correct way. What would you have done in her shoes?

8. Do you think Penny's brief attraction to her coworker, Russ, is a consequence of her grief?

9. Penny fears that Sanjay will resent her if he has to curb his writing to make more money. Do you think her fear is justified?

10. Do you think radical honesty ultimately strengthened Penny and Sanjay's marriage? Why or why not?

ABOUT THE AUTHOR

Photo © 2017 Myra Klarman

Camille Pagán is the #1 Amazon Kindle bestselling author of five novels, including *Life and Other Near-Death Experiences*, which was recently optioned for film, and *Woman Last Seen in Her Thirties*. Her books have been translated into more than a dozen languages. A journalist and former magazine editor, Pagán has written for the *New York Times*; *O, The Oprah Magazine*; *Parade*; *Real Simple*; *Time*; and many other publications and websites. She lives in Ann Arbor, Michigan, with her family. You can visit her online at www.camillepagan.com.